Forget Her

HOLLY RIORDAN

THOUGHT CATALOG Books

THOUGHTCATALOG.COM
NEW YORK • LOS ANGELES

Published by Thought Catalog Books, an imprint of the digital magazine Thought Catalog, which is owned and operated by The Thought & Expression Company LLC, an independent media organization based in Brooklyn, New York and Los Angeles, California.

This book was produced by Thought Catalog. Cover illustrated and designed by KJ Parish. Visit us on the web at thoughtcatalog.com and shopcatalog.com.

Made in the USA.

ISBN 978-1-949759-23-5

*To my fiancé
and the memories we're going
to continue to make.*

CHAPTER 1

An announcement cuts into my movie marathon uninvited. "You can't change your past, but you can cleanse your memories," it says in messy, mismatched fonts. Like a ransom note.

"Jesus. More commercials?" I say in between beer slurps. "We're lucky if our web series gets a single ad break."

Arrow, my miniature dachshund, perks at my voice. He waddles his sausage belly to my side of the couch, abandoning his favorite pillow. I keep it flipped to the plain side to hide the bubble-lettered message about my kid having paws. My mother sewed it as a surprise when I adopted him. One of her subtle guilt trips.

Arrow settles onto my lap as the words on screen dissolve into a beach scene with a barefooted spokeswoman. She looks out of place with her pale, sunken cheeks and long-sleeved dress. I don't recognize her face, but she feels familiar, like a neighbor only seen from peripherals. Someone inspecting apples in the produce aisle or tugging a flopping dog away from a mud puddle.

"I'm honored to announce the grand opening of Endellion Resorts," she says with a Long Island accent, a copycat of mine. "When you purchase a weeklong vacation package at our exclusive island, you'll receive a complimentary Memory Cleansing. This quick, noninvasive procedure will temporarily remove your most traumatic memories. It will help you have a truly stress-free, relaxing vacation."

She pops a monochrome umbrella, tilts the canopy toward the camera, and spins it rapidly enough for the spokes to blur. Dark splotches spit from the center and smack the lens like blood in a B-horror film. A beat later, the camera thrashes side to side, shaking away the grime. The umbrella, remodeled with vibrant purples and pinks, slows to a stop.

Their editing sucks. It looks like one of those local family furniture commercials with jump cuts and green screens. It has to be a scam.

I switch stations, creating a flip-book effect. The same commercial spams every network.

The spokeswoman continues spouting nonsense in a voiceover while a helicopter captures a high-angle shot of the resort. Two separate beaches border opposite sides of an oval island. A U-shaped building with arcade and cafeteria signs sits on a curved end. On the other end, a white wooden boardwalk branches toward rows of bungalows.

A montage follows. Slick, spiraling water slides. Lobster tails dipped in cocktail glasses. Claw machines with colorful, woolly prizes. Each image blinks past at a frame rate reserved for flickering projectors in old monster movies, brainwashing victims with their lids taped open wide.

Fifty photos later, regularly scheduled programming returns, but my interest lingers on the resort. I unlock my cell to check social media, to see whether anyone else finds the concept sketchy.

Endellion Resorts is listed at the top of the trending tab. Friends tag each other, teasing about awkward hookups they want erased. Influencers upload reaction videos with mouth-clasping thumbnails. Trolls patch together memes, Photoshopping the spokeswoman onto characters from campy sci-fi movies about science going *too far*.

I roll my eyes at the strangers with nothing better to do than vomit their opinion onto a screen, but I keep tapping on mine. Another beer later, I cave and join the crowd. I scribble on forums. I sign electronic petitions. I reblog articles about how Memory Cleansing could wreak damage on long-term memory, then toss in my own theories about the company manipulating viewers with a low-budget commercial to come across as unintimidating, harmless.

My coworkers drop question-marked comments beneath each post. They believe I should be at the head of the line to have my mind purged of the childhood stories passed around our studio like cigarette stubs.

They would get along well with my mother. My cell vibrates with an image of her bear-hugging me. I snapped the self-timed photo before she gained sixty pounds, before I slashed my hair into a pixie cut. I tap IGNORE.

I wait until midnight to get rid of the glaring red notification badge. I balance my phone on the cluttered bathroom counter, activate my voicemail, and wet my stale toothbrush.

"Ariadna, honey, it's me," my mother says, sounding tinny through speakerphone. "Did you see the Endellion commercial? We're going to be rich. Rhea Laman is famous now. I have at least two or three graduation pictures with her in them. I wonder how much we can sell them for." She chuckles until it turns into a wheeze. "It's beautiful at the place she built, don't you think? You should see if you can get some days off. We haven't gone on a vacation since The Falls. We deserve a little break. I'm going to submit an application on their website. I have it in front of me right now. It says they're giving away free tickets every week. Fingers crossed we win, but if not, I'm sure the two of us can get a little money together. Call me."

"Graduation pictures?" I repeat, spitting toothpaste foam. I skipped my high school ceremony. A postman delivered my diploma. He crammed the cardboard holder into our mailbox, creasing it straight down the center.

The principal handed Domino hers in person, though. We streamed into blue plastic chairs for four hours to watch my sister prance across the stage in four seconds. My father grumbled about his faraway, out-of-focus pictures, so I took enough post-ceremony shots to pack a memory card. Other families noticed me trampling flower beds, hopping on fountain ledges, and squatting in shrubs for better angles. They thrust their touchscreens at me, requesting the same treatment. A grandmother tipped me ten bucks for my trouble. My first paid photography gig.

I should have added duplicates to a portfolio, but as a junior without any college plans, the idea never occurred to me. If my mother had prints of the woman on the commercial, they must have been from my father's blurred batch. He aimed his bulky, outdated camera at every speaker who graced the stage. Including the valedictorian.

I picture her messy brunette curls and the freckles gathered on her nose like she dunked it in a bowl of pepper. She looked nothing like the woman on the commercial, but a makeup artist could have smothered her freckles with concealer. Bleach could have camouflaged her natural roots. I can't remember what she read from her index cards ten years ago, but I remember discussing it on the car ride home.

"I think that young girl gave a better speech than the woman they paid to deliver the commencement," my mother said from the passenger seat.

My father grunted. "It should be illegal to waste our tax dollars on a reality star. What is she qualified to do? Teach our kids to whore themselves? They got an education to stop them from pole-grinding."

"She's not a stripper," I said. "She was on a dating show. And at least she was entertaining. That valedictorian girl was such a smart-ass. Her whole speech was one big humblebrag."

"She's allowed to brag. She worked hard," my mother said.

My father nodded. "You can learn something from a girl like that."

"Can we stop talking about her, please?" Domino asked, breathing heavily between words, like another panic attack was looming. "Ari is right. That girl thinks she's some sort of genius. She only cares about herself. It's gross. I'm glad I'll never have to see her again. After today, I can finally forget she exists."

CHAPTER 2

My wheels thump over a curb, sending the coupons lodged beneath my visor tumbling onto my lap. The *Twins Spilling Tea* studio shares a lot with a pancake house and a bagel shop, so arriving ten minutes late means parking on the grass and risking a ticket. The last time a cop pinned one under my wipers, I skipped lunch for a week to afford the fine. I cross my fingers, hoping that someone with a soul is on duty.

When I stroll through the front entrance, it jangles like a cat collar. The chime is a relic left over from the previous owners. Before Mr. Ritter rented the space and converted it into a soundstage, it housed a nail salon where my mother would drop me off for mani-pedis. Domino tagged along in our elementary days, back before she started chopping her nails to the flesh. She asked for spider webs and skulls in autumn, candy canes and snowflakes in winter. I stuck to the same color each appointment. A sunset orange. When the salon went out of business, I scoured drug stores and flea markets for the shade but could never find a perfect match.

I slink into the old bikini-waxing area. A craft service cart tips against the wall, cluttered with cereal cups and sesame seed bagels. Brown fast-food napkins are spread under a sputtering, leaking coffee maker. In the center of the room, dining tables are smashed together to resemble a boardroom table.

Mr. Ritter rotates his liver-spotted neck in my direction, tracking my movements to my chair. He waits for an apology the same way my teachers waited senior year, knowing it would be bullshit but going through the motions to maintain some air of authority.

"I'm sorry," I say, searching for an unused excuse. "My dog threw up everywhere. I had to clean the carpet. I didn't want to leave it soaking."

"It won't happen again, I hope."

"I hope not, sir."

He clears his throat like a busted, rattling lawnmower and continues where I interrupted. I pretend to listen, but I have his speech memorized. It hasn't changed since he hired me. *I have a good feeling about today. This segment is going to put us on the map. We have the talent. We just need the views. Don't worry, we'll get there. These things take a while.* His morning pep talks lack practical, real-world advice. Our director is the one who supplies actual pointers, compliments, and criticisms. He plays the part of a boss. Mr. Ritter only holds the title.

When he shuffles into his broom closet office, shoulders loosen. Chairs tilt onto back legs. A wobbling line forms for food. I slather a bagel with cream cheese and chew the halves separately to trick my stomach into feeling full.

"I'm guessing everybody saw the commercial by now?" Harper, our female cohost, asks. "It comes up before literally every video I try to watch. It's like a goddamn virus. Imagine if we had that kind of advertising money here? We wouldn't be eating in a room where chicks used to get their anuses bleached, that's for damn sure."

"Maybe we could try to get that inventor lady on our show," her twin brother says as he shakes cereal into his mouth. Crumbs spit when he speaks.

Harper balls up a napkin and lugs it at him. "When has Ritter ever booked someone under sixty? He only cares about old hacks he grew up watching. Or their wannabe famous grandkids. Anybody who matters doesn't matter to him."

The table murmurs in agreement. Ritter treats our web series like an old-fashioned cable show. He doesn't understand algorithms or SEO, and he won't let anyone explain it to him. Every month or so, rumors about someone quitting circulate, but it never amounts to anything. He took a risk by hiring inexperienced college dropouts. If we put in our two weeks, no other program would hire us.

"If you want to talk badly about the man letting you eat breakfast on the clock, not to mention paying for your breakfast in the first place, do it outside of these walls please. It's disrespectful," our director, Cassidy, says. "In any case, I talked to Mr. Ritter about interviewing the Endellion woman. It took the whole weekend, but he budged. I sent some emails and made some calls, but I haven't been able to get ahold of her yet."

"I bet she isn't doing interviews," our makeup artist says. "I haven't seen her anywhere except that commercial, and every news station has been obsessing over her."

Our wardrobe woman shrugs. "I don't know. It's free money and free promo. She might as well take it. It's only been a few days. Maybe she's getting ready to do the rounds. She could be waiting for the swelling to die down on a new facelift."

"She's not old enough for a facelift," I say. "I went to high school with her. She was only a year ahead of me."

Faces whip in my direction, eyes squinted, brows sewn.

"Call her up," someone says. "Get her on."

I suck cream cheese from a finger. "We aren't friends or anything. I've never spoken to her."

The table lobs questions anyway. *What was she like? Where did she go to college? Is she married? Where is she living now?*

"Jesus, she said she doesn't know," Harper says. She slaps the table to shove herself up. "I'm going to practice my monologue. I want to get it memorized before the guest crutches his way in here."

Cassidy nods. "She has the right idea, fellas. We should start setting up. Take your last bites."

Wrappers crinkle. Knapsacks zip. The twins climb onto our sad excuse for a stage, set up where women in masks once applied acrylics. I veer toward my broken-legged tripod, mount the camera, detach the lens cap, and crank the handle until both the twins fit in frame.

Mr. Ritter recruited them for our premier season, same as me. He scavenged Harper from outside a casting house, mascara leaking into her mouth, one cutlet missing from her bra, screaming lines from a script rolled in her hand. She pounded at the locked door for a second chance and Ritter gave her a new one. When he heard she had a twin, he decided it would be the perfect gimmick.

He found me with a similar method, strolling city streets. He crashed an engagement shoot on the tiered steps of a museum and offered me a job on the spot. I hated freelancing, hated shooting storybook pictures of couples who bickered behind the scenes, but I still turned him down. Train tickets cost too much to work in NYC full-time.

"No, no, I'm looking to build a studio somewhere more affordable," he said. "Maybe in Jersey or on the island. Nothing is set in stone." I mentioned the battered, abandoned nail salon with an AVAILABLE FOR RENT sign near my apartment. I never actually expected him to look into it.

Ritter collected every single person on our crew like strays, rescuing us from rock-bottom. He spent fifty years working social services, trying to break into filmmaking on the side. When the internet gave him an opportunity to build a series from scratch and start a new life, he had trouble leaving the old one behind.

"Ariadna, can we have a quick chat?" Cassidy says, yanking me back to the present. He strides over, blond hair swishing. The split ends reach his chin. "I realize this is outside of your job description, so you're allowed to shoot me right down, but do you think you can try to contact Rhea Laman? Just to see? I'm sure you've picked up on how much the crew has been struggling. This job feels more like an internship sometimes, with how small the paychecks come out to be." He drops to a whisper. "I caught Mr. Ritter sleeping here the other night. I think that's why he caved about Laman. I think he's starting to get it. We need to do something differently."

He has a point. Harper wore sunglasses on camera for two weeks in a row, too broke to fill her pink-eye prescription. Her brother collapsed from heat exhaustion another week when his engine died and he biked to work. Everyone on set could tell a similar story. Everyone could use some extra cash.

"I don't want to pressure you, but a bump in pay would really help me, too," Cassidy says, strumming the ponytail holder on his wrist. "I haven't mentioned anything to the rest of the crew, but my lady is pregnant again. That makes three. We're doing okay now, but diaper prices are worse than gas, so there's a chance we'll be sending our next holiday card from a box by the river."

"Congrats and everything, but I really don't think I'd be much help. Laman doesn't know who I am. I doubt she'd answer me."

"There's always a chance." He gathers his hair in a bun, wrapping and rewrapping the elastic. "I've seen your posts. I know you're against the resort. I'm not nuts about it, either. An interview with the founder doesn't mean we're supporting her company. The more exposure she gets, the bigger chance she'll slip up and say something that screws her, right? We could be the reason her place gets shut down. We could absolutely annihilate the poor woman."

*

I spend my lunch break combing through the internet. Search engines cough up articles on awards Rhea Laman won. An image search pulls up professional photography from press conferences and Photoshopped memes from her commercial. I mine through pages upon pages of fan-made accounts without finding any personal accounts.

When I hit the end of her search results, I switch tactics. I log onto my own social media to message discarded friends from high school, hoping to bum her phone number. Some squeal about how excited they are to hear from me. Others call me out on requesting a favor after a decade of dodging group texts and party invites. Not one person knows Laman personally.

I hunt through my friend list for someone her age who could have had classes with her. I double click on Marzia Moretti, my sister's best friend. She sat cross-legged on our living room rug, doodling on the backside of homework packets, until a baby bump raised her T-shirts. Judging by her profile photo, she squeezed out three more. They cling to her torso like leeches.

I send her a copied and pasted message: "Hey, I know it's been a while since we've talked, but I'm trying to get in touch with Rhea Laman. Any chance you have her contact information? Thanks."

Three dots pop onto her side of the chat box, then vanish. I stare at the screen until it dims from inactivity. She must have changed her mind about answering, which doesn't surprise me. We only hung out one-on-one once, the night of the funeral.

When I showed up at her double-wide red-nosed and red-eyed, her grandfather volunteered to babysit. He juggled sippy cups while we drank straight from our own bottle: a cheap, cloudy vodka. The alcohol convinced us to invite over her junkie cousin who had been apprenticing at a tattoo parlor.

Marzia sketched out a turtle for him to copy onto her seashell-white thigh. I requested a domino, an ant-sized one tucked behind my ear. I planned on draping my hair over it, concealing it from prying teachers and parents, but Marzia improvised with a more elaborate design. Three dominos toppling onto each other, mid-fall. It held too much detail to wedge behind an earlobe. It made more sense on a wrist.

My parents eyed the marks peeking from my sleeve at the church service, but instead of delving into a lecture, they dove for tissues. When they saw the turtle on Marzia in her inappropriate, crotch-high dress, they cried even harder.

Her reply pings onto my screen after work hours, after the twins interview an ancient, doughy comedian who treats every woman on set like an assistant.

"Here you go," her message says along with an email link underlined in blue. "I'm not sure if it's the same still. I did a project with her once in, like, middle school. She's probably changed it by now. And Ari, I know it's not my place to tell you what to do, especially with my track record, but it's probably better to leave the past in the past at this point. I don't think you two need to talk. Not after so long. It's not going to help either of you."

She writes in shorthand, tightening words to numbers. I reread her message twice, thinking I missed something.

"I work for an entertainment program," I type back. "We're trying to land an interview with Laman to talk about her company. What do you mean about leaving the past in the past? Did you and Dominique hang out with her or something?"

I wait for the dot-dot-dot. When it doesn't appear, I check her profile. An error message pops onto the screen. *User not available.* I refresh the page in case it's a glitch, but the message repeats.

She blocked me.

I switch to the tab I used to research Laman and change the search name to Marzia Moretti. Local news sites mention her in reports about DUIs and domestic disturbances, but every social media account is locked, set to private. Without a backup way of contacting her, I shrug away my questions. At least she gave me an email.

I drop the address in a blank document and down a cheap beer before writing out whatever jumps into my head. I type sentimental crap like, "It would be an honor to feature you on our web series since we share an alma mater. We share a hometown. We share a history." I consider name-dropping my sister, but if their relationship ended on bad terms, it might sway her the wrong way.

I smack SEND without bothering to spell-check. The email leaves my inbox with a swoosh.

I tuck away my phone, set on continuing my productive streak. I should haul laundry to the ground floor. I should rinse leg hair from the shower drain. I should scrub dishes, vacuum fur, restock groceries.

Arrow curls on my lap, rearranging my plans. I turn on the television and mute the sound to avoid disturbing his nap. A rerun of *Conspiracy Theory Theater* plays with captions at the bottom, narrated by the original host. My father used to mock the rubber bands tangled in his beard, the aviation cap tied across his chin. He hated the show as much as my sister, but he was much more vocal about it. She let me enjoy my trash TV in peace.

As the episode transitions to a commercial break, my phone shivers with an alert. I intend to check my email, but my mother's contact photo spans my screen. I count out the days since our last conversation. Over a week. Guilt drives me to answer.

"Hey there. Sorry for missing you yesterday," I say.

"You aren't getting any service in that teeny apartment, are you? These phone companies should stop worrying about making screens you can unlock with your face and remember the main purpose is putting calls through. What if it was an emergency?" She clucks her tongue. "Anywho. You have to stop over for a visit. Tomorrow. Or this weekend at the latest, but that's so far away."

It only takes ten minutes to drive to the red stone ranch my mother inherited from her mother. I pass the exit on the way to the studio each morning but avoid making the turn more than once a month.

"Why do you want me over?" I ask. "Is Dad doing okay?"

"More than okay. He has a new set of wheels. You can see them when you visit. And then we could plan out the vacation I mentioned. I did a little digging and found an old letter from Rhea Laman this morning. She must have passed notes with Domino during class or slipped them through her locker like in the olden days. Isn't that funny? Someone who works with fancy computers for a living wrote with a pen instead of sending a text?"

It was funny. Aside from the warning at graduation, my sister never gave any indication of knowing Laman. Her teammates charred marshmallows and hot dogs in our fire pit each summer. Marzia smelled up our bathroom and raided our tampon boxes. Our parents gave us free rein to invite friends over any day, any hour, but Laman never made an appearance.

"Are you sure it's from the same lady?" I ask.

"It must be. It looks like it's ripped from a personalized notebook. It has R-H-E-A printed on the side margins. I've never seen anyone else spell the name like that, only R-A-Y. And that's usually boys. This is definitely girl handwriting. It's written in purple."

"How did you even remember who she was? I was the one who saw her in the halls and couldn't figure it out. Not until you said something."

"It bothered me, how familiar she looked. I flipped through old yearbooks and scrapbooks until I put two and two together. The ones your father took during the graduation ceremony are a little blurry, but the ones you took afterward are beautiful. Really, honey, you should go back to doing engagement photos. Or newborn photos. You could make extra money on the side. And it would give you a reason to get out of that stuffy apartment."

Arrow must sense me tense because he hops from my lap. "What does the note say?"

"I don't have it memorized. I would have to find my reading glasses. It was something sweet. Something about how much they trust each other. Anywho, just let me know when you're coming. I need to know when to cook extra. I'll make chicken. Your favorite."

Arrow paws at the door. I fetch his leash from the counter and hook it onto his collar. "I guess tomorrow works," I say. Dropping by her house after work means a much shorter stay than a weekend visit.

"Wonderful. Make sure you bring the pup. I hear him crying. It's probably because he misses me."

"He misses peeing."

Arrow tugs me downstairs, into a drooping garden scattered with wood chips. Like usual, he ignores the DESIGNATED PET RELIEF AREA, a brittle patch at the back of the complex hopping with ticks.

After he relieves himself, he points his snout toward the sidewalk. I give him enough slack to pull me wherever he pleases while my mother rambles into my ear about bake sales and firehouse fundraisers. I exist on autopilot, mhming and walking, mhming and walking, just trying to survive another day.

CHAPTER 3

Arrow crunches across the driveway, crosses over chipped red step-ping stones, and sniffs at a rabbit statue with gardening gloves. He reacquaints himself with the rest of the plastic lawn ornaments while I scale the concrete ramp to the patio. I wipe my feet as a courtesy, buzz the doorbell as a formality. My mother leaves locks unlatched and windows yawning wide like nothing bad has ever happened to her.

Inside, it looks like a poltergeist has thrust all the furniture against the walls. A futon leaks stuffing in one corner. An emptied wine cabinet collects dust in another. In between, sweatshirts and boxers sag over an untouched treadmill. The empty space in the center gives my mother room to maneuver my father. He slumps in front of the crackling fireplace, fac-ing my sister. One in an urn and the other in a wheelchair.

"Hey, it's me, Ari," I say, knowing he isn't going to speak, turn, or smile. The specialists claim his brain still shows signs of activity, but his arms dangle limp like his jaw. His lips only move when he sucks juice from a straw.

My mother sweeps into the room covered in cooking grease. She drapes an arm around me in a one-sided hug and drops a lipstick kiss on my temple. Arrow leaps at her knees, barking.

"See? I knew he missed me," she says. She pulls a strip of breaded chicken from her apron pocket. He gobbles it and licks her palm for crumbs.

"How did you afford a new chair?" I ask, motioning toward my father. The leather headrest stinks like a bachelor pad. An oxygen tank attached to the back pumps air into his nostrils.

"I put together all the lottery money I'm going to win one day." She chuckles as she cracks the screen door for Arrow. He scampers into the backyard, tail whipping. "Take off your shoes, honey. Relax. You must be hungry for a homemade meal. What's the last thing you ate from an oven instead of warming it to rubber in the microwave?"

I stomp to the fridge without removing my sandals. Its doors are plastered in location magnets. The Grand Canyon. Niagara Falls. Disney World. The Hoover Dam. Vacation pictures are pinned beneath each one. I avert my eyes, swing open the doors, and grab a chilled bottle of wine.

"Don't overflow it," she says, watching me pour. "You drove here."

I carry the glass to my reserved dining seat, the same one since childhood. It wiggles and groans with my weight. The wood on the right leg split months ago, but it feels wrong to steal my sister's chair, and my father's chair has disappeared now that he has a permanent seat attached.

"You know, wine isn't as healthy as everyone likes to pretend it is," my mother says as she simmers peppers on the stove. "You should thank your father for passing down his metabolism. You have no right to look that gorgeous. Me, on the other hand? I'm going to have to join a gym before our vacation. I might not sunbathe, but I'm planning to wear some awfully cute sundresses."

"We're not going on vacation. I can't take off work. And you can't afford a nurse for that long."

"Who needs a nurse? Your aunts are here every week, taking care of your father. They're happy to help me get out of the house, mainly because it means getting out of *their* houses. You know, I bet we could get some incredible pictures on that island. Rhea really outdid herself. I bet Domino would be proud."

"How do you know they were friends? I don't remember them hanging out."

"I think they were friends of friends. She dated Antoni Tan. They might have met through him."

I pause with the wineglass halfway to my mouth. "She dated Antoni Tan?"

She nods nonchalantly, like it makes no difference, like she forgot Antoni was the last person my sister texted before killing herself.

I was the one who found her. All because I couldn't fall asleep that night. My therapist had recommended rubbing lavender lotion onto my wrists as a form of aromatherapy, so I tore apart the bathroom searching for the tube. I couldn't find it in the medicine cabinet, the shower caddy, or the drawers beneath the sink. Domino had complained about sleep trouble earlier in the day, so I assumed she'd borrowed it.

I nudged her door and skimmed a hand over her dresser. I bumped against trophies, medals, and first-place ribbons, but no lotion. Annoyed, I activated the torch on my phone and swept the light across her nightstand and shelves. Still nothing. I tried shining the light onto her pillows to wake her, but a dangling lump of clothes blocked my view. It took a heartbeat to process that the lump was Domino.

I staggered toward her, wrestled her down, and flipped her onto her back. The belt tethering her to the ceiling fan ripped in the process, but a piece stayed wrapped around her like a choker. I untied it and hammered her chest, searching for a thrum in her neck, a flutter in her chest. I whispered her name. I screamed her name. Each second crawled.

When my parents overheard and rushed into the room, the world bumped up to double speed. Everything moved fast. Too fast. Paramedics screeched to our curb, loaded my sister into a gurney, and left us standing helpless in the driveway.

Our neighbors crept onto our property, woken by the blazing lights. My mother fell into someone's arms. My father swung at someone else for *getting off on our grief.* I wandered away as more someones broke up the fight.

Curiosity drew me straight back to my sister's room. I powered on her phone and read through her texts in search of an explanation. Most of her messages were ordinary, unalarming. Aside from the one addressed to Antoni Tan.

It said: "I hope you know this is entirely your fault. I hope you spend the rest of your life blaming yourself for this. I hope what I'm doing makes it clear that I don't love you and never have."

"Who told you Rhea Laman dated Antoni Tan?" I ask my mother, clutching my wineglass tight enough to crack the stem.

"Dated might have been the wrong word. It might have been casual. They might have been together for a few days or they could still be together now. I'm really not sure."

"Who told you?"

She stretches out a long, huffing sigh, like she doesn't want to have the conversation. "Antoni knocked at our door the night before the funeral. While you were getting your tattoo. He was dropping off a fruit basket from his mother. I asked him about the text while I had him in front of me. He acted like he had no idea what I was talking about. I figured he was lying because he was scared of getting in trouble. I didn't blame him. We didn't talk long, but he seemed like a sweet kid. He was polite. He probably turned down a date with Domino or teased her or went *far* with her and then moved onto another girl. You know, typical teenage drama. I'm not saying it's right, but I didn't get the feeling he hurt her any worse than that. Otherwise, I would have called your father outside to deal with him."

"You should have told me."

"I did. It was a blackout night. I guess you don't remember."

Silence crashes over us. Neither of us says a word as she transfers steaming food onto floral plates she once saved for special occasions. She places one beside my wine and one beside her fizzing soda. I stab my fork into the chicken but don't move it toward my mouth, my appetite lost, my thoughts spinning.

After reading the text my sister sent to Antoni Tan, I stalked him on social media. Half his dark, out-of-focus photos showed him smoking joints at backyard parties. The other half were mirror selfies in a plain black shirt, snug against his muscles. I recognized the red and white name tag clipped to the uniform. Ushers wore them at the cinema down the block, the one with stale popcorn and watery raspberry slushies.

I ordered a ticket online, drank to ease my nerves, and kept drinking until my ticket expired. Over the next month, I wasted hundreds on unwatched movies, unscanned barcodes.

When I finally stayed sober long enough to visit the theater, Antoni wasn't working the register, scooping popcorn, or sweeping kernels. I asked the manager when he would be in for his next shift, but she told me my guess was as good as hers. "His parents don't know where he went, neither," she said. "They filed a report, but the police have been calling him a runaway, saying he took off with his girlfriend. If you ask me, though, I wouldn't be surprised if he was keeled over in a crack house right now."

It made me rest easier, thinking he might be dead, too. I convinced myself it was the truth and stopped looking for him.

"I don't want to argue," my mother says, bringing me back to the present. "We're always bickering about the silliest things. This is why I want to visit the resort. I want to have a nice, relaxing vacation together. I want us to get along like when you were little."

"And in order for that to happen, my mind needs to be wiped, right? I have to act like a completely different person?"

"The surgery might make you a little less stressed. A little more upbeat. That shouldn't be a bad thing."

I empty my wine with another gulp. "That place is like popping magical diet pills instead of hopping on a treadmill. It wasn't built to help anyone. It was built to exploit sad, lonely people. Addicts. Divorcees. Widows. Everyone who's excited about Endellion thinks they're going to get closure there, but they have to learn to accept their pain like anybody else. That's part of life."

"Fun should be a part of life, too, don't you think?" She fishes in her apron, pulls out a torn slip of paper, and slides it in front of me like a bribe. "This is what I told you about over the phone. After the commercial came on, I looked through an old yearbook to see if Rhea signed one of the pages. I couldn't find her name anywhere, but I found this letter stuffed into the creases. Your sister was clearly close with her. It feels like a sign we should go to the resort, a sign from Domino. She's trying to tell us something. I know it."

I'm about to spit out something sarcastic about believing in signs, but the water in her eyes shuts me up. I cram the note into my pocket, crumpling it behind my cell phone. "I'll think about it, okay? Maybe we can visit someday. Probably not this summer, but maybe next year."

"Thank you," she says, but we both know it's a lie.

*

Back at the apartment, Arrow snoozes on his pillow, overtired from chasing squirrels. His nose twitches in a dream. His back legs kick against my thigh.

I'm not tired enough to sleep myself, so I scroll through my clogged email. It's piled with cable bills, BOGO deals, and pizzeria coupons. I nearly skip over a reply from the official Endellion account. My message must have been forwarded for an assistant to handle.

"Thank you for contacting Endellion Enterprises," it says atop a watermark of an umbrella. "Unfortunately, our staff is not available for interviews with the press. However, in the interest of supplying the media with sufficient information to spread to their viewers, we are running one-on-one tours of select areas of our premises. You will be guided by Rhea Laman, our accomplished owner and the inventor of Memory Cleansing. See the attached document for directions, our dress code, and your assigned appointment time. We look forward to having you."

I double-click the downloads and scan the details. No weapons. No flash photography. No recording devices.

According to an app on my phone, the drive would cost at least fifty, sixty bucks in gas. I doubt the trip would be worth the trouble, especially since the appointment isn't scheduled for another two months. People would lose interest by then. Her island would be old news, irrelevant.

"That's not true," Cassidy would say. I imagine him as the devil on my shoulder, poking a pitchfork into my excuses. "This technology is invention-of-the-internet big. Rhea Laman is going to be in history books right next to Steve Jobs and Elon Musk. And you have a chance to talk to her. In person. One conversation could change the lives of everyone on set."

I think of Mr. Ritter pumping air into a blue, bubbled mattress. Harper rubbing a swollen, pus-filled eye. Her brother collapsing in the parking lot. Dominique, still in her graduation gown, grumbling about how she wants to forget Rhea Laman exists.

I tug the crumpled note from my pocket and flatten it against my lap. Purple gelled words scrunch together. The ink bleeds from one letter to the next. The message, faded and smudged, says:

"The meeting is the night after graduation. Please come, Domino. I know you're not happy with me right now, but you can trust me. You've trusted me with the biggest secret in the world for four years now. I've never said anything, right? I've never broken my promise. I understand I made a mistake, but I hope you can forgive me for it. I hope things can go back to normal soon."

I wonder what kind of mental gymnastics my mother had to put herself through to consider the note *sweet*. It sounded more *whiny* to me.

The biggest secret in the world must have been a reference to the cabin, the one my sister visited behind our backs. She used to sling a duffel bag across her chest and lie about meeting her teammates for volleyball practice, when really, she snuck into a cabin on the beach known for its drug dealings.

After her suicide, I found a stack of hundreds hidden in her dresser drawer, more money than she could have earned making minimum wage at the library. To protect our parents from the truth, I relocated the stash to my own drawers and rationed it for alcohol. My father had already been hysterical enough and my mother had romanticized the story of Domino dying over her heartbreak. I didn't want to mess with their mourning process. I didn't want to explain how Antoni Tan wasn't some secret lover or unrequited crush. He was a stoner, a druggie. He must have helped Domino deal weed, pills, and powder. He must have gotten her involved in the wrong line of work, introduced her to the wrong people, and she killed herself because of it.

I can't picture someone like Rhea Laman smoking weed, but she might have popped pills to stay awake and study for exams. If she was a customer at the cabin, it made sense she knew my sister's big secret.

I reread her note to test the theory and snag on a familiar word, one I originally overlooked out of habit. *Domino*. My fingers tense. My thumb digs into the paper, piercing a slit through the center.

I invented the nickname by accident. In elementary school, my sister beat me at every game in our football-shaped toy chest. Guess Who. Trouble. Sorry. Life. Dominos were the only exception. Our mother taught us a basic, kid-friendly version where players matched tiles based on the number of dots. It involved more luck than strategy, but somehow, I won every match and rematch.

Losing to someone as incompetent as me drove my sister crazy, so I hid dominos around the house to taunt her. I stuffed them into her dollhouses.

I jammed them into her backpack. I slipped them into her sea turtle lunch box and matching pencil case. She chased me around the house whenever she discovered another one while I sang, "Dominique hates dominos, Dominique hates dominos." Somewhere along the line, the words fused and shifted into nickname territory.

My father scribbled *Domino* on gift tags. My mother swirled it onto birthday cakes with thick, rainbow icing. All three of us programmed it as her contact name on our phones, but we had an unspoken agreement to stick to her birth name in public. We didn't want it overheard at school and catching on. We wanted to save her from embarrassment. Or maybe we wanted to save the nickname for ourselves, reserve it as a family tradition.

My sister, on the other hand, whined about the joke since its inception. She wouldn't have leaked the story to any old person, let alone given them permission to adopt the nickname. She would only tell someone she trusted. Someone she considered family, too.

CHAPTER 4

The two months leading up to the tour are bland, uneventful, excruciatingly average. Aside from the smattering of research I do about the island, my routine stays the same. I film crotchety old stars who refuse to retire. I get guilt-tripped into having dinner with my mother. I circle the dog around the block, letting him lead the way.

Cassidy and I decide to keep quiet about the tour to avoid raising hopes at the studio. I refrain from telling my mother as well, worried she might try to tag along. I keep it vague when I ask her to dog-sit while I spend an evening out of town for work. I offer to duplicate my apartment key, but she volunteers to watch Arrow at her house, which is a relief. Dropping him off works better for both of us. She won't be exposed to the sour milk stinking up my fridge or the rust rings around my toilet bowl. And I won't be exposed to her criticisms about it all.

"How much more is there?" she asks as she helps me unload luggage. "You pack like the end of the world is coming."

I heave a sack of kibble from my popped trunk and add it to the pile on the porch. "Hey, I'm not the only one who spoils him. I know you're going to be sneaking him snacks tonight."

"That might happen. But I'm not going to buy him his own wardrobe."

"I only packed his rubber boots in case it rains. He doesn't like to get wet."

"What about all his other clothes at your place? The sailor hat? The tuxedo?"

"They boost his confidence. He deserves to feel as cute as he looks."

She chuckles the whole way into the house. "He's a spoiled little thing. I can only imagine what you would be like as a mother. You would buy out the toy store."

My smile slumps to a flat line.

"I'm only teasing. I didn't mean anything by it, honey."

"I know." A pause. "I can handle the rest. You shouldn't be lifting weight anyway, with your knees."

"Don't be silly. Your father's oxygen tanks are much heavier than this."

"I'm almost done. I've got it."

"Okay. If you're sure…"

She retreats to the backyard with a whistle. Arrow pads after her to play while I deal with the stack on the porch. I don't want to drop boxes in the living room or kitchen where they would be a wheelchair hazard, so I ferry them to my old room.

I stripped the place bare when I moved into my apartment, not wanting to waste money on a new bed frame or nightstand. My mother loaded the space right up again, mutating it into an oversized junk drawer. Now she uses it to store extra tanks and medical kits, empty canvases and half-finished blankets. I spot my old jewelry-making kit amongst the mess, packed with plastic beads and rainbow strings. One birthday, I weaved the materials into a best friend bracelet for my sister.

I can see her sealed door through my gaping one. My mother moved a few things around after the funeral, but the old layout is seared into my memory. Domino taped overlapping band posters to her ceiling. She carved stars into her bedpost with a pocketknife. She hung a dry erase calendar over her headboard to count down the days until a tattoo appointment she ended up missing.

My father harped on that detail for a month. He dialed the police station night after night, adamant they were wrong about her cause of death. "Dominique was talking about getting this damn turtle tattoo since she learned to shit," I overheard him saying once. "She picked out the design when she was twelve, picked out the artist when she was fifteen. She bugged this real fancy artist to schedule her for months. Months. He does the singers on her walls, girls with their whole bodies covered. My daughter wouldn't have killed herself two weeks before that appointment. You've got to look into this more. She just wouldn't have done it."

I rub circles over my own tattoo, tracing the dominos. Arrow must sense my shift in mood because he scampers into the room, plops beside me, and licks my cheek. Drool rolls onto my chin.

"I'm sorry, buddy, but I need to get the hell out of here." I scratch him behind the ear. "I won't be gone for too long, okay? I'll try to make the drive back tonight. Worst case, I'll sleep in my car and be back by morning."

I kiss his snout and tell him I love him. I leave without telling my mother the same.

*

My phone's GPS guides me around hometown landmarks. An aviation museum. An apple orchard. An aquarium. As the miles slip beneath my tires, the scenery transitions from miles of beach to miles of forests to miles of farmland. There are strips of sand and firework pops one second. There are heaps of hay and gun pops the next.

According to my email, the resort sits on an artificial island halfway between the tip of Long Island and Rhode Island, but there aren't any bridges listed along my planned route. The address must be directing me to a dock.

Once I hit the highway, the drive is mostly a straight line. I pass the exit for the ferry my crew once took to Connecticut for a special taping. The exit for the skydiving center where Domino celebrated her eighteenth birthday. The exit for the animal rescue where I adopted Arrow.

Throughout the drive, hot air sputters from my AC. My side window gets jammed in the closed position. And my radio fails to pick up a signal. My CD player is about the only thing that works, so I replay a rock album caught in the slot. The same songs repeat, over and over, like I'm caught in a time loop.

I reach my destination ahead of schedule. My car crawls beneath a massive Endellion billboard with a leg on each side of the pavement. The shrubs running alongside the private road are trimmed into the shape of umbrellas.

The street ends in a barricade that blocks my way to an underground parking garage. I ease to a stop, expecting a guard perched in a booth to check my ID, but the station is automated.

I follow onscreen instructions, inputting a confirmation number from my email. A slot sucks my license. A flash captures my stare. When a dispenser rolls open, I cast a hand into the compartment. I retrieve a thin, flexible screen with four loops hanging off the side.

I cram the device in my pocket and drive down an incline, creeping underground. The parking garage spirals and spirals, spitting me out in a sprawling, multi-tiered hall. Floodlights dangle from the ceiling like tonsils. Columns stretch toward the ceiling like fangs. A shiver works its way through my spine.

I park in a spot reserved for guests and swipe my flask from the center console. The scotch toasts my stomach, frying the butterflies.

I shove my handbag beneath the passenger seat and stuff the essentials into my A-cup. My phone and car key.

Spray-painted footprints cut me through the employee section. Their cars belong in the junkyard along with mine. Bumpers hang loose. Cracks stretch across windshields. Key scratches carve swears into paint.

Surprised, I snap a quick photo on my phone. With the prices Endellion charges, workers should be cruising around in Mercedes and G-Wagons. Underpaying employees could be the start of a story for *Twins Spilling Tea*.

I follow the chain of footprints to an airport-style metal detector. A glass elevator waits on the opposite side. I step into the machine and extend my arms over my head, matching the diagram on an overhanging instructional sign. The motor purrs as it completes a full-body scan. Convinced there aren't any recording equipment or weapons concealed beneath my clothing, the elevator splits its doors.

I advance into the chamber. The smooth, curved interior warps my reflection. It elongates my forehead. It sharpens my jaw. It turns me into the spitting image of my sister.

Domino only looked older on paper. A growth spurt shot me to her height early and both our chests got stuck at training-bra size. We had the same hair color, skin color, eye color. We shared practically every feature, down to the birthmark on our right hip.

"I'm sick of everyone thinking we're twins," Domino said the summer before high school. "Do you know how embarrassing it is being compared to a middle schooler?"

She spent the season rebranding herself. She replaced her pastel pink dresses with dark crop tops, leather skirts, and chokers. She dyed the tips of her hair blue from a box kit and snipped lopsided, emo bangs. She poured every cent of allowance into looking like a new person, but our relatives still jumbled our names when they caught us from behind. Some of them continued to use the wrong name after the funeral. I chopped my hair to a pixie so they never made the mistake again.

The elevator dings. I step into a bleach-scented lobby with white chandeliers, white walls, white tiles, and a curved white desk. The only color comes from 3D block letters stretched across the back wall, spelling out *Endellion Resorts*. Each letter doubles as a screen. They work together to form a large, cohesive video clip of the island.

I exit the elevator, taking in the rest of my surroundings. A wide hall on my left leads toward bathrooms, a waiting area, and a gift shop. The hall on my right is sealed with glass. The doors on the restricted side are marked differently, with caricatures instead of words. A tap-dancing brain with a top hat. A drowsy brain in a nightcap. A winged brain with a halo.

The receptionist calls out from his semicircle desk. "Excuse me. Miss? Do you need help?"

I wander over and tap my nails on the tabletop. "I was given this address for a tour of the island, but this clearly isn't an island and I don't see any boats ready to whisk me away."

"This is the check-in building where Memory Cleansings are performed," he says. He wets his chalky mouth, discolored from lip balm. "The actual resort is only accessible by submarine."

"Submarine?"

"If we built a bridge to the island, unauthorized visitors would be able to access the land illegally. We had the same worries with cruise ships, speed boats, kayaks, *et cetera*. So we constructed a barrier around the premises. This way, the island is only accessible by diving beneath and passing through a small opening which would be difficult for trespassers to locate on their own. This worked out for the best all around. Without a visible bridge, it gives our guests the impression they're truly alone, far away from the problems of the real world. I know submarines don't sound as cozy as cruise ships, Ariadna, but guests are asleep when they're transported to the island, so safety is our main concern."

I stop tapping. "Who told you my name?"

He rotates his wrist, facing his knuckles toward me. The device strapped to the back of his hand is the same as the one in my pocket, the one dispensed from the machine. His screen displays my miniature mugshot paired with my personal info.

"Your security pass relays your data when you come within a certain distance. It's the same pass used on the island to open resort doors and make purchases. I'm sure Miss Laman will explain more. You can help yourself to coffee in our waiting area until she arrives. It's the first room on your left."

I nod a *thank you* and head where he pointed me. Through the propped door, a man snores in a hardback chair. A woman fingers a true-crime novel, sloppily licking her thumb between pages. A tween pokes at a beeping, buzzing handheld game. A toddler feasts on a wad of snot.

No thanks. I continue down the hall, stopping every few steps to read screens planted between doorways. They resemble bulletin boards, pinned with digital postcards from past guests. One says, "Thanks for bringing my family back together. Endellion reminded us how much we missed each other. We're never going to let some silly fight get in between us again." Another says, "I never thought I could stand a full week with my mother-in-law, but Endellion proved me wrong. This place might have saved my marriage!"

The hall ends in a gift shop. Unlike the lobby, the walls are a mishmash of color. One section is streaked red, then orange, then yellow, then green. Like the underside of a striped umbrella.

The cashier greets me with a stare, charting my movements between overpriced knickknacks. Magnets clutter a steel wall. Hats swing from hooks. Keychains, necklaces, and lanyards dangle limply from racks. For such a high-tech resort, they sell excruciatingly boring souvenirs. A company with the technology to alter memories should have the technology to create more advanced merch than a cow-print phone case. Just like they should have the technology to make a more cinematic commercial.

A door, painted blue, creaks behind the register. "I knew I heard someone out here," a black, bearded man says.

He holds the handle like an invitation, giving me a clear view of the interior. A padded love seat presses against a mosaic window. It faces a sleek leather armchair with a notebook on its cushion. In between, a coffee table holds a cardboard box of tissues.

"I'm sorry." The man does a double take at his security pass. He closes the door until it clicks. "I was expecting to meet with a family soon. Returning guests."

"I'm not a guest. I have a tour scheduled today."

His forehead furrows, but he blinks away the surprise. "How lucky. My parents keep asking to see the place in person. They're hoping to book a vacation next summer."

"They have to pay? That's not part of your employee perks?"

"Oh, I would never expect a free vacation. Endellion gives us more than enough. They provide an excellent benefits package."

I think of the crushed, chipped cars in the parking lot. "Do they really? For everyone? I would think surgeons make more than cashiers."

"I wouldn't know. I'm an in-house psychiatrist. I invite departing guests into my office to discuss their experience while the Memory Cleansing is in the process of wearing off."

"What does this place need a shrink for?"

"I provide families with a safe space to sort through their emotions. I also make sure their memories are fully restored before authorizing their departure."

"Does that mean people have had trouble getting their memories back?"

"Guests leave remembering their experience on the island along with all of their pre-island memories. Nothing is lost. Even if we didn't check in with them, they would leave healthy and happy. However, since we care deeply about every single person who stays with us, the submarines drop them at the docking station outside and they come directly to me. Just to be safe."

I glance at the purple doors saying: SUB EXIT ONLY. The floor plan forces guests to leave through the gift shop. Like a roller coaster exiting into specialty stores selling T-shirts and shot glasses bragging about the ride.

I quirk my eyebrow ring. "It seems pretty unprofessional to have a therapist attached to a gift shop."

"I disagree. It's the most convenient area for all parties. We only have one family scheduled to return per sub trip. And we don't normally run tours, so there isn't any overlap or eavesdropping. I could move my couch out here if needed. It's a pretty private space. Speaking of which, I'm going to have to ask you to…"

His attention trails along with his eyes. He locks onto something to our side, an incoming family entering from the courtyard. A teenager rolls a powder pink suitcase with a pom-pom luggage tag. A graying man, who must be her father, lugs three black duffel bags. A woman lags behind the pair like a sleepwalker. Her purse skims the ground, dangling from her flaccid hand.

The psychiatrist beelines for the woman. He rests a hand on her lower back, steering her toward his office. "I see you were the first to get the procedure. Come with me. Your husband can watch your daughter until they're ready to join us."

"I had such a nice stay," she says, faint as a whisper. "My daughter called me *mom* for the first time since elementary school. She usually uses my first name. It drives me up the wall. I'm not sure if I can go back to her hating me."

The thumping door smothers their conversation. Across the room, the father and daughter browse shelves, oblivious. The girl parks herself in front of a case of cell phone accessories, begging to buy two cases: one for her and one for her boyfriend.

"What do you think? Is getting rose gold for me and navy blue for him too predictable?" she asks. "Maybe I should get us both the marble? But then we might get our phones mixed up."

He laughs. "If it takes you this long to pick a case, we probably should have started looking at colleges in kindergarten."

She rotates the carousel, examining each rack. She unhooks cases, holds them up to the light, and hooks them back again. "You know what? I can't do it. You decide, Daddy. You're a guy. Which one would you want?" She runs a manicured hand through her highlights. "Wait. Do you want one, too? Maybe you and Mom can both get one. I bet she'd like the leopard one to match those shoes she always wears."

She continues rambling, completely oblivious as her father drops his duffel bags, as he doubles over, as his eyes roll to the whites. He steadies himself on a snack rack, gripping the space between taffy boxes and candy sticks, but not even the clatter makes her turn.

It takes noticeable effort, but he rights himself and says, "You're not getting anything. You're lucky you have a phone with how many you've broken."

Her head snaps sideways like he struck her.

My first thought is *that poor kid*. My second thought is *film her*. I left my recording equipment at home, but I crossed through the security checkpoint with my cell phone. I thrust a hand down my shirt, rooting for it. I have my fingers wrapped around the edges when someone says, "You must be Ariadna Diaz."

I swivel toward the hallway entrance, toward the blonde from the commercial. Her ponytail swishes along with her polyester jumpsuit. Her coffee cup reeks of vanilla. "I'm Rhea Laman," she says with her hand outstretched.

I pretend to scratch an itch on my collarbone as I slide my own hand out from my bra. "Nice to meet you. I'd say you look different on television, but it's pretty much the same. Much different than high school, though."

"So much has changed since then. But it's always a pleasure to see someone from my hometown." She eyes my ring as we shake. "When did you graduate?"

"I'm a year younger than you, but you could have had classes with my sister."

"You'll have to ask her if she remembers me. Now, come on, let's give you a tour worth bragging about back at home."

Her silver heels click toward the exit. I hesitate, sneaking a glance at the teenager. She has been mouse-quiet since the lecture, but now she stuffs a polka dot case into her rolling bag, security tag and all. She must have recovered her memories, returned to her old self.

Her father catches her zipping up merchandise and wrenches her arm with enough force to rip it out of the socket. I fight against the urge to record as she swears at him, swats at him, threatens to call CPS on him. If I get kicked out for taping, the guards would confiscate my footage. I would end up leaving without a tour *or* a video.

With tiny, reluctant steps, I follow Laman into the corridor. She escorts me through the whitewashed lobby and into the right-hand, restricted hallway. The glass parts when it senses her security band. Her staff reacts in the same mechanical way, bowing their heads like cult members.

"Since we're working with material as fragile as brain matter, we're extra cautious about contamination," Laman says at our first stop. "We would never want to risk the safety of our guests, some of which are getting their Memory Cleansings as we speak. Unfortunately, that means we can tell you about each room and show you exclusive, never-been-released pictures, but we can't grant you access inside."

Stock photos appear on her security pass as visual aids. Guests greeting their Memory Cleansing technician, smiling wide with digitally whitened teeth. Guests propped on surgical chairs, staring at computerized scans of their brain. Guests reclining in post-op rooms, tilting their heads back in sleep. The photographs all have one thing in common. They place much more emphasis on the posed, Photoshopped models than on any actual procedures.

Laman's explanations are just as vague. She either oversimplifies details without providing any real information (*this is the room where the magic happens*) or overcomplicates phrases until they're too technical to understand.

"I took off work for this," I say after a lengthy stream of psychobabble. "I drove hours to get here. I wasted gas money. And you've been showing me pictures you could have sent in an email attachment. It's a waste on my end. And yours, too. You run this place. I'm sure there are better ways you could be spending your shift."

"Ariadna, I apologize. If I'm being completely honest, you're one of the first few media personalities who have gotten a tour, so we haven't worked out the kinks yet." She cradles her chin in thought. The gesture seems as rehearsed as the photos. "I'm going to take you over to the island, but I do have one room you can explore first, if you would like. It's a few hallways away."

"Anything works."

She leads me through a labyrinth of halls labeled AUTHORIZED PERSONNEL ONLY. The walls are fixed with water fountains, hand-sanitizer dispensers, and employee-of-the-month plaques. The resort only opened eight weeks ago, but hundreds of names are inscribed on gold plates.

Endellion Enterprises must have been a company long before they opened the resort.

"I thought you were the boss around here," I say, studying the names. DAVID DAWSON repeats the most. "You must have been a kid when they opened."

"I'm the current head of Endellion Enterprises, but I'm not the founder. They existed before I was born. They used to be a private company. They got ahold of my grades and invited me to intern for them in high school."

"You've been here your whole life then." Toward the center, her name takes up several slots. Its last appearance is the month my sister died. "What happened in 2019?"

"I didn't get along with the old owners. I parted ways with them after graduation. But I missed the company. I bought them out a while back and finally took them public."

"Interesting. I never read anything about that."

She quiets, silently sipping her latte as we complete our walk. We stop at a door marked with a pink, cartoon brain wearing handcuffs. It parts down the center, granting us access to an immense oval room. A long, curving keyboard wraps around the perimeter. Rows upon rows of circular screens are embedded into the space above. A few are inactive, darkened to black. The rest display footage from different areas of the island. On one, an elderly couple plays tic-tac-toe in the sand with shells. On another, children run circles around a lifeguard tower.

"This is our main security center," Laman says. "These monitors can show me any angle of the island at any hour."

"It doesn't look like anyone is working in here."

"There's a better chance this technology will notice unauthorized activity than a human prone to daydreaming, texting, nodding off on the job. If the program catches anything unusual, it sends out an alert to our security personnel and someone will take care of it. We would rather have our staff situated on the island than cooped up here. It makes guests feel safer when they can see security walking around with them. Besides, I wouldn't want any guards having access to every single camera. That would be an invasion of privacy."

"But you can see everything whenever you want?"

"I can see everything when an emergency entails it."

She dumps her coffee, splays her fingers across a strip of keys, and punches numbers. The combination extends a metal arm, raising the monitor closest to me. The screen broadcasts a live, high-angle view of an Asian family. The mother bumps into the father on the boardwalk. He rubs his arm in pretend pain, breaking character with a grin. Their children, one with a buzzcut and one with green ribbons in her pigtails, suck on fudgsicles.

"This is the latest family who won an all-expenses-paid trip here," Laman says. "I'm sure you've heard about our invited guest program."

I nod. Anyone with internet access can complete a questionnaire and upload a video for a chance to win resort tickets. It works the same as reality-show auditions. Contestants sniffle into the lens, competing to tell the best sob story. Each week, Laman handpicks a household to exploit, and a camera crew piles onto their stoop to deliver the good news. At the end of their vacation, someone edits together a 'heartwarming' before-and-after video for the Endellion website. The internet eats it up.

"These parents are in the middle of a custody battle," Laman says. "She filed several police reports on him, accusing him of domestic abuse. He retaliated with allegations about her collecting unemployment checks with a fake disability. For months, the children have been shuffled between hotel rooms and trailer parks." She fiddles with another keyboard. The camera zooms into the dimples on the daughter, the smirk on the son. "Don't you think these children deserve a break? A family vacation without any arguments? A chance to see their mom and dad together instead of choosing between the two?"

"But only for a week."

"My parents are no longer with us, but you know what I would have given for one Christmas where they weren't bickering? A week is a while for two people like that to get along." With a final tap, the monitor retreats into its cove. "I'm guessing your parents are still happily married?"

"Thirty years this December."

"You've never been through a divorce, then. I'm happy to hear that. That's rare. What about a death? Have you ever lost an aunt, a cousin, a grandmother?"

I fiddle with my ear, twisting the lowest stud. I decided against mentioning Domino in my email, but that happened before I read the letter, before I realized their relationship ran deeper than strangers in the hall.

"The sister I mentioned earlier hung herself," I say, searching her face for a reaction. There isn't one.

"I'm so sorry to hear that."

"Her name was Dominique. Some people called her Domino."

"Losing her must have been awful for you."

She speaks in the gentle, generic way everyone does when they learn about my background. Either she's pretending not to know my sister, or she erased memories involving my sister. I'm not sure which is worse.

"She's the reason I don't understand why anyone who lost a family member would want to come here. They should be scared of forgetting. They should replay the past every night to keep it fresh. I would pay to have my memories of her saved forever, not erased. Screw that."

"No, no, you wouldn't forget she existed. You would forget she's dead. You could get a week off from crying. You could get a break from overanalyzing what you could have done differently to save her. You could get to live the way you would have if she was still alive. It's not all that different from binge drinking or stabbing a needle into a vein. The island is a safe alternative to those toxic, yet common coping mechanisms. What we're doing could reduce substance abuse."

"Or it could create a new kind of drug. One that customers would keep coming back and paying you thousands of dollars for."

She folds her arms. "My mother was an architect. My father was a surgeon. I could have lived comfortably on their inheritance. I chose to build Endellion Resorts because I believe in the cause. I poured all my money into this place because I want to help people. This was the riskier choice. I made it anyway."

"You're right about the risky part. What if the surgery kills brain cells? What if it leads to permanent memory loss? Or creates some new illness that doesn't exist yet?"

"The process isn't as invasive as you think. Memories are never removed from the brain. They can't be deleted from existence. They would need somewhere to go. Think about it this way. When patients are prescribed aspirin after breaking a bone, the medicine isn't going to heal their wound, but it isn't going to make their wound any worse. It's only going to ease the pain for a little while. Cleansings work the same way. They wear off after a week. There's no indication of long-term hippocampus damage. There's no signs of trauma."

"Fine. Maybe not physical trauma. But if someone thought their dead wife was alive for seven straight days and then found out they were a widower when the vacation was over, wouldn't that be like mourning all over again?"

"It's not any worse than waking from a nice dream and needing a second to remember where you really are. You're disappointed to wake up, but you're happy you were able to live in the dream for at least a little while."

"I saw what happened in the gift shop, Laman. That family was a mess. They didn't look *happy to live in the dream.* They looked miserable."

"Endellion didn't make them that way. They were returning to their natural state. In any case, our psychiatrist helps them sort out their feelings." She pokes at her security band with pink, stubby nails. "The family you witnessed should have written their review by now. We usually pare them down for commercial reasons, but you can read the unedited version. Here we are. Have a look."

She slants her screen toward me. The top post is written by the father. It says, "Me and my daughter have a lot of issues. We haven't gotten along since puberty started, but now I don't have to think back to her childhood to recall good memories. I have plenty of good memories from this vacation. Memories that remind us how much we love each other, despite all our arguments. Thank you, Endellion, for giving us a bonding experience we never would've gotten outside that island."

Underneath the post, his daughter rephrases the same sentiment. I read through her sappy, kiss-ass compliments about the resort but only make it through half of the mother's version. In the middle of reading, a notification eclipses the screen. A shrill beeping rings out.

Laman jerks her hand, silencing the alarm. "I didn't realize how late it was getting. Unfortunately, I'm going to have to end our tour here. I have to be on a plane in an hour. More big things are happening soon and happening fast."

"I thought you were going to show me the island. Wasn't that the whole point?" In reality, skipping the deep-sea sub ride is a relief, but I still need to ask her about *Twins Spilling Tea*. I still need to squeeze an interview out of her.

"I know. I apologize. This is highly unprofessional of me."

"No, no, it's cool, I get it. I can only imagine how busy you've been. That's probably why you haven't been doing any press. But my web series is flexible. We could sit down with you any day. Or we could do a video call if it's easier for you. You could do it from the airport or your hotel, wherever, we're not picky. I wouldn't be the one interviewing you, by the way, if you're worried about dealing with me again."

"Don't be silly. It was a pleasure talking with you, Ariadna, and I'm sure your show is lovely, but interviews aren't my priority right now. I've turned down every major network." She pauses in the same rehearsed way as earlier, rubbing her chin. "Of course, I don't want you to feel like you made the drive up here for nothing. How about we provide you with a room? You can vacation here for the week, skip the waiting list."

"I'm not interested in handing this place more money," I say as if I can afford a sparkling water from their vending machines, let alone a basic vacation package.

"I told you money isn't my concern. You're welcome to visit free of charge." She gives a tight-lipped, toothless smile. "Please. I insist. I think you'll change your mind about my work after getting acquainted with the island. You'll see how much good Endellion can do. Maybe you'll even find closure with your sister."

CHAPTER 5

I dial the studio, fingers crossed, hoping that Cassidy answers. His personal number is lost somewhere in a mass work text, unsaved. I never bothered to create a contact page for him or anyone else on the crew. We've shared surface-level stories over peanut butter lunches and wished each other a happy birthday on social media, but our friendship ends there.

He wouldn't know a single thing about me or my family history if it wasn't for an ex-stagehand. She selected my name during a mandatory Secret Santa and cyberstalked me for gift ideas. When she stumbled across an old article, FATHER ATTEMPTS COPYCAT SUICIDE THIRTY DAYS AFTER HIS DAUGHTER, she forwarded a screenshot around the office. Mr. Ritter fired her for fostering an unsafe work environment. I appreciated the gesture, but the night of our holiday party, I was the only one without a gift.

"*Twins Spilling Tea*, the show with the hottest celebrity interviews on the East Coast," Harper says from the other end of the line. She disguises herself with a fake English accent. "May I take a message for you?"

"No, but you can take a bow. When's the audition?"

"Ugh, Ari, hey." She snaps back to her droning Valley Girl voice. "I haven't had any auditions in months. I'm just embarrassed we can't get a real secretary around here. Imagine a guest calling and *me* answering. The *host*. The *main* dish?"

"What a disaster."

"Shut up. There's a betting pool about why you're not on the schedule, you know."

"Can I have in on that? I could use the cash."

"Cute."

"So what was your guess?"

"That you got kidnapped. It would really help me out if this was a ransom call. Ugh. Hold on. Cassidy wants to cockblock us."

Static crinkles as the phone is passed from one person to another. "Sorry about that," our director says, speaking low to avoid being overheard. "I didn't think you'd be calling. I thought you would wait to tell me what went down in person. I hope it's good news and not I-got-kicked-out-and-could-use-some-bail news?"

"Somewhere in between. I didn't get a chance to talk Laman into an interview. She gave me a quick look around, but she didn't show me much. This whole tour was bullshit. She invited me to stay at the resort for a week to make up for it, but she has to be bluffing. I mean, why would she offer me a resort room for free when there are thousands of people applying to get in? She knows I would never agree after the way we were talking."

His pause drags. I glimpse my cell to check if the call has disconnected. "Are you there? Cassidy?"

"Sorry. I'm just taking a look at our film schedule. I'll figure out a way to get coverage for you. We'll miss you here, obviously, but we'll figure something out."

"What? No. I'm on my way out the door. I'm not staying."

"Why not? How long has it been since you've taken a break? Ari, there's a bet going around about you for a reason. You've never cashed in on a vacation day as far as I can remember. Or a sick day."

"Neither have you. Or anyone else on the crew."

Skipping a shift means sacrificing a paycheck, and no one can afford that kind of luxury. I've slogged to the studio tipsy, hungover, constipated, and coughing from the flu. I might have missed a few morning meetings, but I've never missed an actual shoot.

"What if we pay you?" Cassidy asks. "It's a work trip, so we'll pay you the same as if you were here filming. If this leads to something big, you'll get a bonus on top of that."

"It's not like she's not going to change her mind about doing an interview if I keep harassing her. I doubt she'll visit the actual island. I doubt I'll run into her."

"We don't need her. We'll interview you. Someone who will tell us exactly what it was like on the island. The uncensored story. Everyone else who has walked out of there gushes about it like they've had some sort of religious experience. You'll be the first person visiting who didn't spend hours writing out applications and begging for a visit. You'll give us a different side of the story. People will want to watch that."

His argument makes sense. In two months of business, at least two hundred families visited the island. There should have been someone with a complaint by now, but every review has been five-star. Just like the reviews plastered along the halls.

"What do you want me to do, Cassidy, expose the place? Get it shut down?"

"We don't have that kind of power. We run a chat show. We're not hard-hitting journalists. The toughest questions we've ever asked guests are how they get their cats to pose for selfies. The whole point is to draw in viewers, to give them an honest review of the island. If we happen to smudge this woman's reputation in the process, oh well. You said you didn't get along, right?"

"She seemed sketchy. The whole tour was sloppy, like she'd never given one before. Nothing about her sat right with me."

"Let's figure out what she's hiding then. Aren't you curious?"

Curious doesn't even begin to cover it. The woman wrote my sister a long, intimate letter a decade ago and acted like she didn't know her a minute ago. She spent her high school years, the same years she had a secret friendship with my sister, interning for a company that messed with brain chemistry. I doubt the two details were linked.

But what if they were?

"You win," I say. "Just don't hire anyone better than me to cover my shifts while I'm gone. I don't want to come back and find out I was replaced."

*

A single-file line has formed at the front desk. I wait behind a woman in an NYPD uniform who stinks of smoke. I step back to avoid breathing in the smell. From my position, I can see into the waiting area. The father and son from earlier flip through a motorcycle magazine, balancing the spine on a shared armrest. They look more comfortable without the girls, who must have been summoned for their Memory Cleansings.

A thump steals my attention. The officer has smacked her hand down on the desk. "If you think I'm leaving, you're out of your mind. The next closest Transfer station is in Jersey and I don't feel like road tripping."

"It doesn't matter which station you use," the receptionist says. "The rules are the same. You were here earlier in the week. We're supposed to space out the appointments. They're not supposed to be an everyday thing."

She lifts an index finger to shush him, but it has the same effect as the middle one. "I'm not going to fight with you, sweet pea, but I'm not going to beg you, either. You can either let me through without a hassle or you can call up your boss and have her let me through. The only difference is whether you bother her or not. I heard she's been busy."

"She's the one who created the restrictions. To protect both you *and* them."

The officer sprawls her elbows on the desk like she has all the time in the world. The man rakes a hand over his bleached hair, but he repeats the rules. They bicker back and forth, rephrasing themselves, caught in a cycle.

It only ends when the receptionist notices me watching, eavesdropping. His voice trickles to a whisper as he says, "I'll authorize your entrance into the hall today, but I won't bend the rules again."

"You take this job too seriously," she says at full volume. She shoves herself away from the desk and marches toward the sealed corridor. A click of his keyboard grants her access through the glass, but she stops a few footsteps later to input a code into a password box. It unlocks a door marked with an angelic, winged brain. During our tour, Laman called it the employee lounge. She skipped over its photos.

"Miss?" The receptionist waves me forward. "You can leave your security pass here and exit the way you arrived. Did you enjoy your look around?"

"I had so much fun that I'm not going anywhere."

I give him a brief rundown of my too-good-to-be-true deal. Throughout my story, he bounces his attention between me, a laptop, and a tablet.

"I'm sorry," he says when I finish. "Miss Laman must be mistaken. We're booked solid. If we allowed you onto the island, I don't know where we would put you. We have to...Huh."

"What? Is there an empty room?"

"Yes. My mistake. I should have known better. Miss Laman always has a plan." He scrolls, taps, and swipes. "This shouldn't be too difficult, then. I just need to find your video application. Do you remember the date you submitted it? I see a Maria Diaz but not an Ariadna. Or is it Ariana?"

"I never submitted anything."

"You never submitted anything." He sucks a breath. "Okay. Without processing a payment, the system needs to treat you like an invited guest, like a winner of our weekly contests. I can bypass the video message, but I'll have to set you up with the written portion of the application." He hands me a spare tablet with a cover, stand, and stylus. "We're sort of doing this backwards, but this is the application form. Complete this, press submit, and then the program should give me permission to finalize your arrangements. You can take a seat in the waiting area and get started."

I remain standing and skim the application. It begins with the basics. Name. Age. Relationship status. Phone number. I list my medical conditions and medications. I check boxes for gender and pronouns, blood type and allergies.

Then come the essay questions. *Where did you hear about Endellion Resorts? Why do you think you should be chosen as an invited guest? Are there any specific memories you want Cleansed (feel free to use as much or as little detail as you would like)?*

I scribble N/A across blank lines and thrust my tablet at the receptionist. He mentioned my mother's name when searching for mine, which means she followed through on submitting her form. She spilled our private, personal stories in the hopes our family would look pathetic enough to get picked.

I wonder which memories she went through all that trouble to erase. Her memories of the urn and the wheelchair, obviously, but what about older memories? Does she want to forget the nights my father stumbled home from the bar, leaving his dented red car in the parking lot like a beacon, and she had to walk five miles to drive it back so none of the neighbors noticed it missing in the morning? What about the nights she dragged me, swearing and sweating, from those same bars because old drinking buddies of my father decided I had gone through enough trauma to earn myself a spot on their tab before it became legal?

"You need to wear your security pass on the island morning, noon, and night," the receptionist says, saving me from my spiraling thoughts. "The rest of your devices will be stored in this building until your return. Your phone. Laptop. E-readers. Music players. You won't need them. You can use your pass to order wine to your doorstep, magazines to your lounge chair, aspirin to your bedside. Anything you need."

I draw the device from my pocket. It looks like a fingerless, palm-less glove. I tug my knuckles through four tiny loops, leaving my thumb free. The touch screen spans the space between my knuckles and wrist, molding to the skin. I make wide circles with my hand like I'm working out a cramp, but the device clings at any angle.

"This won't get ruined in the ocean?" I ask, flexing my fingers.

"Our devices are waterproof and heat-resistant. You could submerge them in a hot tub for hours and they'll still work as designed. Instructions will loop on channel seven of your resort room television, but it's pretty self-explanatory for anyone with a touch phone. You shouldn't have any trouble with—"

A whistle slices through the lobby, cutting him off mid-sentence.

The policewoman strolls out from the angel door. Her hands dangle loose and unclenched. Her lips pucker in song.

"She's in a much better mood," I say once she disappears into the elevator. "What the hell happened in the break room?"

The receptionist clears his throat. "She was just paying someone a visit."

CHAPTER 6

I tap a restless rhythm onto my armrest. The digital clock on my security pass says 6:00 PM, which means it's been three hours since my last sip of alcohol, two hours since stepping into the waiting area, an hour since I had the room to myself.

Imprints of the previous family remain. A snot stain on the cushion. A Binkie stranded in between chair legs. A motorcycle magazine slanted atop an otherwise neat pile of celebrity gossip. The tabloids remind me of my mother, which reminds me to make a call.

"Honey, are you on your way home?" she asks after we exchange hellos.

I push off the armrests and pace the room, crunching the phone between my shoulder and cheek. "It turns out I'm going to be staying longer than I thought. If you run out of food for Arrow, the store on the corner carries his brand."

"Don't worry, he's not going to go hungry while he's here with me. Hold on. He wants to hear his mama."

She must crouch to his level because I hear a tail thump, an excited whine. I coo his name and babble about missing him, wishing he could take the trip with me.

When my mother reclaims the phone, she says, "Where did you say you are again? I watched the show this morning. It seemed like a regular episode in the regular studio. Or was that one taped yesterday?"

I nibble my lip, flaking the color. Technically, I never lied about where my boss sent me. When I told my mother about traveling upstate for work, she filled in the blanks on her own. She assumed the crew scrounged together enough money to film on location, like the week we boarded a ferry to Connecticut. Or the week we took a train ride into the city. Those were our two highest-rated webisodes, but we couldn't afford to make a habit out of them.

"I'm not here to film anything," I say, reluctant to snowball the lie. She would find out the truth after my interview aired anyway. I would rather blab about my assignment now, over the phone, and mention the weird way Laman reacted when Domino came up in conversation. My mother might have a good guess about what's going on.

Before our back-to-back family tragedies, she was the only one who took my worries seriously. I had been a weird kid, a conspiracy theorist. My father mocked the stickers slapped over my laptop lens to prevent the government from spying on me. He taunted me for stockpiling cans and batteries beneath my bed in case of nuclear winter. Domino followed his lead, teasing me about being *paranoid* even though she was the one who would waste an hour rewording an email, cower at answering a phone call, analyze a text line by line.

My mother understood where I was coming from because she fell into the same trap with celebrity gossip. She skimmed grocery store tabloids whenever she carted past, reading articles about 90s singers being replaced with clones and famous actors joining the Illuminati. She sat through every episode of *Conspiracy Theory Theater* with me, even when I outgrew the show and stopped believing the theories.

"My director sent me away to do research," I admit to her. "He wants me to give a report about my experience here when I get back."

"A report? Like a journalist?"

"Something like that."

"This is so exciting, honey. Let me know as soon as they put the episode online. I'll have to send an email to your aunts so they can watch. Maybe you can replace one of the hosts. Or they can add a third. *Twins Spilling Tea And Me.*"

"I'd rather be behind the camera, believe it or not."

"But I bet you'd be a natural on screen. You have such a pretty face. Paparazzi will be following you around soon, I bet. You won't be able to walk out the door without seeing flashes."

"It's a once-in-a-blue-moon thing. It's not that big of a deal."

"Don't be silly. You're stepping up in the world."

Whether she meant to insult me or not, it kills my temptation to confide in her. She can wait until the interview to hear about Laman. She can find out from a pre-recorded version of me she won't be able to interrupt.

"I'll be gone for a week," I say when she pauses long enough for me to edge into the conversation. "I don't know when I'll be able to call again, so don't freak out if you don't hear from me."

A low battery warning flashes as we say our goodbyes. Stranded without social media, I page through the magazine pile with slick, sweaty fingers. Despite the AC rattling away in a corner, my entire body boils. I'm dying for a drink, but my only options are water from a standing cooler or a cold cup of coffee. I'm not in the mood for either.

Too distracted to read, I tap my feet and drum my nails until my security pass buzzes. An arrow materializes on the screen, acting as an indoor GPS. It directs me across the blinding white lobby and unlocks the sealed hall. I proceed to the indicated room. Its door is marked with a cartoon brain carrying a wand in one stick-figured hand and a top hat in the other. During the tour, Laman referred to it as *the main Memory Cleansing hub, where the magic happens.*

I shove inside. A dainty brunette inputs data into a complex-looking computer system. The massive screen is cut in quarters. Each square holds a different perspective of a brain. A top view, bottom view, and side views.

"Hello, hello," the woman says with a toothy grin. Pencils are threaded through her bun. A smiley face sticker clings to her lab coat. "My name is Cara. With a C."

She wafts toward a high-backed chair, inviting me to take a seat. Instead of four separate legs, a solid base sits flush against the floor. Mechanics must be contained inside because wires spool out from a fist-sized hole in its backside. They snake up and into a helmet leaning against the headrest, hinged back.

I sit on the edge of the seat, half my butt overhanging. "You're not another therapist, are you? Do I have to tell you every horrible thing that's happened to me, so you can Cleanse it?"

"Oh no. It's nothing like that. You don't have to give me any personal information. Most people like to keep their damp, dark memories between them and their diaries." She uses tweezers to flatten an ice-cold strip of plastic against my skull. "Believe it or not, that little thing is going to monitor your brain activity. Your helmet is going to take care of the rest. You know, a decade or so ago, it was only possible to measure serotonin levels in the bloodstream. Most of that serotonin was stored in the gut. However, Endellion has found a way to detect it in the brain."

She motions behind herself, at the monitor, and continues. "The handy-dandy computer over there will show me the memory portion of your mind. Right now, each section is empty, but once your helmet drops down, different sections will get illuminated with either red or green. The green means there are traces of serotonin. In other words, when you have thought of these memories in the past, they have made you smile a big wide smile. But the red areas are the memories that get you all stressed and panicky. Those are the ones we want to get out of there."

"What's stopping you from taking more memories than the ones pinpointed on your screen? Or stopping you from putting something new inside my head?" I scan her up and down. She reminds me of a circus clown hiding barbed teeth beneath a painted smile. "How do I know you're not going to brainwash me into buying from your gift shop or posting a good review online or coming back in another few months?"

"If you read the fine print on the paperwork you signed, it explains how we take away plenty of memories, but we only insert one. It makes you think you checked into a regular hotel for a regular vacation. If you knew you went through this whole process and had memories removed, then you would be desperate to figure out what those memories were. Like when a song is stuck in your head and you can only think of the melody but not the words. Or when you wake up from a bad dream and can't quite remember the details. It drives you insane. It's all you can think about. Knowing you've forgotten something, anything, would ruin your vacation."

She thumbs a button. A retractable arm angles the helmet outward and upward. It hovers centimeters above my scalp. "You have to keep in mind your memories are never erased. They're only scribbled over. That means you could jog them if you had an inkling about what was going on, which would ruin the whole purpose of your vacation. The implanted memory is meant to avoid all that."

"And when does that thing get removed from me?"

"It disintegrates after your week of fun in the sun is up. Like stitches."

"And it's the same with the memories? They return after a week on their own, no surgery?"

"Yup, yup, yup." She returns to the centralized monitor and cranks a knob, twists a key. "Just to be blue-sky clear, we never open up the brain. We work with electrical impulses. Nearly imperceptible shocks."

"Will it hurt?" I ask. My spine straightens against the chair back. I picture the surgery backfiring, my brain decaying, my mother grinding steaks in the blender to spoon-feed both me and my father.

"You can tell me in just a second. I need you to lean all the way back and sit perfectly still, please and thank you."

The helmet sinks toward me with a creaking whine. It resembles an antique diving bonnet, bulbous and copper. Except there isn't a viewing port. When the material drops to my chin, it darkens my world to black.

I flinch, expecting an onslaught of zaps and jolts, but a tingling warmth spreads across my temples. Aside from the lingering ache warning me it's been too long without a drink, my head feels fine.

The process reminds me of my freshman year brain scan. Our school district was chosen as one of fifty across the country to test unreleased, experimental machines. They were built to *assess our personality constructs* and *predict career paths*. Half of our school signed up as guinea pigs. We assumed picking electives and applying for colleges would be easier with our futures mapped out for us. Our parents rushed to sign permission slips, hoping to brag about giving birth to a future CEO or politician.

Our principal held an assembly for all the volunteers. Rows of acne-crusted students clicked pens and tugged backpack straps, eager to receive their results. The machine sat in the center of the stage, looming over us.

"We didn't have laptops on every desk when I was younger," our principal said into a microphone clipped to her suit. "My teacher had to drag us to the computer lab to access the internet. One day, she gave us a multiple-choice aptitude test. We had to input which subjects we preferred and how we spent our weekends and how our best friends would describe us. I guess I gave too many answers about loving animals, because my results encouraged me to become a dairy farmer." She paused for laughs. "The point is, the test I took was inaccurate. It was something to joke around about at lunch. Unfortunately, you don't have the luxury of laughing about your results. This scan is going to tell you which field of work is best suited for you, but it will also tell you whether you suffer from depression, anxiety, bipolar disorder, or schizophrenia. It will tell you whether you are in the top percentage to commit a violent crime or fall into substance abuse. It will tell you more about yourself than you might want to know."

Feet stopped tapping. Notebooks stopped rustling. Gum stopped snapping. We'd never thought of it that way.

She gestured backstage, beyond the machine. "There's a laminator behind the curtain, so you can hang your scan on the fridge forever along with all the A's you're going to get this semester. There's also a shredder. I realize you're all excited to share your results on your Instagram stories, but you shouldn't feel pressured to show anyone the paperwork you're given. If you don't want to look yourself, no one is forcing you. This test is much more accurate than the one telling me to become a farmer, but that doesn't mean your future is written in stone. It doesn't mean you have to pay attention to what this scan tells you."

Seats were unassigned with four different grades mingled together, but she called students in alphabetical order. When my turn arrived, I climbed onto the stage and took a seat facing the audience. Domino sat toward the back, bookended by teammates.

The scan took two minutes total. My helmet rose as my results inched from a slot like a photo booth printing a strip. The principal handed it over with the edges folded to protect my privacy and called out the next name. Dominique Diaz. She speed-walked down the aisle as I disappeared backstage.

I stood halfway between the shredder and laminator, unfolded my results, read the first two words, flipped it upside down, and flipped it back. I was working toward reading a full line when Domino split the curtain.

"Those were the longest two minutes of my life," she said. "I was sitting by the exit. In the last row. You know how long it took me to walk to the stage? Everyone was staring. And why'd they have to make us sit there, facing everybody? They could have put the machine back here. I wouldn't have signed up if I knew I'd be in front of the whole fricking school."

"You got through it, though. You always do." I bumped her arm with mine. "So what are you going to do?"

"I'm going to kill myself. I looked like an idiot."

"I meant about the scan."

"I'm not getting rid of it after going through all that. Why? You don't want yours? What did it say?"

"I didn't look at it." I frowned as she fed her results through the laminator. "You're supposed to be the one who overthinks everything. Why aren't you overthinking this? You're not worried about the results saying you'll turn out an alcoholic like Dad? Or telling you you're going to spend the rest of your life working at a fast-food place?"

She shrugged. "I've never understood the way my brain works. This might help. And if it can tell me what kind of career works best for me, that's one less decision I have to make, one less thing to be anxious over."

"I don't know. I don't want anyone telling me how to think, what to do, who I am."

"But it's from inside your own head. It's basically you telling yourself. You're not scared of yourself, are you?"

I fiddled with my paper. "The whole thing just seems like cheating to me. I don't need some machine controlling me. I can figure life out on my own. I mostly signed up to skip class anyway."

I dropped my results into the shredder. The paper crinkled and crunched.

During an empanada dinner later that night, my mother whined about how much she'd been looking forward to bragging about my results. She gave a tag team lecture with my father, who ranted about me wasting the school's time and tax dollars.

I expected my sister to save me from the scolding by whipping out her results, but she admitted she came home empty-handed. She must have changed her mind after talking to me. She must have shredded her scan, too.

*

The helmet climbs, exposing my nose stud, my brow barbell, my industrial piercing. The transition to bright, glaring light spots my vision. I blink away the dots.

"There you go. Easy peasy," Cara says. "As you can tell, the process doesn't take effect immediately. We've placed the implanted memories and Cleansed memories on a timer. That gives you an opportunity to walk your pretty little caboose into the next room where you'll be misted with a sedative. Don't let that term scare you. It's nothing like a dentist cupping your mouth with a mask. You might have noticed we counter our futuristic technology with the familiar to avoid overstimulation. That's why there are paper magazines in the waiting room, mall elevators in the lobby, minimalistic decor in our halls. The next room is going to feel like a sauna, nice and relaxing. When you wake up, you'll be on the island and the process will be complete. All your bad memories will be gone along with your memories of Endellion, including what you've gone through today. Isn't that exciting?"

"Thrilling."

"One last thing before you leave me. Do you have a phone on you? A laptop? An e-reader? I'm going to label and store anything electronic for you. Don't worry, you'll get it back in shipshape as soon as your vacation ends."

"I would rather hold onto my stuff. I don't have much. I didn't pack a suitcase."

She raises a sympathetic smile. "Unfortunately, we can't risk guests calling anyone on the mainland because the procedure makes them think this is like any other resort. We don't want them finding out they had memories erased because then there's a risk of those memories returning. It's the same with social media. There are resort ads everywhere, so visitors have limited internet access."

"Can't other things trigger memories, too? A scar or something?" I rub at my wrist, at my tattoo.

"The brain ignores familiar stimuli. It's called habituation. Can you feel the weight of your shirt pressing against your torso throughout the day? No, sir. You're used to it, so your brain doesn't think about it. Not unless someone draws attention to it. And, remember, guests are flocking here because they don't *want* to remember. Denial is a powerful force. But a phone can be much more powerful, so hand it over, missy."

"Fine. It's dead anyway." I dig into my bra, toss her my cell. "Can I get out of here?"

"Of course. We're finished for now. Enjoy your stay."

I follow the fresh set of arrows on my security band to another door. This one is marked with a snoozing brain wearing a nightcap and slippers. A cutesy way to symbolize knocking guests unconscious.

The lock clicks when it senses my arrival. I step through the threshold and it clicks again, bolting itself.

A three-sided, cushioned bench wraps around the room. A basket of rolled blankets sits by the door. I bypass the pile, tuck my knees beneath my butt, and lean against the bare rosewood walls.

A rumbling builds in the panels, vibrating my back. As it strengthens, the sedative hisses from ceiling vents. I clamp my mouth on instinct, sipping short breaths through my nose.

I don't want to think about the medication snaking its way into my lungs, so I drop my attention to my security pass. The GPS arrows have been replaced with resort photographs. They capture guests sipping from fishbowl margaritas, flipping salted hair, and sunbathing in strappy bikinis.

The slideshow transitions to snapshots of Laman advancing in age. The caption scrolling across the bottom promises to give a behind-the-scenes look at the *visionary who led us here today*. The montage shows her as a baby wearing a SMART COOKIE onesie with chocolate chips printed across the chest. As a toddler inspecting ants with a magnifying glass flipped in the wrong direction. As a teenager organizing papers in an office. As an adult hunched over a desk cluttered with microscopes and beakers.

I swat at the image, reversing back to the teenage photo. A pinch magnifies the background. The pixels blur up close, but I can make out another teenager standing beside the pile of papers, pen in hand. My sister. A maple leaf pin weighs down the collar of her army jacket. Swooped bangs cross the center of her forehead. A scar dissects her only visible eyebrow.

I remember that scar. She tripped during a charity game senior year, banged her head on the bleachers, and cleaved a cut above her eye. The match took place only a month before her suicide. Thirty days.

My father fixated on the timestamp, obsessed over it. He was the only one in the family left who considered conspiracy theories bullshit, but he created the biggest conspiracy of all by claiming Dominique never would have hurt herself.

"Look at these. She couldn't have been faking this," my father said shortly before his own suicide attempt. He held his touchscreen and swiped through social media photos snapped from my camera. They showed Domino bumping the ball, conspiring with her coach on the sidelines, and high-fiving teammates with a tan bandage on her brow.

"You don't know what you're talking about," I said, slapping my notebook shut. My summer school teachers had stopped checking my homework anyway. "You never know what's going on in someone's head. Look at all those celebrities. All those comedians. They're millionaires, they're married with kids, and they do exactly what Domino did. A smile in a picture doesn't prove anything. You don't know what you're talking about."

He clenched his square jaw. Talking back to him should have earned me a scolding, but the suicide softened him as much as my mother, my classmates, my cousins. I could sleep until noon or drop F-bombs without repercussion. Everyone pitied me too much to get pissed at me.

Their tiptoeing got old fast. Pretty soon, I stopped answering texts. I stopped showing up at family functions. I stopped leaving my room for anything other than a drink.

"Think logically," I said to my father. "A lot of people with anxiety end up with depression. It's just the way brains work. Ask Doctor Q. It makes sense, whether or not you want it to make sense."

"You're right. Her doctor. She would know." He darted back and forth like an untrained sniffer dog. He yanked papers from refrigerator clips. He rummaged through junk drawers. He hunted through moist, soggy garbage bags.

"Are you two getting along okay?" my mother asked, shuffling inside. Rosary beads clinked in her palms. "You're making a racket."

My father grunted as he dug deeper in the recycling can. "I'm looking for the looney bin number. I need to talk to that shrink. She'll say everything was fine. Domino cut back appointments. She was fine."

"You can't start calling her at two in the morning like you do with the cops," I said, slipping my phone deep into my pocket. If he was sober, he would have realized her name was at the bottom of my contact list.

Doctor Q treated me, too. She tucked me in her geometric office for forty-five-minute spurts to listen to me vent about insignificant teenage drama. My teachers flunking me. My sister raiding my closet. My friends suddenly caring more about boys than books or music or movies.

My father stripped cabinets bare searching for the number right under his nose. He missed the business card pinned to the fridge and the address book in the junk drawer. He didn't bother to search her name online or check her company website, either. I think he wanted an excuse to tear the house apart.

A few more whiskeys hammered the interrogation idea out of his head, but it stuck in mine. During my next therapy session, which turned out to be my last, I asked, "Did you know she was going to do it?"

Doctor Q adjusted her bright orange shawl, tightening it like a safety blanket. "I assure you every possible step was taken to ensure her safety. There wasn't anything more me or my staff could have done for your sister."

"That wasn't the question."

"Ariadna, honey, I wish there was something more I could say, but I have to protect all of my patients' confidentiality."

"She's dead. She's not your patient anymore. I am. And you're supposed to help me get through trauma, right? I've known you since I was in first grade. Give me something. I won't tell my parents. I won't tell anyone."

She took a long, wistful look at her LIFE IS TOUGH BUT SO ARE YOU sign. Her eyes glistened with water. "Dominique never made any direct threats. She never hinted at anything that would cause me to involuntarily commit her. But it would be disingenuous to say the news surprises me. She was in a bad headspace during her last few sessions. We discussed returning to our old schedule with multiple meetings per week. I can't provide details, but she was certainly struggling with anxiety and loss and..." She swept under her eyes with a finger, careful not to ruin her liner. "I'm sorry. Losing a client is never easy for me. Although it's nothing compared to the pain of losing a sister or daughter. I provide family counseling if your mother and father are seeking help in the grieving process. None of you should go through this alone."

"Thank you," I said, dry-eyed and numb. "I appreciate you telling me."

I meant it, but the part about keeping our conversation between us was a lie. I repeated every word to my parents over a cold pizza dinner. My mother listened with her cross necklace clasped in a trembling palm while my father stared into his whiskey. When I finished, he abandoned his drink, abandoned his slice, abandoned his chair. He abandoned us the next night too, on a bigger scale, with a tattered rope he trusted not to tear.

A whiff of the anesthesia coursing through the sauna would erase the memory and the guilt that goes along with it. It would make me forget how insistent my father was about Domino being murdered. And it would make me forget the photograph on my security pass, snapped only weeks before her death, signing papers for a woman who ran the island where I was about to be imprisoned for a week.

I leap toward the exit. I pound the metal with both fists, begging for someone to let me out, but the shouting backfires on me. Tainted air pools into my open mouth. It weighs my arms, anchors my lids, clouds my mind. I collapse on the floorboards, still screaming, as the Memory Cleansing starts to work its magic.

CHAPTER 7

A memory foam pillow cradles my scalp. A fuzzy, cotton-candy blanket warms my feet. I stretch my arms toward the ceiling with a yawn and notice a device clinging to the backside of my hand. It reminds me of the magic bands at Disney, meant for unlocking rooms and buying fast food. I roll for the nightstand, planning to use my cell phone to fill in missing gaps. I land on a remote instead. It activates a theater-sized television.

The first channel plays a welcome video. I press an up arrow to skip it. The second is formatted like a TV guide, listing resort activities. I skip again. The third shows a pastry chef squeezing icing onto cake pops. Skip. Skip. Skip. Skip. The first useful channel, seven, loops cartoon instructions on how to download apps. Fun facts scroll across the bottom like a news ticker: *Did you know you can use your security pass in place of your remote on your resort television?*

The device on my hand must be my security pass. I activate its entertainment app and click to kill the TV, but it reverts to the same rest screen as my pass. A monochrome umbrella twirling, creating a hypnotic swirl.

I wriggle out of my cocoon of blankets and swing my legs onto the white oak floors. The room feels fresh, unfamiliar. I remember inserting my credit-card chip for a receptionist, but I must have blacked out before climbing beneath the covers.

I sweep my gaze across an egg-shaped mattress, a headboard carved with roses, a window-wall of ocean. No suitcases in sight.

I step through an open arch separating the bedroom from the rest of the suite. A black leather couch faces the same continuous window wall along with a kidney-shaped coffee table. Disposable cups are piled on top, clear plastic rimmed with gold. A Bible rests on the bottom shelf.

"You've got to be kidding me," I say after checking the coat closet. Other than a pair of sandals, the shelves are completely empty. Either the front desk lost my bags when I dropped them with a bellhop or I lost them on my own. Either way, I need a drink.

In the kitchenette, each appliance has been rolled with white paint and ornamented with black, tasteful line drawings. A palm tree climbs up the side of an espresso machine. A regal sandcastle wraps around a toaster.

I tug open a full-sized fridge decorated with ocean waves and a dolphin in mid-jump. The shelves are cluttered with miniature liquor bottles, snack packs, and microwavable meals. On the counters to its side, there are bowls of coffee pods and granola bars. I grab a berry flavor and wash it down with vodka.

Before scouring the resort for a clothing shop to make up for my lost luggage, I swerve into the bathroom. I plan on mopping away any leftover smudged makeup but come across a blank wall where a medicine cabinet should be mounted. I nudge the door closed to check for a full-length mirror. There's only a metal rack strung with towels.

I roam around the room, trying to improvise, but every reflective surface fails on me. The kitchen appliances are painted, opaque. My television fades into an animated rest screen instead of darkening to black. My security pass does the same exact thing.

Even the window wall refuses to catch my reflection. I can't make out my face, only a leaping fish, a swooping seagull. The tropical scenery looks crisp, clear, cinematic. It takes me a moment to put two and two together, to realize there are no panes or sills. The window is an illusion. Another screen with a pre-taped recording of an ocean.

Feeling claustrophobic, I kick on my sandals and risk walking around with raccoon eyes. I step outside and crest the short bridge connecting my resort room to the boardwalk. Turning left would lead me to a dock posted with guards in electric-green uniforms, so I turn right, toward the main plaza. A few footsteps later, the white wood transitions to white stone.

The broad patio stretches between two beaches. In the center, hot tubs bubble. Pool filters gurgle. Martini glasses clink. I could continue forward until I hit the U-shaped building in the distance but stop for a drink first.

A family hogs the barstools, so I spread myself out in a lounge chair facing the pool and people-watch. Two kids slap water in a relay race. Another scoots down the spiral slide, his trunks slipping from his backside. Beyond the pool, a wooden set of stairs leads to one of the beaches. A lifeguard whistles from her tower. Toddlers rattle plastic shovels. Teenagers boogie board. Women burn tan lines into their skin.

A couple disconnects from the crowd and advances my way. They swing clasped hands in a choreographed stroll, only slowing their stride to kiss. When they reach the pool, they call out in Korean to collect their children.

"Don't you feel like you're missing out?" Harper asked once in between takes. She had been interviewing an elderly couple celebrating fifty years since their first onscreen kiss. The whole crew fawned over their disgustingly adorable love story.

"There are plenty of asexuals who date," I said as I repositioned my camera for the next segment. "I'm just not one of them."

"I guess you spend a lot of time alone then, if you know what I mean. Or wait. I guess you don't need *alone time*."

"My showerhead would disagree."

"Wait. What? How does that work?"

Every answer drew two more questions, like my lifestyle was too complex to comprehend. I received a similar reaction when I drunkenly mentioned my first and only dating experience to my mother. A floppy-haired boy from sixth grade had asked me to the spring formal, and my friends pressured me to accept. We held limp hands in the hallway and texted about our favorite bands, but I never hung out with him outside the schoolyard. On the few occasions we kissed, it felt like shoving my lips against a foam football, hard and soft all at once. I broke up with him before our relationship reached the two-month mark.

My mother, who weeps at romcoms and soap-opera weddings, should have passed down the romance gene to at least one daughter. But Domino never snuck anyone through her window after hours, either. She never got caught with a hickey bruised across her neck. She never uttered the name of a boy during meals or movie nights.

My security pass chirps as I slurp the last of my poolside drink. A notification instructs me to swipe right for a refill. I swipe. It takes sixty seconds for a man in a deep V-neck to recycle my mojito.

"How did you do that?" I ask, squinting up at him. He blocks the sun with his torso.

"We use white rum, club soda, mint leaves, and a tablespoon or two of white sugar."

"I mean, how did you know where to find me?"

"Your pass sends your coordinates directly to my screen." He gestures to the tablet clipped to his belt. A tracking dot notes my location.

"Don't you think it's pretty creepy guests are getting GPS tracked?"

"Phones off island do the same thing. Except they don't bring you booze."

He has a point. I flick aside the decorative miniature umbrella and sip as the sun reddens my cheeks, wets my neck, fries my legs beneath the denim. I dab the cold glass against my forehead, but it doesn't stop the sweating. I sprout armpit stains on my only shirt.

Desperate for the swish of air conditioning, I book it to the closest door along the U-shaped strip. A cafeteria. Fish scales are carved into white wooden tables. Chair backs are curved in the shape of pale seashells. Seafood and pasta stations display menu choices on ivory surfboards suspended from the ceiling.

The bland layout draws attention to the walls. Unlike the screens in my resort room imitating an ocean view, these mimic an aquarium. Salmon dart around coral reefs. Seahorses bob. Eels writhe. Out of nowhere, a mermaid whips across the scene, thrashing her rainbow tail. A group of children point at her, hypnotized by the fantasy thrown in the middle of a humdrum reality.

I circle around them to heap a cheesesteak, nacho fries, and a water bottle onto my tray. My security pass tallies the cost. It bings a reminder the payment will be charged to the credit card on file, which belongs to an unfamiliar name. Rhea Laman. The same person who screwed up my luggage must have screwed up my account information.

I drift toward a single table and dig into my freebie meal, eavesdropping on surrounding families. I zone in on a pair of parents, a teenager in a motorcycle jacket, and a toddler with a runny nose. In between bites of ice cream, they take turns piecing together a silly story, contributing one word apiece. When their nonsense tale ends, they transition into *Going On A Picnic*.

My family tweaked that classic game on road trips. Instead of listing alphabetical foods, we switched the topic each round. We would list game shows or celebrity couples or boy bands or wild animals.

On our drive to Niagara Falls, my mother twisted in the passenger seat to help brainstorm. "We can try *names you would never name your baby*," she said. "Like Mildred. Agnes. Moon Unit."

"Don't give examples." Domino giggled. "That's cheating."

I shrugged. "It doesn't matter. I'm going to win this one anyway. I'm not having a baby, so I can list any name and it will count."

My mother clucked her tongue. "I hate when you talk like that."

"What? You know it's not my thing. I would rather have a farm. Chickens. Some cows, maybe. Babies don't pull their weight. I'd have to give *them* milk. Not a fair deal."

"Smart kid, smart kid," my father said, chuckling.

"Don't encourage her," my mother tutted. "You'll grow out of that way of thinking, Ari. Your children will be the greatest thing that ever happened to you. Just like you two were for me. I couldn't live without my girls."

Chair legs screech, snapping me back to the present. The storytelling family rises from their table, crumpling napkins and disposing of plastic spoons. A heat burst hits me as they swing open the entrance. Reluctant to face the sun again, I toss my own garbage and escape through a side door. It connects the cafeteria to the next area along the strip, a recreation room.

A yoga instructor lunges forward with outstretched arms. Rows of students struggle to imitate the basic, beginner pose. Men in stained tank tops use their hem to blot their foreheads. Women in sports bras sip from infused water bottles. They pant and wheeze on rubber mats.

I avert my eyes to check out an electronic corkboard near the exit. The screen mimics old-school flyers tacked with pushpins. Each poster announces a resort activity. Sandcastle competitions. Scuba lessons. Henna tattoos. Camera rentals.

I enlarge the last option. Clickable tabs list schedules, age restrictions, and sample pictures. The next photography session starts within the hour, so I sit cross-legged on the floor and fiddle with apps on my security pass. I play puzzle games. I read e-magazines. I swipe through meal delivery options.

When students trickle into the sunshine, the instructor rolls each of their mats herself. She stows the pile in a trunk labeled *yoga gear* and un-latches another labeled *photography equipment.*

"Do you need a hand?" I ask.

I help her unload cameras as she runs me through the rental process. All of my photographs will be available to upload on my computer back at home, free of charge. For an extra fee, I can print them onto keychains and magnets at the gift shop.

When we finish setting out the gear, she hands me a tablet prepro-grammed to a rental form. I scribble an electronic signature, which promises to pay for any damages and grants the resort rights to use my photographs in promotional material.

I brace the sun with a camera slung over my neck. I photograph wind streaks in the sand, cone-shaped shells, and brown, skittering crabs. I frame a handful of candid shots before the shore is invaded by amateur photog-raphers. Parents call out poses for their children to strike, positioning them like mannequins. Shutters chink. Bulbs flash.

My mother dubbed me the designated photographer for family por-traits and holiday cards, but I've always preferred action shots. My sister click-click-clicking a pen in concentration while solving crossword puzzles. My mother scrawling *I love you* notes on napkins to pack in our bagged lunches. My father dragging on a cigarette, puffing out smoke rings bigger than his scuffed wedding band.

I scale the wooden steps to escape the congestion and cross the patio to the secondary beach. It holds the same white sand, the same crystal ocean, with one key difference. Instead of open space for swimming and sunbath-ing, the area is loaded with inflatable slides, jumping platforms, and obstacle courses. I snap candids of kids cannonballing, teenagers surfboarding, and adults parasailing.

It takes an hour to run out the memory card. When I return my camera to its trunk, my skin glistens red. I ask the woman in charge where to pick up sunscreen, a change of clothes, and some deodorant. She points me toward an all-in-one shop. It's only two doors down, but the thinning bar distracts me. I snag a stool next to a big-bellied man with sunburn on every exposed inch of skin.

"Finally," he says, smacking the countertop. "Someone who looks like she can handle her shots. I'm sick of throwing back whiskey alone."

"I feel like it's more margarita weather," I say, lifting a finger toward the bartender.

"Come on. We could meet in the middle with tequila shots?"

"I don't think so. I need something chilly to sip on for now. It's been boiling all day."

"Your fault for packing jeans on a beach trip. My husband did the same thing in Finland. Brought three suitcases of V-necks and bitched about the cold."

"Hey, I'm on your side. I don't know what I was thinking."

I redirect my attention toward the bartender. She rattles a cocktail shaker and pours, letting the liquid cascade in a lime waterfall. According to a chalkboard sign, she pairs a new trick with each order. She juggles strawberries. She tosses bottles. She sets shots on fire. I keep requesting different combinations to see what else she does, how she adds to her routine.

"Christ on a crutch," the sunburned man says. "If you drink like this in paradise, I wouldn't want to see how you drink after a shit day."

"Are you telling me to slow down?"

"I'm telling you there's no way I'm catching up if you keep moving at that pace."

"Fine, I'll take a break, stretch my legs a little." I hop onto the patio. "Have some of that tequila waiting when I get back."

I roam into a strobe-lit arcade. Pinballs whistle in rhythm with throbbing neon bulbs. Skee-Balls rumble and thump into pits. I thread between empty strollers and children on sugar highs, setting myself up at a knockoff version of an old arcade game. Instead of Pac-Man, an umbrella gulps down enemies, its canopy opening and closing like a mouth. I die on the first level.

I move onto pinball, then slots. Points accumulate on my security pass after each round, but I barely hit double digits. I'm about to call it quits when I stumble across a machine right up my alley. A virtual beer pong game. It's targeted at children, rebranded with a PG name. *Toss-a-cup.* I earn the high score on my first go. A random woman overhears the congratulatory bells and buys us a round to celebrate.

The night ends with a guard nudging me awake. I squint at my surroundings, registering the deserted patio and lidded hot tubs, the lifeless pool and inky black sky. At some point, I must have wobbled back to the bar.

"I didn't realize it was so late," I say with a slight slur. I stumble to my feet, trip over a pair of sandals I must have kicked off earlier, and careen toward the pavement.

The guard lunges to prevent my fall. My vision steadies for long enough to read his name badge. Elliot Avidan. "I just wanted to make sure you got back to your room safe," he says, holding me upright.

"I don't remember my room number. I don't know if I looked at it." I smack my security pass, activating random apps. "It's probably on this thing, right?"

"You're in room twelve." He raises his own pass. "It's on this thing, too."

"How much stuff about me is on there?"

"Not much. Just your Social Security, number of sex partners, whether or not you sleep with socks on."

"I'm too wasted to tell whether you're kidding," I say, staggering toward the boardwalk in bare feet. I grip the wooden railings for balance.

"Sorry. It's just your name, room number, photo, and if you have any allergies or medical conditions we should be aware of during your stay. Whoa, be careful where you're walking."

He tries to steady me, but I shrug from his touch. "It's okay. I'm good. You can go. I doubt babysitting drunks is your favorite part of the job."

"It's not the worst."

"Yeah, what else do you have to complain about? Do you have to scrub urinals or something?"

"I didn't mean it like that. Working here has been great. The insurance is great. No exclusions, which is great."

"What part isn't so great?"

"Oh, uh, nothing major. Early shifts are early. Late shifts are late. My sleep schedule is all screwy. It's hard to get any rest."

"Right."

We walk side-by-side as a wind gust rustles trees, ripples water, rattles buoys. The sudden drop in temperature pricks my skin. Goosebumps pepper my arms.

When we reach my bungalow, my security pass automatically unlocks the room. I cross into the attached kitchen and say, "Thanks for the help. And thanks for the shoes. I didn't realize you were carrying them."

"No problem." He drops the sandals on the welcome mat but lingers with his hand cupping the doorframe. I can't close it unless he unlaces his fingers, unless he backs away from me.

"I can handle myself from here," I say, sobering up as my guard rises.

"Good. You should get some rest. If you're not feeling a hundred percent in the morning, you can order aspirin to your room. Breakfast, too. You might be better off spending the whole day inside, giving yourself a break from drinking."

I nod, acutely aware of how dark it's gotten, how few guests are awake, how alone we really are on the island. He could easily power his way inside and pin me down. I would have nowhere to run, except the ocean.

"Don't forget you're alone here," he says. "You're on vacation, sure, but that doesn't mean nothing bad can happen to you. Right?"

He doesn't wait for a response. He uncurls his fingers, takes a step back, and retreats down the deserted boardwalk, letting the darkness swallow him whole.

CHAPTER 8

I lounge poolside, sipping a cocktail to chase away my hangover. The sun beats onto my skin, but the warmth is welcome. Swapping my denim jeans for a high-waisted swimsuit has made the weather bearable.

I hunted through the all-in-one shop after waking in a stinking sweat. I browsed through white T-shirts with *Endellion* printed across the chest and yoga pants with the same branding across the cheeks. I settled on a subtler collection with thumb-sized umbrella logos. I should have restricted myself to the necessities, especially since my security pass was linked to the wrong credit card, but I splurged on nail polish. It was the same shade I'd hand-picked during manicures with my sister growing up, the shade I'd struggled to find in stores for over a decade. I bought one for me and one for her, a small souvenir.

I plan on dipping into the bottle as soon as my fake nails lose their glue. Until then, I tap my tips on a lounge chair and people-watch. The Korean couple perches on the pool edge. They dangle their long legs, playing underwater footsie. On the shallow side, their children fumble to serve and spike a volleyball. They double hit. They fall short of the net. They scream out LOVE along with nonsense scores like PEACE and HATE.

A pang hits my chest. My sister mastered every sport, from horseshoes to cornhole, but she never wanted me to play with her. She complained about me balancing badminton rackets on my palm and making swooshing sound effects when shooting baskets. It was the same with board games.

She flipped out when I moved chess pieces too early or checked my phone during her turn. "You're not taking it seriously," she would say. "It's no fun winning against someone barely trying. You have to pay attention. You have to notice the details."

I don't notice the inflated beach ball arching toward me until it flutters against my foot. The young girl fumbles to hitch her leg over the pool edge to chase it. She loses balance halfway through and falls backward with a plop. I scoop the toy to stop her from trying again.

"You have to hit it with your wrists," I say. I stand to bounce it back the proper way. "If you're serving, make sure to throw it with the opposite hand you use to write. That way, you can hit it with your writing one. You'll have more control."

"Do you play?" a slightly older, scrawnier boy asks. He wrenches the ball from her hands and balances it against his stomach to float. Her lower lip curls toward her chin, eyes brimming, but she bats away the tears.

"My older sister does. I've watched a lot of her games, so I've picked up some pointers here and there. She's pretty good. By the end of high school, she won more trophies than she could fit on her dresser."

"I have a trophy," the girl says, smiling with gums.

The boy rolls his eyes. "They're only ribbons. Field day ones. Everyone gets them. Even the fat kids."

"Whoa, watch your fucking mouth."

The swear leaves my own mouth before I can process it. The kids exchange mute, wide-eyed glances. Their parents stare across the water, but they must not be able to hear me.

I backtrack before anyone can tattle. "I'm just saying, your sister doesn't deserve being spoken to like that. You should have her back. You're lucky to have her. I can rely on my sister for anything. It should be the same way with you two."

The clichés bubble out of me, but in reality, I hurled much worse insults at Domino at their age. I called her a whore when she got her first period and teased her about the gap in her teeth even though we had the same one. We brawled over movies and Happy Meal toys, bunk beds and shotgunned seats, but most of our arguments involved leftover food. My father would intercept us mid-argument and say, "Girls are supposed to fight over boys and dolls. You two are defective." He meant it as a joke. Neither of us found it funny.

My mother solved the problem with a pair of permanent markers. "If you only eat half of an animal cracker box or a fruit box and you want to save it for later, scribble a big mark on top." She assigned me orange and Domino green. We marked our territory in the fridge, then moved onto drawing on clothes hangers and teddy bear tags. Our father threw a fit when we marked the couch cushions, drawing squiggles straight down the center.

In the middle of my poolside speech, the children lose interest. The boy pinwheels his pruned hands, trying to catch the attention of another woman on the boardwalk. The ball pops from his stomach with a splash. "Hey lady, thanks for the toys," he calls out to her.

She sips from an oversized coffee as she clacks across the patio. "You're welcome," she says without shortening her stride. Her blonde hair is pulled into a tight ponytail, squeezing her scalp. Her feet are squashed into heels that look just as uncomfortable.

"Do you want to watch us play?" the boy asks as her back is already turning. "I can probably score a point."

"I wish I could, but running this place isn't always fun and games. Relaxation is reserved for my guests. But I'm happy to see you kids enjoying the net. Volleyball has always been a favorite of mine."

She advances toward the U-shaped building. As she walks, the slits running up the legs of her floor-length romper billow out. Each step highlights her frail, birdlike bones.

I jog to catch up. "Excuse me," I say, following her into a restroom. "Did you say you run the resort? Maybe you can help me out. I think someone lost my luggage. My room's completely empty."

She addresses me through a stall. "I'm sorry. That's unacceptable. There must have been some sort of mistake. I'll look into it for you right away."

"Awesome. Thanks."

"It's the least I can do. We'll have it sorted ASAP." The toilet flushes. The door swings out. "I certainly hope this inconvenience hasn't ruined your stay."

"It's annoying, but it's not the end of the world. I just bought a bunch of clothes to hold me over until the end of the week. The store sold all the stuff I needed."

"We can reimburse you for that."

I don't mention the cardholder name attached to my security pass, the same one attached to her name tag.

"Has everything else been up to your standards?" she asks.

"Yeah, for sure, this place is nice. Different. I'm used to fast-paced vacations. My family was always running from park to park until our feet bled, trying to get on every ride. Either that or driving from landmark to landmark starting at six AM. I've never been much of a beach person."

She soaps up, rinses, and retouches her lipstick. There aren't any mirrors over the sinks, only splotchy paintings, so she uses a compact to check her progress. "I was the opposite. I spent almost every day on a beach back in high school. I found a nice secluded spot nobody else touched. I would hide myself beneath an umbrella on my way there, so no one would recognize me and come start a conversation."

I tug at the patch on my bathing suit, the monochrome umbrella. "That explains your logo."

"It's beautiful, isn't it? I'm a fan of simple, monochrome patterns. Like your tattoo."

"I don't do tattoos. Piercings are more of my thing."

"Maybe I need my vision checked. Because that most definitely looks like a tattoo from where I'm standing."

I follow her eye line, expecting to see a misidentified mole or birthmark, but a dark blotch stains my skin. Like a bar stamp. The server must have branded me last night. I must have forgotten.

I twist the faucet and thrust my arm under the stream. Water cascades over the markings, but the ink doesn't smudge or smear. I scrub with my knuckles to erase each line. That doesn't work either.

My mind churns. So does my stomach. But there must be some sort of explanation.

Before I drank myself into a blackout, I skimmed through flyers for sandcastle competitions and camera rentals and henna art. I must have stumbled from the arcade to the rec room. I must have plopped into a chair and had my skin stained.

I draw my arm closer to inspect the color. On amusement park vacations, Domino dragged us to henna stands. Artists dyed the backside of her hand orange, but her ink faded to a reddish-brown as the sun beat down and the day wore on. My markings are a few shades darker, closer to black. Closer to the hue of an actual, permanent tattoo.

"Are you feeling okay?" Laman asks. "Do you need a glass of water? A noose?"

"What?"

"Do you need water? Or juice?"

I toss my head, trying to concentrate, to visualize the bulletin board, to recall whether anything about tattoos was pinned amongst the flyers. I dig my nails in deep to flake ink, to peel edges, but nothing changes. The scratching only loosens my acrylics and irritates my skin. The area grows red and blotchy, but it doesn't hurt. Not as much as it should.

A new tattoo should have stung. It should have bled.

I close my eyes to summon up a lost memory of a tattoo parlor on Long Island. I picture orange walls with framed samples of praying hands and pierced hearts. I picture an artist applying a faint, blue stencil to my wrist. I picture a buzzing needle, stabbing lines into my flesh dot by dot.

My eyes flap open as I shake out my wrists, shake out my nerves. That scene isn't a part of my past. It's stolen from videos my sister showed me. She was the one who wanted to cover herself in ink, not me.

One morning, she sat cross-legged on the bottom bunk, scribbling a sea turtle onto her thigh with black eyeliner. I watched her in reverse, staring into the full-length mirror taped to our door.

"Why would you want to do that to yourself?" I asked, swinging my toes from the top bunk. "Piercings take two seconds, pop-pop, and the holes close if you don't want them anymore. Tattoos aren't like that."

"Yeah. That's the whole point. You have to pick something you really care about because you're stuck with it no matter what. Removing them is super painful."

"I don't know, I guess there's nothing I care about enough to put on me."

"What about a doggie?"

"I already have Dalmatian earrings. With a tail sticking out the back. Remember?"

"That's true." She contorted her leg in different directions, admiring her amateur sketch. "What about Mom and Dad then? You care about them."

"Not enough to put their name on my body. I don't like anybody that much."

"What if they died?"

"Maybe. But that's the only reason I would think about it. Otherwise, it's a no from me."

Another memory tumbles loose. Me, flopped in the backseat of our family car, fiddling with a plastic prayer card. The tattoo peeking from my sleeve was red and raw and itchy. Fresh. As we peeled out of a funeral-home parking lot, my father swore beneath his breath. My mother dabbed at her mascara with one hand and held the wheel with another, zigzagging the tires across the street.

The seat next to me was empty. Domino wasn't sitting in her usual spot. But dominos were on my wrist.

My head rushes. The bathroom tilts sideways as my knees buckle and tear against tile. Through blurred vision, I can make out Laman ducking to my level. She reaches out cold fingers to shutter my lids like a corpse. I lose consciousness as she slips away, as more memories bubble to the surface, as the stitches snap.

CHAPTER 9

I pop painkillers to chase away my headache, but it remains like a sword digging in one ear and corkscrewing around my skull. After my memories stormed over me, after I collapsed onto the bathroom tile, someone must have shuttled me back to my bedroom. I can't remember whether Laman or one of her guards tucked me into the sheets, but I remember everything else. Her commercial. Her email. Her tour. Her technician, who mentioned memories could be jogged under the right circumstances. Circumstances I happened to fit.

I think back to an episode of *Conspiracy Theory Theater* centered around hypnotism. The audience fidgeted in their velvet seats, shrinking to avoid being singled out in the crowd. The hypnotist calmed them by explaining only participants who willingly volunteered would be susceptible to his powers of suggestion. They would only believe if they wanted to believe.

Memory Cleansing must work the same way. Paying guests with RIP tattoos unloaded their life stories in audition tapes. They filed formal requests to visit the island. They begged to be brainwashed. If someone pointed out their memorial tattoo, they would avert their gaze and shift topics. But me? My subconscious *wanted* my memories jogged. Laman must have underestimated me.

Unless I was the one underestimating her.

Triggering me on purpose makes absolutely no sense, but she hasn't made sense from the start. She conducted a private tour with me, a nobody from a failing, fluffy talk show, when she could have been meeting with a network name. She granted me early access to a resort with a historically long waiting list. She assembled a volleyball net in broad view of the lounge chair I'd adopted for drinking. She drew blunt, blatant attention to my tattoo. She practically reached into my skull and unlaced the stitches herself.

I fling my sheets to my ankles and hobble toward the front door. I plan on hunting Laman down and demanding answers, but my legs pulse with each step. Dried blood is crusted across a kneecap. The other is swollen and discolored, a rust yellow. I brace myself on a countertop, out of breath from the short walk to the door. I need to rest. I need to think.

I crutch myself to the fridge. I stockpile enough mini bottles to numb the pain, collapse on the sofa, and cast my mind back to high school. Laman orbited outside my social circle, but we occasionally crossed paths in our one-story school. She skittered from class to class in a draping skirt that dragged against tile, a sweater two sizes too big, and an overstuffed backpack with a clutter of keychains. Kids gossiped about how she lived on the rich side of town but dressed like she came from the trailer homes.

I don't know much else, other than she earned valedictorian, which means her course load was stacked with AP and honors courses. Domino was placed in regular classes, so they must have met in an elective course. They must have frosted cupcakes in home economics or chucked footballs in the gym. Unless I was right about her being a customer, unless they met at the cabin on the beach.

I stumbled across the hideout by accident. A free messenger app our whole family used had automatically updated and added a friend tracker. Before my sister adjusted her privacy settings, a dot with her initials appeared on a 2D map. It planted itself on a beach when she was supposed to be at practice.

I still believed her lie. I assumed her teammates had moved the match outside. Domino looked funny enough as an emo in cherry-red gym shorts, so I could only imagine how awkward she would look in a two-piece. Sand would cling to her stubbled legs, worm its way into her belly button, dust her stringy hair. It would be a nightmare. I straddled my bike, planning on surprising her with a photo shoot as payback for borrowing a pair of Converse without permission.

When my tires cruised onto sand, I skimmed the shore for a net or an airborne ball. College boys in cutoff shirts sipped cheap beer. An unleashed dog sprinted after a Frisbee. Children carved out a shallow moat that the tide kept refilling. But no one on her team was in sight.

I double-checked my map. It placed Domino at the far end of the beach, a tumbledown area made of more dirt than sand. I followed the tracking dot to a row of wooden posts spearing the ground, warning NO ENTRY BEYOND THIS POINT. No one was around to enforce the rules, though. Families gathered in the clean areas without glass shards and cigarette stubs, the areas where fit lifeguards flirted with cougars and let underaged teens get away with drinking.

I slunk closer to the cabin with my phone primed to call 911. Used needles were scattered around the entrance. A black umbrella leaned against the doorway. I chickened out of knocking but gathered enough courage to peek through a speckled window. Domino's gym bag squatted on the floor. The map was right. She was here.

I texted her a casual *how's practice?* to test whether she would spill the beans. I heard the muffled alert along with mumbled voices. A minute later, an alert came through on my phone.

Same as always, she said. A lie.

I left in a huff.

"You know, I saw you today," I said later, slouched on opposite couch arms. Our parents puttered outside, gardening and grilling while we caught up on summer reading assignments.

"You're seeing me right now," she said, crossing her eyes.

"I meant at practice."

"You saw me at practice?"

"Yeah. On the beach."

She stiffened. Her cheeks lost color. "Are you going to tell anyone?"

"I don't know what I would tell them, really. I only looked through the window quick. I'm not exactly sure what I was seeing."

"Right." She twiddled the tassel on her bookmark, staring at the strings. "I would have told you sooner or later. I just never knew when to bring it up, so it seemed easier not to say anything. I understand if you're mad. Or weirded out or something. I get it. I'm a bad sister. I'm sorry."

She stuttered through each sentence. Her breathing grew short and ragged.

"Calm down," I said to stop her from spiraling into a panic attack. "I really don't give a shit. I'm sure when I'm a moody goth teenager I'll keep secrets from you, too."

Before she could stammer out an answer, the backdoor rolled. My mother sloshed inside with muddied boots. "Dinner should be ready soon," she singsonged as she peeled away sunshine yellow gloves. "I'm going to get washed up if one of you wants to win Daughter of the Year and set out the silverware."

I volunteered, practically sprinting from the room to give my sister space. I could see her through the doorway, tracing the same paragraph with her finger again and again. In the time it took for our father to finish browning the burgers, she only turned the page once.

I spent weeks slipping *beaches* and *volleyball* into conversations, giving her smooth segues to explain herself, but she never took the bait. I didn't want to push too hard and upset her again, so I let the matter drop. I stopped thinking about the cabin, stopped caring about the cabin. Until her suicide.

The week of her funeral, I stumbled onto the beach choking the neck of a vodka bottle. Black bits flaked from my tattoo in a bread-crumb trail, landing in between chewed coffee stirrers and torn sugar packets. I flashed my phone light from corner to corner, illuminating the litter. A ring caught my attention, dropped into a broken floorboard, covered in grime.

I tossed my bottle with the rest of the trash, pinched the ring, and blew cobwebs from the center. Domino had worn rubber bracelets with band logos, stretchy chokers, and skull earrings. She never sported any rings, but it looked like her style. Black. Studded. Simple. I seesawed it onto my index finger. A perfect fit.

I twirl the same ring, now old and discolored, from the resort room couch. I stare out the window at the simulated ocean view while reprocessing something Laman said before my memories returned. She said she spent almost every single day on a beach back in high school. She said she carried an umbrella for privacy, to avoid being seen.

If she spent that much time in the cabin, it couldn't have been to pick up pills. I twiddle with my tongue piercing, rethinking the narrative I've been telling myself since Domino died.

If my sister hadn't been selling drugs in the cabin, how did she earn her secret stash of money? From Endellion? Laman interned for them in high school. And according to the photo from the sauna, my sister signed papers for Laman in high school. Maybe they used the cabin as a research center? But then how did Antoni Tan factor into the equation? How did the suicide?

I'm tempted to scour the resort for Laman and shake answers out of her, but she must have fled the island by now. I should do the same. I test my strength, placing weight on one leg, then the other. They carry me into the washroom where I roll deodorant onto prickly armpits, change into a loose sundress, and pop on a bandage from a med kit beneath the sink. The beige strip only covers a third of the damage.

I limp toward the dock, planning to talk my way onto the next sub. Between my injuries and the elderly couple stuck in front of me, it's a painfully slow trek.

"I don't think my jaw has ever been this sore," the older woman says, wheeling a puffy suitcase. Her husband must wink or waggle his brows because she tuts at him. "I mean because of how much I've been smiling."

His liver-spotted fingers wrap around hers. "I sure do love that smile. You have a better one than any of the girls here, dentures or no dentures."

"You're such a sweet talker. You haven't changed since the night we met."

In the distance, I spot the sub waiting with its hatch unscrewed. I pick up the pace, swerving around the old couple whose delusional love story is ending soon.

"What do you need?" the guard asks when my feet hit the dock. She squints at her security pass. "You're not on the list."

"I know, but I don't feel great. I took a fall the other day."

"I'm sorry to hear that. I can send a medic to your room for a checkup."

"I'd rather get out of here."

Her head shakes once, a firm *no*. "You're not scheduled to leave for another few days."

"What's the difference? Someone else can start their vacation early."

"It doesn't work like that. We run on a strict schedule."

"You don't understand. I really need to go home."

"I really need you to step aside."

Her scowl warms to a smile as the elderly couple totters up to her. She checks their information, transports their suitcases into the stomach of the sub, and guides them down the ladder.

"Come on," I say when she resurfaces. "They're not taking up much room. Neither will I. I don't have any suitcases. You can squeeze me down there easy."

"Fitting you isn't the issue. I have to follow protocol."

"Isn't keeping people safe part of protocol? I don't feel comfortable here."

Her head tilts. "What do you mean? Has someone been bothering you? I can file a report. We don't tolerate abusive behavior here."

I hesitate. Confessing that my memories returned prematurely might get me shipped off for another surgery. "Forget it. I've just been having a rough morning. I'll get over it."

I hobble toward the plaza in search of a new plan. Everything looks different than yesterday, when my memories were rosy and silver-lined. Now, the cartoon signs look more childish than charming. The guards look more intimidating than kind.

One of them emerges from the side of the strip, beaming. He reminds me of the woman on the mainland who argued with the receptionist. The woman who stormed through the angel door scowling and came out whistling.

I creep to the edge of the U-shaped building for a closer look. A skinny, paved path is hidden by shrubbery. It curves around the backside of the property.

I check that no one is looking and sneak down the trail. I pass boxes coiled with power cords. A network of pipes. A row of dumpsters.

On the flipside of the building, there are three doors. I peek through the window on one. It leads to a storage room tucked behind the rec room. Another leads to a kitchen attached to the cafeteria. The last is missing a window. It has a symbol instead. A winged brain wearing a halo, the same as the employee lounge on the mainland.

A long, telescopic security camera swivels above me, but I risk drawing closer. I unhinge the cover on a metal box, revealing a pad of numbers.

I type in the year Laman delivered her graduation speech. A single bulb blinks red. I try her birth year. Another blink. I estimate the date the resort opened. Blink. Blink. Blink.

I rattle through anything and everything I think she might deem important enough to use as a passcode. I test the date Domino was born and the red light returns. Then I tap in the day she died. A lock clicks. The door hisses in invitation.

I take a long, lingering look into the camera. Breaking in feels too easy. It feels like a trap.

I enter anyway.

The room is split by a ceiling track curtain. A razor-thin laptop rests on a wheelable surgical table along with an untouched plate of eggs. File cabinets and double-doored medical cabinets hug the surrounding walls. I cup a hand over frosted glass, peering into the closest one. Its shelves are cluttered with a rainbow array of candles, perfume bottles, and incense sticks. Green Apple. French Lavender. Caramel Pumpkin. Trademarked scents are mixed in between, with labels like Endellion Ivy, Endellion Breeze, and Endellion Almond.

The adjacent cabinet is piled with cardboard boxes. Random bits and pieces protrude from their tops. Plastic nose pieces. Coiled wires secured with twist ties. Cylindrical tubes engraved with MEMORY SCENT TECHNOLOGY. A heavy brass padlock binds the doors together, protecting the stash.

"Are you back already?"

I freeze. The voice comes from a few feet away, the opposite side of the curtain.

"Are you back?" the man repeats with a gasping, wheezing cough. It takes a few clock ticks for him to compose himself. He doesn't sound threatening. He sounds sick.

I tiptoe close enough to peel away the curtain. The hooks scrape and screech against their metal rod. Directly across from me, in the hidden section of the room, a chunky computer spills thick, tentacle-like cables into two metal chairs. On a shorter side wall, a bloated IV bag sags over a hospital bed. A mess of chocolate hair peeks from the covers.

"Jesus Christ. Are you okay?" I scurry over and ease the blanket to his chest. A ratty, tangled beard climbs across sunken cheeks. Broken blood vessels darken his eyes to red. "What happened? What's your name? How did you get here?"

His overgrown brows furrow. "I'm not sure."

"About which part? About how you got here?"

"About any of it."

"Did you have a Memory Cleansing? Did it go wrong? Did they hurt you and lock you in here so no one could see?"

"Hurt? Me? No." He rubs his runny nose. Snot sticks to his knuckles. "I cause the hurt, mostly."

"What do you mean? Who did you hurt?"

He clears the rasp from his throat. "My wife. She threw the wrappers in the wrong trashcan. The one in our bathroom. She knew the cat kept knocking the lid off. She knew I would see. She couldn't do anything right, not even cheat. She was almost as dumb as the boy we caught smoking dope out in PA. That poor, stupid kid." The new story comes with a subtle shift in his tone, like he's playing hot potato with his voice box, passing the microphone off to another character. "It's not like I wanted to hurt him. I have boys of my own. That's why I wasn't going to wait for him to strike first. I wasn't risking my babies growing up without their daddy. Anyone would have done the same thing as me. Anyone. Of course, the worst was that sweet little girl last winter." Another shift. Another character taking control. "I tried to knock a hole through the second-story window, but her parents had installed shatterproof glass. They wanted to protect her from a break-in. They never expected a fire. I was right there. I could see her holding her little stuffed dragon to her chin, wailing and wailing, but the guys at the fire station couldn't get there soon enough. I couldn't save her without them."

He crumbles into thick, sloppy tears. His beard catches more snot.

"Did someone put those thoughts in your head?" I ask, latching onto a bruised hand. "Are you sure those are your memories? I don't think one person could do all those things. I don't think you're remembering right."

He squirms beneath the sheets. His dilated eyes spread and squint, spread and squint, like the question hurts to think about.

I try again. "When you heard me come in, you thought I was someone else. Who usually comes in here?"

"Friends. They like it here. They like me."

"Is Rhea Laman one of your friends?"

His cheek twitches. His eyes flutter to the whites. Panicked, I press my palm against his caved chest. His heartbeat races. I rock his shoulders to wake him, but he shows no signs of stirring. His snores rattle like a broken bike chain.

I gawk at his gaunt, gangly body, trying to align his reaction with the woman on the mainland. She emerged from a room with the same symbol, serene and smiling. If they underwent the same procedure, they should've had the same results.

I rub the laptop on the surgical table to life, hunting for some sort of explanation. A password box spans the screen. I guess different versions of *Domino* bookended by numbers. On guess ten, a TOO MANY PASSWORD ATTEMPTS message freezes the screen.

The monitor lodged between chairs has the same blinking password box and the medical cabinets are locked tight, so I head toward the file cabinets. I unroll the top drawer, expecting to sort through manila envelopes stuffed with guest applications or resort blueprints.

Instead, dozens of video chips are crammed into plastic storage organizers. Each one is tagged with the date of filming. I rummage for the day Domino died, the month, the year.

Heavy footsteps stop me.

"Maybe I should wait. I feel weird going against her rules," a man says. It comes from the opposite side of the steel door this time. The security camera picks up the audio and relays it through an internal set of speakers.

"Don't be a puss," a woman says. "Everyone does it. We made an agreement. Whenever an alert about this place goes off, we ignore it. There's no chance Laman will find out. Either way, it doesn't look like anyone is scheduled to guard this place today. That's how much of a damn anyone gives."

I whirl in every direction, hunting for an emergency exit, a vent, a window.

"I just know I could have waited on this one." The man sighs. "It's like when a fly is buzzing through the room. You don't need it out, but you *need* it out. Does that make sense?"

The lock clicks on the only door. The handle twists sideways. I swipe the most recent video from the drawer and bury myself in between the bunched-up curtain and cabinet.

I can see their hazy outlines through the fabric. The woman, dressed in a green guard uniform, taps a wordy password into the computer. The man, strapped with a hairnet, plops himself onto one of the metal chairs flanking the monitor.

"This place is fancy," he says, nodding his approval. "My other Transfers were done on the mainland with thirty-two or thirty-three. Her room was half this size. With roommates."

The woman stomps toward the bed. "This is number one, The Original. He's my favorite. He never curses or chomps down like the others."

She clamps onto his frail wrists, heaves him from his stained bedsheets. He crumples like a rag doll against her bosom, murmuring the same question over and over. It takes three or four tries for anyone to understand him.

"Did the lady leave?" he asks. "Did she leave?"

My stomach clenches. I brace myself to be found, but neither worker turns or tilts a head.

The man only grunts. "Laman? She was here? I thought she was marketing the Memory Scent tech in Cali."

"Who knows? None of these crooks make any goddamn sense. He's talking gibberish."

"I thought the first batch of these guys weren't criminals."

"Does it really matter?" She flings The Original onto the unoccupied chair. With a practiced rhythm, she binds his ankles, neck, and torso with broad leather straps. "You want to tell the story? Get it off your chest before getting it off your mind?"

The man scratches beneath his hairnet, rips the cap from his scalp, and fiddles with it as he speaks. "Eh, it's the dumbest thing. I was assigned to one of the Endellion Enterprise stations on the mainland. I don't know if you've ever been to the conference hall they built, but there's a concession stand where we sell chicken fingers and hot dogs and personal pizzas, kid stuff. I guess I programmed the oven wrong yesterday because the place ended up bathed in smoke. I'm lucky I didn't burn the whole place down. Makes me feel like I'm getting old, like I can't do a simple job right. I would rather not think about it."

"I hear you. Let's get rid of that sucker."

The woman enters a string of commands into the monitor. As her fingers dance across the keyboard, helmets rise from the backs of both chairs. They tilt into position and drop, covering the men to their chins.

With a few more keystrokes, the monitor in between them hums awake. One side of the machine sucks like a vacuum. The other side whooshes like a leaf blower.

I risk peeking out from the crumpled curtain. The tubes connecting the chairs to the main monitor are wrapped in screens. Ones and zeros flicker across them like ping pong balls in a lotto machine. They travel from the officer to the computer to The Original.

My pupils flick between the numbers and the helmets, the data and the brains.

During our tour, Laman told me memories couldn't be destroyed, only temporarily repressed. The closest thing to erasing them permanently must be transferring them from one mind to another. That would explain why the officer on the mainland came out whistling and The Original has been whittling into a corpse. A worker gets rid of a memory. The Original gains a memory.

"Lord, that's better," the man says after the machine completes its cycle and the helmets rise.

The woman unbinds The Original and chucks him on the bed with his gown unflapped. "This sucker could cure heroin addiction," she says. "I haven't smoked a single cigarette since getting hired here."

"They could have marketed this place as rehab."

"Eh, it's better as a resort. Nobody wants to admit they need a shrink."

"But they won't shut up about needing more vacation days."

"Exactly."

I stay crunched in my hiding spot, waiting until the door thumps, until the footsteps fade.

Once I'm alone, I crawl out from the curtain with the video chip balled in my sweating palm. I could inspect the cabinets some more, but I want to get the hell away from the hulking machine and the helmeted chairs and the poor, tortured soul sprawled unconscious in a hospital bed.

CHAPTER 10

I plug the stolen chip into an SD slot on my resort television. The camera pans across an audience. Badges glint on chests. Guns sag in holsters. Hundreds of police officers watch Laman walk onto the stage. Half of them wear official NYPD uniforms. The other half wear the electric-green, Endellion kind.

"I'm Rhea Laman, owner of Endellion Enterprises," she says into a bendable microphone. A coffee cup balances on her podium. "It has been an honor to partner with law enforcement, to provide you with the same benefits every Endellion worker receives: the ability to transfer your unwanted memories into the minds of rapists, murderers, and child molesters.

"It's likely that, before we came along, some of their minds had already developed a series of false memories as coping mechanisms to deal with their traumatic pasts. That is to say, the implementation of false memories is not an unnatural one. Every brain is capable of creating false memories on its own.

"The storage capacity of the brain is limitless. A single mind could house hundreds, thousands, millions of pieces of data. That means one convict can help millions of officers do their jobs better. In the same way teenagers who have never had their hearts broken can love with an intensity no one else can, officers who are still starry-eyed and hopeful can perform better than officers who have turned bitter from experience. Of course, this is old news to you. I'm sure you want me to get to something fun, something new."

The audience chuckles and murmurs their agreement.

"Since you all took the initiative to come down here today, I'm going to let you in on what we're exploring next. Olfactory memory."

A projector sprays a 3D brain onto the curtain behind her. She uses a laser pointer to indicate different areas.

"The olfactory nerve is located near the amygdala, which is linked to emotion. It's also near the hippocampus, which is linked to memory. This is why scents can trigger memories better than any other sense *and* why those memories can trigger strong emotional responses. When someone smells the scent of cinnamon, for instance, they might remember the cookies their late grandmother used to bake and get misty-eyed. When someone smells the lavender perfume their ex wore, they might get aroused. This happens naturally every single day."

She clicks to the next slide. Sketches of a prototype span the screen. I recognize the bits and pieces. They stuck out from a cardboard box in the cabinet with a chunky brass lock.

"I'm honored to introduce Memory Scent technology. You only need one appointment at an Endellion location to prep your brain for unlimited uses. During your appointment, we'll insert artificial associations between emotions and our unique, copyrighted scents. That way, we'll all have the *same* associations and can pump our branded scents through a room like this one to experience sensations together.

However, inside of your own home, you can use *any* scents that have personal meaning to you. With the help of this portable, easy-to-use device, you'll be able to alter your mood whenever you wish. When you're anxious, you can make yourself feel at ease. When you're scared, you can make yourself feel safe. When you're lonely, you can make yourself feel loved."

She finishes with a demonstration. She plugs a thin wire into a tube like a set of headphones. The opposite end branches into a nose piece similar to the one my father uses for his oxygen tanks. The scent, which she inserts in the main tube, travels through the wires with a press of a button.

"Hundreds of officers have gotten their associations inserted at past conferences," she says as the projector flickers and fades. "If you're interested in doing the same, please form a line in the back of the auditorium."

*

I scroll through applications on my band in search of an email app, a texting app, a carrier pigeon app, any link to the outside world. A built-in Endellion Caller allows guests to walkie-talkie workers and other guests, but off-island calling features are unavailable.

I could dial someone on shift, but I don't trust any of them after what I witnessed beyond the angel door. My only option is to put my faith in another guest, someone scheduled to leave, someone who could deliver a message for me.

I tear apart my room for a sheet of paper and a pencil, but I might as well look for a stone slab and a chisel. The whole island runs on technology. The corkboard in the rec room is an electronic imitation. The chalkboard signs at the bar are cleverly disguised tablets. The only books and magazines available are digital, pre-programmed into security bands. Except one.

I dart to the coffee table to borrow a blank page from the Bible, then rifle through my shopping bags for my new nail polish. I sweep the bristles across the page. They form thick, wobbly shapes. The letters bleed together.

A detailed letter warning about the secret surgeries is never going to work. I need to keep it simple.

I tear out a fresh page and draw a large, goopy phone number. While the polish is uncapped, I spiral a thick mark on a hazelnut vanilla coffee pod. If Laman performs another Cleansing on me, a whiff of the coffee she carries with her everywhere should trigger memories of her luring me here and lying.

When my note dries, I step outside on the lookout for suitcases. There should be one more round trip before the night ends. One family. One chance.

A batch of obnoxious children holler *Marco Polo* in the pool. Two toast-burned teenagers poke tongues in a hot tub. A Korean couple hogs extra barstools with a set of bright blue luggage.

I sprint over and park myself between them, careful to make eye contact with them both. "Hi, how are you? I was wondering if you could help me out with something."

They exchange blank looks.

"Since you're heading back to the mainland, I was wondering if you could get in touch with someone for me. It's important." They stare at the note thrust toward them but make no move to grab it. "There's a number on here. For a man named Cassidy. I just need you to give him a quick message. I would ask someone else, but it looks like you're the last ones leaving today and this really shouldn't wait until tomorrow."

"Nan ihaega an dwaeyo," the woman says. The man responds with even more syllables.

"I would translate for you, but they're not going to help," their son says. He hangs onto the back of a barstool like a set of monkey bars. "I didn't translate when you swore at me the other day, either. Daddy wouldn't be too happy."

"Oh. Yeah. Sorry about that. I wasn't myself."

"Who were you?"

"It's just a saying." I take a knee. His mother eyeballs me, but she lets the conversation continue. "Hey, are you allowed to use the phone at home? Do you know how to call someone?"

"We have our own cellphones. I have emoji keyboards with Spider-Man and The Flash and Black Panther and—"

"That's great. Do you think you can give someone a message for me as soon as you get your phone back? It would help stop bad guys from doing bad things. You would be like a superhero, too."

He perks, bouncing on the heels of his light-up shoes. "What would I have to do?"

"Something very, very important," I say, stalling. When his mother turns to order another drink, I wedge the note into his backpack. I stuff the video chip along with it. "Make sure not to lose those. Call the number on the paper and ask for *Cassidy*. Tell him Endellion is not safe. There are bad people here. There are crimes. Make sure he doesn't contact the cops. The cops can't be trusted, either. Is that too much to remember?"

"Nope. I'm good at memory games. Like that shell one. I always find the pearl. What's that other thing?"

"A video. Let him know *Ari* left it for him as evidence. As a clue. I'm sure he'll find a way to get it from you. He can have you mail it or download it or something. You two will figure it out. Does all of this make sense?"

He starts to repeat the details back to me, but his sister interrupts with a high-pitched whine. She cowers behind the neighboring stool, eyes round and watery. "Where are the bad people?" she asks, pressing two tiny fists against a wobbling mouth. "Are they here now?"

Their mother notices the tears. She slams her drink, mutters something that must be a curse, and storms toward the dock, dragging her children by the wrists.

The father lingers to chug her leftover drink. Instead of swallowing, he tilts his head down and spits in my face.

Their surgeries must be wearing off early.

"I'm so sorry about that, miss," the bartender says, ripping napkins from a dispenser. "Endellion doesn't approve of that kind of behavior. Here. I'll put together a special drink to make up for it."

I swat away the saliva skidding down my cheek. "That's okay, maybe later," I say, promising myself to stay awake. Alert. Alive.

I beeline to the public bathroom to wash my face. I hope the germs are worth it. I hope the boy gets in touch with Cassidy.

I scrub myself with a rough brown paper towel while staring at the watercolor over the sink. The abstract painting makes less and less sense the more I try to figure it out.

I'm about to pump more runny pink soap onto my towel when my security pass shivers. An alert rolls across the screen. VIDEO CALL FROM RHEA LAMAN. My fingers snap into fists, but I keep my face neutral as I press *accept*.

"Ariadna, I wanted to see how you were doing after your tumble the other day," she says. Extensions form a single, Rapunzel-length braid down her chest. Heavy eyeliner swoops toward her plucked brows. "I heard you were thinking about ending your vacation early."

"I was considering it."

"I'm sorry to hear that. I hope you'll choose to stay with us a little longer."

"It doesn't seem like I have a choice. I tried to get on a sub. Your guard wasn't crazy about the idea."

"Yes, well, we do things a certain way around here. But I don't understand why you would want to leave. This doesn't have anything to do with what Mister Tan told you, does it?"

"Tan?" I choke on the name. "As in Antoni Tan?"

Her old boyfriend? The last person my sister texted before stringing a rope around her neck? *I hope you know this is entirely your fault. I hope you spend the rest of your life blaming yourself for this. I hope what I'm doing makes it clear that I don't love you and never have.*

Laman nods. "I heard you snuck into his room."

Blood whooshes to my head. I lean against the sink to stop myself from collapsing.

The man banished to a hospital bed, with his scrawny arms and bushy, tangled beard, looks nothing like the high school version of Antoni Tan. In his social media pictures, he wore hockey shorts around thick, solid thighs. He buzzcut his hair, razored his chin. He was an average kid. *A kid.*

"Did you dump someone else's memories into Domino like you did to him?" I ask. My entire body shakes, itching to wind my hands around her throat, to carve the smile from her face. "Is that why she killed herself? Because she thought she was some horrible person? Because you stuffed fake memories in her head from one of your cop friends?"

"Endellion is financed by the government. I've been forced to create a relationship with the police force over my career. I'm not thrilled about helping them, either." Her voice never hardens to match mine. She stays infuriatingly calm.

"By helping them, you mean dumping their memories into your old classmates?"

"Into criminals. Antoni was the original, the exception. I didn't realize what was going to happen to him. Everyone since then has been transported to Endellion locations from maximum-security prisons. These men and women are given much better care in our facilities than in the penitentiaries we rescued them from. We give them adjustable, pillow-soft mattresses instead of concrete slabs. We give them fresh-cooked meals instead of bread and water. All in all, they're treated more like guests than felons."

"Bullshit. Antoni is starving to death. And what you're doing to the cops is just as bad as what you're doing to the criminals. You realize erasing their mistakes makes it easy for them to do the same thing all over, right? If they can shoot a kid and get away with it, what's stopping them from doing it again?"

"Their commanders should be stopping it by firing them. Unfortunately, that never happens. It's been like that for decades. It's never going to change, which means what I'm doing isn't causing any real harm." Her mouth ticks to the side. "It might not be the perfect plan, but as long as we're working with them, we can keep this place running. They would shut us down otherwise. I can't afford for that to happen. Not for a few more days."

"Why? What happens then?"

Her fingers dart into frame. She fiddles with her security pass until a lock clicks. I assume the sound has come from her side of the screen, but then the hissing starts.

I crane my neck toward the ceiling vents. A light mist sprays from the slats, mingling with my oxygen.

"What is this? What are you trying to do, Laman?"

I bolt to the door and wriggle the handle. It doesn't budge. I ram my shoulder against the metal once, twice, three times. A blinding pain shoots down my arm, but the door stays standing.

Laman exhales, drawing my attention back to the screen. "I was going to do this while you were sleeping, so you weren't as frazzled. But I think it's best if we get it over with now. Luckily, the whole resort is prepared. The bathroom works just as well as your resort room." She offers a soft smile. "Don't worry, it's not going to hurt you. It's the same anesthesia used on the mainland, meant to make you sleepy. You might want to sit down, though. You don't want to bang your head if you fall again."

"Screw you." I rip off my band and chuck it, killing the video.

I press an ear against the exit. I don't hear any water slide splashes or clinking glasses or screaming children running across the plaza. That means the room is insulated, soundproof. Screaming would only waste my voice.

I scan my surroundings. I could clog the vents with toilet paper or towels, but the padding wouldn't restrain the scent for long. Either way, the grates are elevated, unreachable.

I would have an easier time accessing the windows set over each toilet. They're too tight to squeeze myself through, but I could ventilate the room with them, buy myself a few extra minutes.

I pinch my nose and scramble into a stall. I climb onto the toilet seat, straddle the bowl, and stretch an arm across the panes. My nail grazes the lock but my legs wobble, still sore from my first fall. Right as I unhook the latch, my knees buckle. One foot lands on solid ground. The other plunks into toilet water.

I hop backward to untangle myself. I prop myself against the stall for balance and shake out my leg, drying my dripping sandal.

I try to remount the bowl, but with one hand holding my nostrils closed and one foot still dripping with water, I immediately lose my balance. I slip off the porcelain. I crumple onto tile.

The fall knocks the wind out of me. I breathe in a deep, gasping breath. Completely exposed, the anesthesia travels fast. It slackens my limbs. It slows my heartbeats.

My vision goes last. It fades to black as a single thought runs through my mind. *I wonder if she drugged Domino, too.*

CHAPTER 11

I wake to the shrill beep of a heart monitor. Beside it, an IV feeds me liquid from a sloshing, bottom-heavy bag. I try to yank the wire snaking into my veins, but my arm stays anchored in place. The same thing happens with my legs.

I hoist my head high enough to spot the problem. Cords wind around my ankles and wrists and chest, binding me to a surgical table.

Laman bends over me, shining a penlight into my eyes. Her teeth are a shade whiter than when we met on the mainland. A push-up bra deepens her cleavage. "Do you really think Domino killed herself because of me?" she asks.

It takes me three tries to speak without hacking. "You messed with her head. You must have."

"I never wanted anything bad to happen to her, Ari."

"You weren't at her funeral. Or any birthday parties. She never mentioned you."

"We stayed away from your house. It was too risky. We would sneak into a cabin on the beach most evenings. Once in a while, we would get dinner a few towns over. Or take the train to the aquarium."

My monitors chirp a warning about spiked blood pressure, elevated heart rate. "Is that where you would have your Endellion meetings? I saw the picture of her signing papers with you. You used her as a guinea pig, didn't you? You did something to her."

"I understand why you would assume that, but I would never hurt your sister. Not after four years together."

The medication slows my thoughts to a crawl. "What do you mean, together? Weren't you dating Antoni Tan?"

"Not until the end of senior year. That was after your sister tossed away the ring you're wearing right now. Antoni was only a rebound. He was a way to make Domino jealous, so she would want me back. Or a way to prove I didn't want *her* back. I'm not sure. Memories change, you know. Whenever you think about the past, you're not remembering an actual memory. You're remembering the last instance you remembered the memory. It's like a game of telephone with yourself." A pause. "You look confused, but bisexuality isn't all that complicated. It's brain chemistry."

"She never said…" I stumble to complete my thought, any thought. Endless questions tingle on my tongue. "You weren't doing surgeries on her in the cabin? Or selling drugs?"

"Of course not. Domino never took drugs. Other than marijuana, obviously, but more than enough studies have proven it's safer than alcohol." She chews on her lower lip, inspecting me. "I'm sorry. I thought you knew most of this. She told me you saw us at the cabin. You never contacted me after her death, so I assumed you only saw *part* of me and wasn't sure exactly who I was."

I flash back to that night on the couch. I called Domino out about keeping secrets, but I dropped the subject when she spiraled toward a panic attack. I never asked her about the cabin again. I should have asked her again.

"What happened to her, then? Why did she kill herself? Why was she signing those papers?"

"I only wanted the best for your sister. I was devastated when she died. I dabbled with the idea of suicide myself, but I realized I needed to make it up to her. Fix my mistakes."

"You built this whole place because of her? Why haven't you used those machines on yourself? Why haven't you forgotten about her by now?"

"I would never want to forget her. I guess we have that in common."

Wheels rattle against tile. Laman rolls an overbed table toward me, positioning the tray inches away from my stomach. The surface glints with a scalpel, forceps, and a wide range of needles.

I jerk my wrists, trying to work myself free. The bindings nip at my skin. They carve grooves into my flesh. "Domino wouldn't want you to hurt me, Laman. She wouldn't want you to give me another one of your bullshit surgeries. I don't know why you bothered to have me go through a Memory Cleansing in the first place if you were going to jog my memories a few days after I got here."

"This next procedure is complicated. All our past trials failed, so we've been extra cautious with you. We've been monitoring your brain waves with a micro camera Cara inserted on the mainland. We wanted to see what would trigger your memories, whether you would be able to retrieve them in full. Now that we have adequate information, we can prevent you from being triggered in those same ways after this next surgery."

"What do you mean all your past trials failed? You mean people died doing what you're about to do to me?"

"Unfortunately, progress requires sacrifice. I'm sure you've heard of the Milgram Experiment or The Stanford Prison Experiment or The Monster Study. They were all morally reprehensible, but they helped us learn much more about the human psyche."

"I get why she never told us about you," I say, still thrashing. "She knew she could do better."

Her smile falters, but she quickly composes herself. "I easily could have kept you asleep and performed this surgery against your will, but I wanted your consent, your blessing." She props a tablet on my table, using its cover as a stand. "This might help you understand why your next procedure needs to happen."

She presses the triangular *play* button. A close-up of my mother spills across the screen. A dark spot stains her collar from swiping snot and tears. Red puffs outline her eyes. In the corner, a date flickers. Two months ago, almost to the day. It must be her application tape.

"My name is Maria Diaz," she says, over-enunciating each consonant for the camera. "I live in a cottage on Long Island with my husband. He's in a wheelchair, unable to walk or speak or eat solid food. He blamed himself when our little girl passed. He tried to punish himself for failing her, but he only ended up making me and my other daughter suffer more. I've been worried about her lately. About the way she's handling everything.

Even before the suicide, my husband was an alcoholic. He was never violent enough to file a police report or take my girls to a hotel, but there were some holes in the wall we had to spackle and dishes we had to replace. We tried not to argue around the girls, but I'm sure they heard a thing or two through the walls."

That was an understatement. We could hear every creak, every curse. Domino crawled into my bunk during their whisper-scream arguments, our thumbs stuffed in our ears, la-la-laing until we fell asleep nuzzled like swans. In the morning, during ham and egg breakfasts, we chickened out of asking our mother what had happened. Everything felt okay in the daylight.

"I signed my girls up for therapy when they were in elementary school. I used to bring them to Al-Anon meetings at least once a month as well. That's a support group for families of alcoholics. They teach the Twelve Steps there. I wanted my girls to learn them early. They say children of alcoholics usually marry an alcoholic or become one themselves and Ariadna is never going to marry. I don't want her to end up like her father, but she always has a glass of something in her hand. I think it's because she's so stressed. She stopped going to therapy after her sister died. She stopped seeing friends, too. Now she doesn't really do anything except work. I don't want to make her stress worse, so I never complain about the hospital bills or the demand letters or the husband who I would have divorced after the kids left the house if it wasn't for his accident.

"I should probably be harder on Ari. I could hold some sort of intervention, but I don't want to scare her away from me. She's why I want to come here. A trip to Endellion might bring us back together. It might help her get better. It might give her a reason to change. Please. She needs this. She needs help. I don't want to lose my second daughter. I don't want to go through that heartache again."

Tears prick my eyes. The medication loosens my muscles, making it impossible to hold back my emotion. Thick, sloppy drops slope down my nose and coat my tongue with salt.

I could have driven my father to more appointments. I could have cut down on alcohol. I could have called Doctor Q. I could have given my mother less to stress over when she was already dealing with enough.

"Did you ever feel like the wrong sister died?" Rhea asks, cupping my shoulder.

I flinch but can't shake her off me.

"Did you ever pray about taking her place?"

"I'm an atheist," I say.

"Ari. You understand the question."

"There's no point in thinking about stuff like that. It doesn't make a difference."

"Maybe it does. You and your sister have similar DNA. I can take her memories, her essence, and put it in you. I can replace you with her."

It doesn't sink in at first. I don't think I've heard her right.

"You said it yourself back when we first met, Ari. Memory Cleansings are pointless because they only last one week. I think your mother deserves more than a temporary vacation. She deserves the daughter she lost. She deserves to have Domino back."

I rattle my head, more confused than anything. If she operates on me, it won't actually be my sister banging around in my brain, resurrected from the dead. It will be my imitation of her. In my body. With my voice. Pretending. Like Antoni Tan, convinced he's a dozen different people when he only has their history.

"I'm going to ease her into her new identity," Laman says. "I'm going to keep her in the dark at first, away from your mother, away from the mainland, just to be safe. I'm concerned about sending your body into shock by Transferring all of your memories in one large bulk, so we're only going to Cleanse for now. Every week. We'll gradually work up to Transferring. Maybe into Antoni. We had him moved to make room for you in here, but we'll bring him back. He deserves some nicer thoughts. Once he passes, there will be no going back. That's when we can give Domino the truth. She'll have to accept it. So will your mother."

"This is psychotic. You can't just... It's not going to..." My thoughts are too disconnected, too disorganized, to bunch into words. The drugs coursing through my system aren't helping. They turn my tongue to lead, my mind to mush. I keep starting to protest and stuttering to a stop. Technically, I never tell her *no*.

"This should put you to sleep for the procedure," she says. She fiddles with the IV bag, unleashing liquid. It funnels down the tube, vanishing into my veins. "My best surgeon will be in shortly to begin. Don't worry. You're doing the right thing, Ari."

PART II

CHAPTER 12

A machine measures my heartbeat in squiggles. An IV drip-drip-drips into my veins.

"Domino? Are you in there?" a woman asks. Her ghost-white hand squeezes mine. I follow a trail of veins up to a freckled neck and puffer-fish lips.

She looks too old, too plastic, to recognize. The nickname is what gives her away. I trusted my girlfriend with the infamous domino story thinking she would be on my side, but it backfired. She called me Domino as a joke at first, a harmless tease. I scolded her but could never hold back my smirk for long. Hearing her use the name my parents and sister called me made her feel a little more like family.

On our first anniversary, I officially embraced the name. I dug up a pair of dominos from a cobwebbed chest in the attic, drilled holes in their tops during tech class, and strung a lanyard through the center. Rhea clipped the makeshift keychain to her backpack zipper. Everyone could hear her jangling down the halls, but she never minded the attention. I think she wanted people to ask about the present, ask about me. But I swore her to secrecy.

"I missed you so much," she says with the husky rasp of a smoker. Strange. She's always stayed away from bongs, blunts, cigarettes, anything with a flame. Maybe she's been crying, then. Maybe she's been screaming.

I squint around the room. "Which hospital is this?" I ask. A cream curtain bends around my bed. Metal chairs connect to a monitor pressing against a windowless wall. The only light flickers from naked fluorescent bulbs.

"You're on an island facility. Domino…your family was in a car accident on the way home from Niagara." She pumps my hand like a heartbeat. "It wasn't their fault. It was raining. They didn't see the construction signs and tipped into a gully. The windshield shattered. The engine exploded. The paramedics saved your mother, but the accident left your father paralyzed and your sister…she didn't make it. I'm so sorry."

I blink. Blink again. "I've been in a coma?"

"For around ten years. I know that must be scary to hear, but I'm here with you. I'm going to make sure you're okay."

She rubs a thumb over my knuckles and waits with her head tilted, like she expects an outburst. I only nod. The news is unsurprising, like I had already known deep in my subconscious. It hurts, but it feels right. It's the room that feels wrong with its towering metal machine. It's Rhea, with her creased, aged eyes.

"Where's my mom?" I say, staring at the door like she might burst through with her arms spread. "Is she here?"

"I've been trying to get ahold of her. You'll be able to talk soon."

"I want her with me." I lean weight on my arms, trying to prop myself into a sitting position. A yelp shoots out. I glance down to see cotton gauze spiraling across my forearm. It winds four fingers together. The thumb pokes out like a turtle head.

"Be careful. You need to let yourself heal." Rhea presses a button, slanting my bed to a forty-five-degree angle. "How do you feel? Aside from the wrist?"

"My head hurts. It feels like a cat is clawing at me."

Her lips bunch to the side. "We should bring you someplace more comfortable. I sent some of my cleaning staff to prepare a room for you. It should be ready by now if you'd like to sleep in a real bed. I'll call for a wheelchair."

"Your staff? Do you own the hospital?"

She pokes a screen strapped to her hand. "It's not a hospital."

I struggle to follow along as she whizzes through a decade of missed milestones. After earning valedictorian in high school, she graduated from Princeton with honors. She won prize money from regional, national, and worldwide neurochemistry awards. She inherited some more money when her parents passed, both from surgical complications.

She used her fortune to buy out a relatively unknown company, Endellion Enterprises, the place she secretly interned for in high school. She built an island resort in their name to bring families closer together, a way of honoring the dead in her family and mine. At some point, she convinced my mother to release me from the Long Island hospital where I'd been withering away in a coma. She helicoptered me onto the island where her private doctors provided me with specialized treatment which led to my recovery.

I peek at the IV bag, swimming with goop. "How strong are these drugs? Shouldn't I feel worse than this?"

"There have been a lot of advancements in the past decade. A lot has changed."

I have an endless supply of questions, but the door claps. Wheels whimper. A man with a goatee black as a storm cloud pushes a wheelchair to my bedside.

Without warning, Rhea scoops her arms beneath my pits. She repositions me while the man holds the chair steady. When my soles are planted firmly on the footrests, I grab the joystick to tilt and roll.

Rhea tuts at me. "Easy," she says. She nudges the goateed man aside and grips the rubber handles herself. She guides me around the spread curtain, giving me a glimpse at the other side. There are file cabinets, medical cabinets, laptops, and a stout guard guarding it all.

Aware my girlfriend isn't going to let me man the controls anytime soon, I uncurl my fingers from the joystick. I flop my hands onto my lap and notice my ring—along with a set of long, pointed acrylics.

Rhea must catch me staring. As we bump along a back alley lined with dumpsters, she says, "I know you hate those things, but when you were starting to come out of the coma, you kept scratching at your IV. I was worried about you hurting yourself. I read a study about how women with excoriation disorder—that's a skin-picking disorder—attach artificial nails to prevent scratching, so I gave it a try. And, before you freak out, you lost some of your hair during our procedures. But it's growing back and the fake nails can be taken off, so it's nothing to worry about."

"You could have at least made them black," I say, running them across my scalp. There's stubble on one side and a pixie swoop on the other. "I'm scared to see what I look like. I don't know if I'll recognize myself."

"I think we'll keep you away from mirrors for a while. I wouldn't want to send your body into shock."

She navigates us down a narrow path that curves around the building. Only two wheels fit on the concrete. The other two snag on hedges. The goateed man keeps dropping to the ground to untangle branches, dirtying his slacks.

The three of us emerge on a broad, tiled plaza stinking of chlorine. Children splash in an underground pool. Hairless men soak in hot tubs. Women in wide brim hats sip on colored cocktails with toothpick umbrellas.

"What made you want to build a hotel when you were winning chemistry awards?" I ask, surprised she would approve of a place like this, let alone run it. "I can't remember you ever taking a vacation with your parents. And you went ballistic when I visited Canada."

"I made a point to avoid them as much as possible, you know that. And I only complained about Canada because it was our last summer before senior year. I didn't want to spend a week without you."

"I texted you nonstop, though."

During our road trip, I angled the screen toward the window, praying the reflection wouldn't ricochet off the glass. I had listed Rhea under a fake name, but she sent selfie after selfie with her face in full view.

The first shot arrived after we crossed country lines. I sent her a message saying, "We're officially a long-distance couple. Goodbye America." She replied with a picture of herself holding a printout of the Canadian flag taped to a popsicle stick.

She sent fitting selfies throughout the trip, timing them along to our itinerary. When we grabbed breakfast, she sent a picture of herself dousing pancakes with maple syrup. When we took a boat tour wearing plastic blue ponchos, she sent a picture with her hair drenched from the shower. When we tossed hats at a hockey game, she wore a plastic pail like a helmet. She made the distance between us feel small, indiscernible.

In return, I texted her pictures of the promise ring she gave me for our anniversary. She bought it under the assumption I would wear it at school like she did with her keychain, but it felt more comfortable in my pocket. I only slipped it over my knuckles when we visited the cabin.

"Are you embarrassed of me?" she used to ask even though she was the smart one, the rich one, the one with a future.

Dr. Quinta assured me her other LGBTQ patients had the same reluctance about coming out, but I insisted she had it all wrong. My situation, my hesitation, would be the same if I were attracted to guys. I had seen the way my best friend, Marzia, got crucified after reaching second base in middle school. When our classmates found out, rumors spread about her sneaking into the locker room for quickies and cheating with every player on the football team. Once we moved up to high school, even more brutal, reputation-ruining gossip circulated about anyone with a boyfriend, anyone with a crush.

Keeping our relationship a secret saved us from classmates placing bets on when we would break up and friends begging for details about our sex life and parents interrogating us across the dinner table. It was easier to keep quiet. It made more sense.

"Here's your temporary home," Rhea says as she clicks the wheelchair over a final set of boards. She parks me in the living room and dismisses the goateed man so we can talk one on one.

"Is this your place?" I ask. A black leather sofa faces an oversized window with an ocean view. A sleek silver coffee table balances on curved legs. A marble bathroom peeks through a cracked door.

"I don't make a habit of sleeping on the island," she says. "In fact, I have to get back to the mainland soon."

A chill shoots through me. "You're leaving me alone? I just woke up. I still have a bunch of things to ask you about."

"I know. I wish it could be different. I hate this more than you do. Unfortunately, I have a packed schedule."

"You said it's been ten years. You're really going to leave me after ten minutes?"

"If I could cancel, I would, but this isn't something that can be put off. Don't worry. I'll send someone to watch over you. I'll make sure you're comfortable."

"I don't want someone else watching me. I want you. I just woke up and don't know what's going on and—"

"Domino. Please. Don't make this harder on me."

I wince. She never raises her voice at me. She knows it sets off my anxiety. "Sorry," I mutter. "I guess it's fine. Being alone for a bit is probably a good idea anyway. I really need to pray or cry or sleep or…I don't know. My mom should be here in a bit either way, right?"

"As soon as we get ahold of her." She drops a kiss on my crown. "I'll see you later. I love you."

"I love you too, Stingray."

She takes small, tentative steps toward the door. When it sighs shut, I roll myself to the window. My pulse races at the thought of being stuck here alone, but the push-and-pull sounds of the ocean trick me into feeling close to home.

Our neighbors lined their bumpers with BEACH BUM decals. They dangled seashell necklaces from their mirrors like dice and strapped surfboards to their roofs. Our parents were the only ones in town without a vehicle permit for the beach. Neither of them understood the point in mindlessly lounging around the ocean.

Dad picked up extra shifts at the power plant whenever someone called out sick. Mom quit working when I was born, but even when she spent hours on the couch watching trashy TV, she multitasked with a crochet needle, a sewing kit, or a grownup coloring book.

I try to age her in my mind, to picture her with deep-set wrinkles and shaggy gray hair. If she was the only one who made it out of the accident intact, it must have taken a toll on her. It couldn't have been easy to aid Dad and mourn Ari on her own.

Tears swell at the thought of my sister. She was too young to die, too artistic, too packed with potential. She had a knack for preserving in-between moments most cameras missed. She caught me running to my room in a towel, dotted with pimple cream. She caught me honking into tissues. She caught me cupping my mouth mid-burp. When she wasn't actively trying to embarrass me, she caught me puffing on winking birthday candles. Or swinging my arms, serving volleyballs. Or staring into the mirror, tracing my lashes with black liner.

I fiddle with the adhesive holding my bandage together, wondering what made me lucky enough to outlive her. If the accident stopped her heart and disabled our dad, I'm surprised my skin isn't slashed with scar tissue. All

I spot are a few unfamiliar freckles and stretch marks, evidence my body has matured over ten years. The only injury is on my wrist.

I pick at my bandage like a stubborn roll of tape, seeking to survey the damage. A fake nail snaps in the process. I wriggle the rest loose and toss them into a sloppy pile on the coffee table.

With naked fingers, I unravel my wrap layer by layer. When I uncover my wound, the sight squeezes my lungs dry. My wrist is blackened, charred, bubbled with heat blisters.

I try to calm myself with a grounding exercise Dr. Quinta taught me in therapy, listing out five things I can see, four I can hear, three I can smell, two I can touch, one I can taste. I log my surroundings. I can see the sun cresting over the water. A seagull swooping for fish. A limp, crumpled bandage on my lap. Speckles of dried, dark blood. Burned leather skin.

The damage couldn't have been caused by a ten-year-old accident. It looks recent, alarmingly fresh.

I haphazardly rewrap my bandage and hunt for a cell phone to get ahold of Rhea. The coffee table is empty aside from a Bible. The living-room walls are smooth and cordless. The nightstand in the bedroom only holds a remote and a twisty helix lamp. There's nothing in its drawers, not even dust bunnies.

I try the kitchen last. I fling open cabinets, rummaging through snacks, silverware, drink stirrers, and an assortment of coffee pods. A fat patch of orange graffitis one of their foiled tops.

The smudge pulls my heartstrings corset-tight. Rhea must have remembered my childhood stories and spiraled color onto the cup to remind me of my sister.

I insert the pod into a pocket of the coffee machine. I nearly topple from my chair while filling the cavity with water, then thumb the *brew* button. The coffee gurgles and sputters from its spout. A warm, sweet aroma wafts into my nostrils. It smells like home.

Rhea drank three lattes per day. She crammed restaurant sugar packets in her purse. She left liquid rings across countless school desks.

Once she smuggled a cup into an aquarium in spite of the NO FOOD OR DRINK BEYOND THIS POINT sign.

"What happened to my miss goodie two shoes?" I asked once we split the entrance fee and cleared the front desk.

"Calm yourself. It's not a big deal."

"Who are you fooling? It's a milestone moment. I've never seen the golden Rhea Laman do anything bad before."

"Legal and illegal aren't the same as good and bad. Sometimes the right thing is the illegal thing."

"Like jaywalking to push a kitten out of the way of a moving bus?"

"Or speeding to get your dying son to the hospital."

"Or sneaking in a latte because you're a sad, hopeless caffeine junkie."

"To be fair, it's the best kind of addict there is."

She consulted the map at the main entrance. With our arms linked, she weaved us around eel tanks and hurricane simulators and ice cream vendors, heading for an exhibit she knew I'd love.

A miniature waterfall cascaded into a stone circle. A sand-colored turtle camouflaged itself on a rock. Another waded through the pond with only its shell scraping the surface. My favorite, a leopard tortoise, waddled until he plunked into the water to join his friends.

"I'm surprised you've never owned one," Rhea said, watching me with the same fascination I watched the turtles.

I rested on ripped jeans, resisting the urge to stroke their shells. "Ari would kill for a dachshund, but I don't really want any pets. Turtles are happier outside. They're my spirit animal, you know."

"What would you say mine is?" Rhea asked, even though she considered astrology and MBTIs and love languages to be pseudoscience. "Maybe an otter? An angelfish? You better not pick a shark."

"More like a stingray. Get it?"

She frowned, unamused. As revenge for calling me Domino, I assigned her random, punny nicknames. *Ray of sunshine. Hurray. Do-Re-Me. Raisin.* Stingray was originally meant as a one-off to add to the list, but it stuck because of a touch tank we found further into the aquarium.

We dunked our arms into the water to skim the smooth, rippling wings of a dozen stingrays. As a light gray one glided beneath my fingertips, I said, "I think I was right before. These do remind me of you. They're one of the cutest things I've ever seen. But they're dangerous. Their tails have venom. See? It says on the sign."

"If that's the case, I guess you shouldn't upset me." She flicked water onto my face.

I dried the drops with my sleeve. "Of course not, I would never mess with a wild animal."

The memory shatters when a fist strikes the resort door.

I stiffen. Since we learned about stranger danger in elementary school, I made a habit of ducking beneath windows and army-crawling to my room whenever a salesman knocked. I employ a similar method now, wheeling away from the window.

Unfamiliar with the controls, my chair moves clunky and slow. The front door creaks before my tires bounce into the connecting room. The goateed man enters on his own, pushing a room service cart. Boxes are stacked on its lower level. Chinese Checkers. Backgammon. Scrabble. Battleship. Boggle. The upper level holds a domed dish.

"Miss Laman was unsure whether you would be able to take down anything solid, but she decided to send over a platter, just in case." He tips the lid open like a mouth. Skinless chicken, brown rice, and yogurt pack the plate. "She also requested a specific set of board games for you. Unfortunately, it looks like they're all multi-player. There are some others stored in the rec room if you would like. Or a pack of cards, perhaps?"

"No, it's okay. I'm not really in the mood for games." They weren't meant for playing anyway. Rhea sent them as a romantic gesture, as a nod to the week we first officially met. Another way to make me feel more comfortable.

The goateed man swings open a closet strung with shirts, shorts, and dresses. He stores the gaming bundle on the lowest shelf and transfers the meal tray to the kitchen counter, beside my steaming coffee.

"You'll also need one of these," he says, presenting a thin, floppy device. He helps me equip the loopy straps. "You can use it to read e-books, to play puzzle games, or to order food to your room."

"Can I use it to call Rhea?"

"You can make calls as long as the other person also owns a pass. But Miss Laman is away at meetings, so you might get transferred to another department. Or put on a waiting list. Anything you need, you can ask me."

"Do you know when she's coming back?"

I roll closer to spy at his device. He unlocks the screen with a six-digit passcode and pulls up a calendar. "My apologies. There might be a technical error. I don't see a return scheduled. She has a televised presentation tomorrow, but the rest of the calendar is blank."

"You mean it could be a few days? I figured she'd be back later tonight."

"Miss Laman is a workaholic. She had to be in order to get where she is today. She moves around a lot, but this week is especially hectic. Is there anything else you need until her return? A tea? Aspirin? More blankets?"

It takes a dozen different versions of *I'm fine* to convince him to rattle away with his cart. I pick at tiny slivers of chicken, lick a dot of yogurt from my pinkie, and take a single sip from my mug. The small dose of caffeine gives me the jitters, like an addict in withdrawal.

Restless, I nudge my kickstands out of position and push off my armrests. My kneecaps crack when weight is placed on the joints, but I hold my balance. I circle the room, limping away the pins and needles prickling my calves.

I add my high-speed recovery to the growing list of questions for Rhea. Technology must have advanced while I was in my coma, and she loaded my body up with drugs, but I still find it bizarre that I can walk unbothered after a decade spent prone in a hospital bed.

I roam outside to clear my head, to stretch my legs, to breathe the salted air. I follow echoed shouts to the main plaza where a group of kids race end-to-end in the pool. Their parents shout over the slapping water.

"You're doing amazing, kiddo," a father calls from the sidelines.

"Come on," another says. "You're almost there. You can win this right now. Go, go, go."

Dad screamed like that at my volleyball games, loud and unfiltered. The principal escorted him off the premises once for cursing out a referee. She had issued me a yellow card, which would have been fine if she hadn't made a show of calling me out. She prolonged my embarrassment, making sure all eyes were set on me, so my father did the same to her.

When I reunited with him outside the auditorium, he spoke between cigarette puffs. "That pig give you any more trouble?" he asked. I shook my head and he shrugged. "Worth it, then."

Mom tamped down her excitement during matches to avoid embarrassing me, but she let loose on phone calls. I overheard her with aunts and neighborhood friends, boasting about her daughter *who belonged in the Olympics.* Ari mocked her in a high-pitched voice—but she came to every single game with her camera.

I redirect myself away from the cheering parents and stamp down slats onto crisp, crunchy sand. A seagull hops toward a stray fry. Children squeak in swim shoes and water wings. A burned man kicks over his beer while setting up an umbrella. I drift toward him to help dig the stake into the ground.

"Thanks. I always get clumsy around the same point I start getting tipsy," he says. The umbrella blocks us from speaking face-to-face until the canopy is popped. When he orbits to my side, he chuckles. "Oh, hey, you look good. I'm surprised you're on your feet right now."

I raise a polite smile, wondering how many strangers know about my situation. "I'm a little surprised, too. Maybe it's a miracle."

"Must be. I thought you'd be hung over for three straight days after how much you drank the other night. I saw a guard bring you back to your room and everything. You probably don't remember that."

I fidget with my ring, regretting the decision to socialize. "I'm not much of a drinker. I wasn't around the other night. You must be getting me mixed up with somebody else."

"Could have sworn it was you. Ariana, right?"

My stomach drops. Teachers mispronounced my sister's name at the start of every school year. One instructor called her Ariana until the second semester, so she convinced everyone in class to call *him* a different name. She received a week of detention, but he never made the mistake again.

"My name's Dominique," I say, struggling to hold eye contact with the sunburned man on the beach.

He scratches his chest hair. "Huh. I guess I was pretty drunk the other night, too." He ends the conversation by spreading himself out on his beach towel, face down.

I stumble toward the shoreline. I try my best to focus on the scenery, to empty my thoughts, to forget about my sister. It doesn't work. The roar of the water reminds me of the morning we sat in the front row on Splash

Mountain. Ari threw a hissy fit about getting her hair soaked after waking up at six AM to straighten it.

The memories keep coming—the summer she nailed up flyers volunteering to wash neighborhood dogs, the weekend she pranked me with a rubber band over the faucet, the night she stood in a downpour to take pictures of a baby deer crossing our road.

I'm so consumed by the past I almost miss the goateed man. He takes careful steps with his dress shoes, shaking out his pant legs whenever his heels sink into sand.

"I was notified you left your room," he says, cupping a hand on his forehead to blot out the sun. "We didn't think you'd be up and walking around this early. You caught us by surprise."

"Was I supposed to stay in there?"

"You're not a prisoner. You're free to explore the resort. But for now, Miss Laman is having your tracking information sent to me. She would like you to be accompanied whenever you leave your room. To make sure you're safe."

"I feel fine. There's really nothing wrong. I can call you on this glove thing if I need you, right?"

His hand drops to his chin, stroking the hair. "I can't go against orders."

"Maybe I should call her. I'm sure she'll answer when she sees it's me."

I swipe through the main menu and activate the Caller App. The directory lists employees in alphabetical order. I double tap on *Rhea Laman*.

The call goes straight into a recorded message without bothering to ring. "You are number 0023 on our waiting list," an upbeat robot says. "Miss Laman, or one of her colleagues, will get back to you as soon as possible. Thank you for your patience."

The screen flickers back to the main menu. A white light shines steadily in the corner.

"No luck?" the goateed man asks, even though he could hear the answering machine for himself.

I shake my head. "I'll hang out in my room until she calls back. I don't want to get burned anyway."

My babysitter shadows me onto the boardwalk. He doesn't leave my side until my feet hit my resort room floors, until the white light on my band vanishes.

"I don't know why she sent someone after me," I say to myself, alone in my room. "She knows I hate strangers."

I unstrap the device and toss it onto the coffee table. The white light returns.

Curious, I tug the straps onto my fingers. The light disappears. I yank the device off again. The light shines.

The GPS chip must do more than track my location. It must sense temperature, body heat.

I wrap the glove in a bundle of blankets to test whether I can trick its sensors. The light glows through the fabric, a shining pinprick. Frustrated, I try notching the electric stove to its lowest setting. I rest the glove on the range. Still white.

A fist knock-knock-knocks. I flinch, switch off the stove, and scramble for the screen. Its heat scorches my fingertips. I fling it across the counter and thrust my burn under ice water.

The goateed man peeks his head in the kitchen. "I should have mentioned, if you take your security pass off, I'll get false alerts and will have to check on you. The device is weather-resistant, so you can shower with it on. You don't have to take it off to wash your hands."

"Sorry, I didn't realize. I didn't want to ruin it." I dry myself with a dish towel, stalling to let the glove cool.

"No, miss. It's my fault. I should have been clearer with you."

Once I tug each strap into position, we exchange another round of goodbyes.

I plop onto the couch, tossing and turning and smacking pillows, unable to make myself comfortable. I feel like I'm trapped under a microscope. At the same time, I feel sick with loneliness.

I wish I could call my mom, but the glove only gives me access to Endellion staff. I redial the only person on the island I know, fingers crossed she answers. I want to ask about my wrist, the sunburned man who called me Ariana, and the goateed man she ordered to stalk me.

I receive the same chirpy, robotic message. I should probably be pissed at her for ditching me and dodging my calls, but it's difficult when she's the reason I've risen in the first place.

I exit the phone app and launch a digital store. I download a food journal, a maze game, a workout tracker, a joke generator, anything listed as free. I click and click until the device runs out of data. When I finally get around to testing one of the apps, it takes a full minute to load. When I try another, it crashes within seconds.

Deleting an app or two should make the device run faster, but the delay could be a good thing. The clogged screen could jam the GPS signal. It could give me a chance to explore the resort without a babysitter.

Or it could have absolutely no effect. I failed my only computer course in seventh grade.

I shared a cubicle with Marzia, which was my first mistake. We took turns on an outdated computer facing a corner wall. While the rest of the class typed on covered keyboards to memorize their finger positioning, she streamed music and played Flash games on pages too obscure to get blocked. I convinced her to switch tabs whenever the teacher looped around the room to check our progress, too paranoid to play along.

Marzia could have made it through the semester without getting caught, but she got greedy. She pulled up a sex toy shop to brag about ordering a vibrator on a school computer. The page automatically downloaded a virus that turned the screen a ghastly bright blue. When our teacher traced back the issue, I refused to pin the blame on Marzia, so she flunked us both on principle. It was my first and only *F*.

I open a browser on my security pass and insert website names Marzia taught me into different tabs. A movie torrent site. A porn site. A lingerie shop. They're too old and irrelevant to be blocked, stuck in the stone age with neon purple backgrounds and lime-green fonts. Each site comes with a handful of pop-up ads. They slow my screen to a crawl.

I worry the device will send out an alert about being corrupted, but the indicator light stays dimmed. My door stays sealed.

I creep outside, dividing my attention between the screen and the boardwalk. No matter how much distance grows between me and my resort room, the light never flickers or flares. I never stumble across the goateed man, either. Judging by his polished shoes and pocket square, his workdays involve more air conditioning than ocean breezes. Without my GPS ratting me out, I should be able to explore the resort undetected.

I beeline for the horseshoe-shaped building at the opposite end of the island. I expect walking to come easier as my body adjusts to being awake, but I feel worse than an hour ago. My muscles twitch. Sweat drips into my eyes. My head swims with dizziness.

I sag onto a barstool to rehydrate. The server offers me a beer, but I turn it down in favor of water. I uncap the bottle and chug.

"I'm glad to see you're drinking healthy today," a guard says, dropping into the adjacent seat. "Unless you poured some vodka in there."

"I don't think I can drink. I'm on medication."

"Ahh. I thought that might be the case. I saw Gomez and Laman wheeling you around before."

"She was worried about me walking on my own. She's always been pretty protective of me."

"You two are friends?"

I start to nod, but it feels unfair to lie after everything she's done for me. "We're actually dating. At least, we dated in high school."

We officially met in our ninth-grade health class, the only period our schedules overlapped aside from lunch. Our teacher arranged us into four-person groups for a research project on contraceptives. Before we created an email thread to split apart tasks, Rhea finished the project solo and sent us the finished files.

Too shy to confront her in person, I smoked a bowl and emailed her back about wanting to earn my varsity team grades right. "I don't understand the issue," she said. "You should be happy you don't have to lift a finger."

"There's definitely a finger I'm ready to lift," I typed and erased. We went back and forth over whether we should restart the project from scratch or hand in what she had completed.

"Do you want to flip a coin?" she eventually said. The sarcasm bled through the screen.

"I'd rather play you for it. Any game you want. You can pick."

I expected her to choose a hoity-toity game like chess or blow me off completely, but she chose Battleship. During our lunch period, we borrowed a box from an art teacher with a jumble of kiddie games in her closet. Rhea capsized first, despite firing at odd-numbered squares to maximize her potential of getting a hit. It was refreshing to compete against someone with a strategy instead of someone like my sister who would fire at random and accidentally pick the same squares twice.

After our group rewrote our presentation as a team, Rhea and I continued to meet, just the two of us. We played card games, dice games, any games we could scavenge from the art closet. In forty-five-minute spurts, our relationship escalated from friends who hugged a little too long to friends who held hands as a joke to friends who French kissed.

"What happened to your arm?" the guard asks, prying me from my memories.

I lower my head, embarrassed. I should have drilled Rhea for as many details as possible about the car crash to the recovery. I should have nagged her to stay and clear up my missing history.

"I'm not really sure," I say, "I was in a coma."

"A coma?"

"For ten years."

"Christ. I'm sorry to hear that. I hope you feel better soon." He bites his lip like he wants to say more, but he springs from his barstool. I catch his name tag as he leaves. ELLIOT AVIDAN.

I finish my water and stroll into a random door along the horseshoe. I end up in a blinding arcade with neon signs and skinny, flashing machines. I weave around clumsy toddlers and their tipsy parents, trying to avoid thinking about my own parents. I fail at every turn. The slot machines remind me of the birthday when Mom hit the jackpot and bought me a life-size turtle plushie with her prize tickets. The air hockey table reminds me of the night Dad accidentally sent a puck flying across the board and smacked me in the jaw.

I veer toward the more modern games without any memories attached. There are a variety of zombie games, games inspired by phone apps, even a simulation beer pong game. I skim their high scores. Three-letter initials spell out joke names. ASS. POO. PIG. On the final machine, a set of initials spell out ARI.

My heart stops. I stare at the scoreboard, paralyzed, until a pimply teenager bumps me aside to play. I shuffle forward in a daze, assuring myself the initials are only a fluke, a coincidence, an unhappy accident.

I stumble upon a row of old-school games altered with umbrellas. Pac-Man with a bright yellow canopy gobbling enemies. Frogger with an umbrella blowing across city streets. Pong with raindrops instead of bouncing balls. I wonder whether the collection is meant to pay homage to our relationship.

I wonder the same thing about the pair of bathrooms along the back wall, differentiated by cartoon brains. The male wears unlaced sneakers and a cape. The female reads a book over her cat-eye glasses.

Junior year, our school district was chosen to test out state-of-the-art brain-imaging equipment. After my scan was completed, I met up with Rhea in a cove beneath the EMPLOYEE ONLY staircase. Another same-sex couple, a few potheads, and a guy cheating on his girlfriend took turns using the space. We bumped into each other on occasion, but we kept their secrets and they kept ours.

After Rhea read my results, she begged to hang them in her locker the same way other girls posted heart-shaped pictures of their boyfriends. It was a way to flaunt our relationship without anyone realizing. Like our pet names. *Domino* instead of honey, darling, baby. *Stingray* instead of sweetie, snookums, hot stuff. "It's so much better than a picture," she said. "I like your face, but I like your brain more." The compliment made me cave. I had studied the papers top to bottom on the walk over, so I had no use for them anyway.

It's hard to accept that memory—every memory—is at least a decade old. It feels much more recent to me. The juxtaposition gives me a splitting headache. The twinkling, buzzing arcade doesn't help matters, so I skip to the opposite side of the building.

In the rec room, a quiet, well-behaved group plays Trouble. While they pop dice and slide pieces around the board, I read through a bulletin board. Its flyers advertise resort activities. Diving lessons. Portrait sessions. Synchronized swimming. Parasailing.

I tap an option. A portfolio of information spans the screen. The main tab gives a brief description of the activity along with age restrictions, meeting times, and locations. The middle tab contains a list of frequently asked questions. The final tab stores pictures of past sessions.

I swipe through pictures of tourists dangling beneath a pink parachute, their feet skimming the sea. I switch to the scuba diving page and flick through underwater shots of swimmers surrounded by rainbow fish. The portrait page is set up slightly different. It includes extra pictures taken by guests with their rental cameras. There are close-ups of sand crabs, artsy angles of shells, posed photos of families shooting peace signs and devil horns.

In one photograph, a father carries his diapered son across the shore. A woman behind their heads snipes my attention. I pinch the screen to zoom. One eye is covered by a camera. Half her nose is blocked. But she looks like Ari with her hair pulled back.

"Sometimes, your brain plays tricks on you," Dr. Quinta said session after session. "Just because you feel like a screw-up doesn't mean it's the truth. Just because you have a hunch someone hates you doesn't mean it's reality." Just because the woman in the photograph looks like a grownup version of my sister doesn't mean she's still alive.

I think back to the sunburned man. He called me *Ariana*. He swore he knew me, swore he saw me yesterday. In school, teachers mixed up *the Diaz girls* every semester. Our own parents swapped our names on occasion. The man could have made the same mistake. He could have gotten drunk with Ari while I was asleep and then mistook me for her on the beach.

I twiddle my ring, second guessing my second guessing. As much as I want to believe my sister is alive, Rhea wouldn't have lied to me about a death in the family. If she would actually answer her phone, she could clear the air about the suspicious things that have been building up—the sunburned man, the high score, the picture on the corkboard screen.

Determined to get ahold of her, I return to my room to fiddle with my warped security pass. I exit spam tabs. I delete apps. I clear data. I approve software updates.

While waiting for the longest update to load, I sort through board games in the closet. I unbox an old favorite and dump the tiles from their drawstring sack. I stuff the empty pouch with soaps swiped from the bathroom. Three miniature bars fit inside. The sack is small, but it's heavy enough to create the illusion of protection. Like my pepper spray.

Dad bought a bottle for me and a bottle for my sister when we started walking to the bus stop on our own. Ari tossed the container into the bottom of her bag along with dried-out pens and cookie crumbs. I clipped mine to a keychain where it was easy to grab in case a neighbor inched too close or a door banged in the middle of the night. I never aimed and fired at anything more than a shadow, but I would rather be *over*prepared.

With that same better-safe-than-sorry mindset, I flop my soap pouch in between my legs. I pull the strings taut as my security glove finishes its upgrade. It beep-beep-beeps with missed message notifications, but before I can get a closer look, an incoming call overrides them. A popup asks me to slide left to *dismiss* and right to *answer*. I swipe right.

"I tried getting in touch with you all afternoon," Rhea says, spanning the screen. Her pupils are dilated, over-caffeinated. "I was about to send Gomez over to check on you."

She must mean the goateed man. My original plan involved calling him off, but after the last few hours, he's the least of my problems. I would rather collect info while I have her on the line—and keep my GPS loophole a secret.

"I just woke up when my pass started buzzing," I say. "I didn't hear anything until now."

"Good. Good. You had me scared for a minute. But I'm glad you've been getting some rest. Are you feeling okay overall?"

"Not really. I'm kind of freaking out. I'm trying to figure out what happened. With my family. With my accident. Some things aren't lining up. Like my wrist. How did I get this burn? It couldn't have been from the car crash. It looks new."

"We used a lot of experimental treatments on you in the hopes of waking you up. Some chemicals didn't work as well as others." She scratches at her chin. "I'm sure you must have a million questions, but you have to remember, you haven't been awake for twenty-four hours yet. It's natural for you to feel disoriented. I hate that I'm not there with you to make the transition easier, but what I'm doing on the mainland is more important than my feelings. If it wasn't, you know I would be there, right? If this wasn't life and death, I wouldn't have left your side for a second."

"I know that. And I know you want what's best for me, so you might be scared to tell me some things to protect me. But I want to ask you something important and I want you to be honest." I rephrase the question in my mind a dozen different ways before asking, "Was Ari on this island?"

Rhea stiffens. I worry another error has frozen the screen—but she vacuums in a deep, shivery breath.

"Was she here, Rhea? You can tell me. Did she not want to see me? Are you keeping her away from me for some reason?"

She strokes her chin, rubbing her thumb along the jawline. "I know it's hard to accept your sister is gone. I'm not sure what caused you to suspect she's been on the island, but anything you've seen is just your mind playing tricks on you. I'm sorry, Domino. I should have guessed you'd go through a denial phase. I can send someone over if you'd like to sort through your feelings with a professional. I probably should have done that earlier, but I was so focused on your physical health that I guess I overlooked your mental health."

"I don't need to talk to a therapist. I need to talk to you. You still haven't explained—"

"As soon as I get back, we can stay up until 2 AM so all your questions get answered. Does that sound good? I'm sorry about my rushing around, but the chaos should be over by tomorrow night. Try to get some more rest until then. I love you, Domino. I'll see you soon."

She disconnects the call. Her image is replaced by a clear, decluttered home screen.

I clutter it up again. I reupload apps. I open browser tabs. I revive glitches.

I want to trust her, my girlfriend, my first love, the only person on the island I actually know. But she spent the whole conversation massaging her chin. She did the same thing whenever I called her out on counting calories or skipping meals or curbing her appetite with coffee. It's her scheming face. Her lying-through-her-teeth face. Her not-even-*you*-deserve-to-know-the-truth face.

CHAPTER 13

I roll my wheelchair around the side of the horseshoe hidden by shrubs. I stop every few feet to untangle my snagged wheels from branches and pluck leaves from spokes.

Around the backside of the building, the narrow, concrete strip thickens into a wide patio. A stout, heavyset guard keeps watch outside a door marked with a haloed brain. My hospital room.

I only snuck a glimpse of the interior when Rhea wheeled me around the curtain, but I saw several file cabinets and a computer. A library of information. If I can't trust my girlfriend to give me straight answers about my accident, my injuries, or my sister, I'll uncover the truth on my own.

"This space is employee only," the guard says. "I'm going to have to ask you to turn around."

I roll closer and repeat words I practiced in my resort room over and over. "I'm sorry. I've been looking everywhere for a lost and found. No one could help me, but they said I might want to check the dumpsters back here. I can't find my bracelet."

"There's no reason to worry about something so small on an island so pretty. The gift shop should have something to match any one of your dresses."

"I can't replace it. My sister gave it to me. When we were little. She twisted my favorite colors together. Baby blue and pink and this gorgeous mint green. I wore it everywhere. I only took it off to shower." Tears bead in my eyes, the story half-true. "When I got to high school, I stopped wearing it, but I kept it in my drawer for safekeeping. I had a full-on meltdown when it went missing. But it was only because my sister had stolen it back to dye the strings black. So it would match my new clothes."

I picture the bracelet collecting dust in my drawer, the strings frayed and faded. Of course, the drawer might not exist anymore. Our house might not exist anymore. A lump clogs my throat. A tear slopes down my nose.

"Calm down, sweetheart," the guard says. He rolls his sleeves as he marches toward the dumpsters. "I'll check it out if it's that important. I'm not jumping in there and swimming around, but I'll take a good long look." He hauls the lid and secures it with an attached stand.

"Thank you. So much. I appreciate it."

I park my wheelchair behind him, leaving a gap between us, enough space to stand. As he digs through steak bones and dirty diapers and hot-dog water, I grope for the pouch lodged between the chair back and my own back.

I clutch the cloth tight and rise slow, steady, silent. I reel my arm back, prepared to sling it against his skull, but I chicken out halfway. My arm falls limp. My bag flops against my hip.

In my middle-school days, I burned myself with a straightener. I ran a razor against my thighs. I ripped out clumps of hair. I thought hurting someone else would be easier than hurting myself, but he didn't do anything to deserve it. He agreed to help me.

I drop the sack and wheel to his side. "Any luck?" I ask, grabbing the edge of the dumpster, pretending to use it as a crutch to stand upright.

"So far, I've found an earring and a broken flip-flop. But I'll keep looking, sweetheart."

I tighten my hold on the metal. Unlike the industrial green dumpsters outside schools and restaurants, this one is constructed of solid steel. Our family spotted the same kind on vacation in Wyoming. They were scattered around Yellowstone National Park to deter bears.

The skinny kickstand is the only thing supporting the thick, iron lid. It sits an inch away from my fingers, tantalizingly close. Dislodging it would be quicker than swinging the sack. It would be easier to write off as an accident, too.

But it wouldn't make me feel any less guilty. I glance at the guard rooting around in the trash, muddying himself to the elbows for me. Maybe telling him the truth would convince him to unbolt the entrance.

Or maybe he would turn me away. Maybe he would call Gomez to collect me. Maybe he would keep me separated from my sister.

I can't let that happen. I squeeze my eyes shut, knock the stand, and draw my hand toward my chest. The cover falls with a clatter. It grazes the tip of my index finger, shaving the skin.

When my eyes open, the guard is crumbled on the pavement. Blood blossoms under his hair, in the spot where the lid must have connected with his skull.

"Sorry," I whisper, lapping blood from my own finger. "Sorry, sorry, sorry."

I kneel to his level to check for a pulse. A beat thrums in his neck. *He should be okay,* I tell myself as I unhook his security pass. I unlock the touchscreen with the same passcode the goateed man input when checking the company calendar.

The main menu opens, granting me full access. I scroll through timesheets, group chats, email chains, and file-sharing applications. I keep searching until I come across a spreadsheet of codes.

Four-digit numbers fill the first column, separated by dashes. Locations are listed in the next column. In the final column, multiple occupants are crammed together. The on-island location is the only one without a current resident. In red letters, it says, ANTONI TAN, DECEASED.

I frown. A pothead named Antoni Tan sat in front of me in psych class. He blasted rap through his headphones, mooched gum off me, and copied my test answers.

I didn't realize Rhea knew he existed until I asked who she would date out of all the boys in our grade. She assured me she had no interest in anyone else, but I kept bugging her until she spit out a name. His name.

"Wait. I'm so confused. I thought you had good taste, considering…" I motioned to myself. "Antoni is nice, I guess, but he's not the brightest bulb. He's only in a few honors classes because his coach pulled strings."

"With men, the attraction is more sexual than romantic for me, so I just picked someone pretty. A symmetrical face. Muscular body." She played with the ring on my finger, rolling it around and around. "I told you. I don't want anyone else. He would drive me mental after a week with him. Speaking of which… I'm going to go mental a week without you, Miss Canada."

"You'll survive. Maybe you'll be with Antoni Tan when I get back."

"Not funny."

"What do you want me to do? I don't think you'd fit in my suitcase, Stingray."

"You know what I want."

I huffed out a sigh and dug in my backpack for my cell. She had been bugging me to add her to my contact list since we started dating. I slipped love notes into her locker to make up for good morning texts and sent her emails from a private account, but with the Canada trip coming up, she wanted more immediate access to me.

"Don't worry, I know you don't want anyone to know about me. I'll be discreet in case your mom snoops through your messages."

She typed her information into my phone. When she tossed it back on my lap, still opened to my contact list, I burst out laughing. The first name, right before Ari, was Antoni Tan.

"I'm stuck dating him now?" I asked.

"He's a lucky man."

"He won't be getting lucky with me."

She joined in with the laughter, letting out the giggles and snorts she saved exclusively for me. I was the only one who could bring out her carefree side, her silly side. I thought that meant something back then—but apparently not if she's been hiding secrets from me.

I inhale through my nose, exhale through my mouth, and input the code into the keypad. A lock clicks.

I enter the vacant room and approach a laptop shining with a password box. I scroll through the stolen security pass for another answer key. I type the jumble of letters with care, afraid one wrong touch will lock me out or trigger an alarm.

The desktop unfurls. PDFs and JPGs and MOVs litter the screen, eclipsing generic palm tree wallpaper. At the bottom, an app in the shape of an eye bounces on a dock. I ignore it for now, locate the most recent video, and smash *play*.

A petite, porcelain woman addresses the camera. Mechanical pencils crisscross her bun. A smiley sticker curls up from the lapels on her lab coat. "I'm in the process of prepping for Memory Transplant 63. Patient A is currently under sedation. Her BP reads 120 over 80. Her heart rate is slightly elevated at 100 BPM. All vitals are stable. Note there is no body present for patient B, who is currently encapsulated in a series of binary code retrieved from a brain scan taken at the approximate time of death ten years prior."

I don't understand what she's saying, what anything means. I search the background for signs of Ari, but the doctor hogs the screen. I fast-forward here and there, jumping through her gibberish.

"Are you ready, Cara?" Rhea asks when she strides into frame.

The woman talks through a toothy smile. "Yessiree. However, there is one itty bitty hiccup."

"What kind of hiccup?"

"We can't Transfer all of the Ari memories into the patient *first* because there would be nothing left in her mind. It would be too dangerous. It could send her to heaven. That means we need to Transplant the Dominique memories into Ari before anything else. For a short period, while her body is unconscious, their memories will be pooled together." She flips pages on a clipboard. "Our next step is to get rid of the Ari memories. Unfortunately, I'm worried Transferring them too soon would place too much stress on the brain. It would be much safer to temporarily Cleanse the Ari memories at the same time we're Cleansing the memories you didn't want Dominique to remember—the breakup, the suicide. You'll still achieve the desired results. The only downside is that there's a teensy-tiny chance the memories could be restored because they're not permanently Transferred. They're only temporarily Cleansed."

Rhea crosses her arms, her pinkie tap-tap-tapping. "I don't like it. If she's triggered, she could remember her life as Ari."

"It's much more likely she would remember the repressed Dominique memories because of the precautions with the camera we took earlier. We know how to avoid Ari triggers." She hugs the clipboard against her chest. "It's the best I can do. For now. In a few weeks, we should be able to complete a Transfer as long as her vitals are strong and there aren't any complications. Everything unwanted will be gone. Permanently. We just have to be patient."

"Any other glaring issues you waited until the last second to tell me?"

Cara pauses, clears her throat. "Yes, as a matter of fact. I know you requested for The Original to take on the Ari memories. Unfortunately, when we moved him from this room, there were complications. He might not last much longer. From what I've heard, he's been stubborn as a mule, refusing food for weeks. It's inevitable, really. So we might have to place the Ari memories elsewhere."

"He's still my first choice. I want every possible measure taken to keep him alive." Her blinking picks up pace, like she's warding off tears. "In any case, don't forget to remove the piercings, nails, tattoo, and any other obvious markings while she's under."

"Can we cover the tattoo with a bandage for now? A single laser treatment isn't going to get rid of the design. It can take anywhere between six to ten sessions to…"

"No. It needs to be removed."

"I'm sure I can sort something out, but it would be much easier if we weren't under such a strict time constraint. I wish we had a few more days."

"And I wish we could have brought her in two months ago when she first emailed me, but we weren't ready then. We're barely ready now. Leaving it to the last second like this has been a wreck for us both. My schedule is packed. When the Transplant is complete, I'll be lucky if I get to see her for five minutes before I have to jet off again." She swivels away from Cara, away from the camera. "You're doing this because I trust you. Don't screw it up. This one isn't allowed to die."

"Yes, ma'am. You can count on me."

"Good. Now show me how to wake her up. Before you begin the surgery, I'd like to get her consent. In a private conversation."

"Right. Of course." Cara fiddles with her security pass, deactivating the camera. The screen goes blank.

I fumble to drag the marker back to the beginning to replay their conversation, to make sense of what they're saying. They mentioned a suicide ten years ago. They mentioned transferred and transplanted memories. They mentioned *my life as Ari.*

An unsettling theory takes shape. It seems impossible, but it would explain the sunburned man on the beach, the high score on the beer pong game, the photograph of my sister. It would also explain why Rhea won neurochemistry awards and switched her career to real estate.

She didn't give up science to build a resort. She incorporated it *into* the resort.

I pat myself down, searching for unfamiliar scars, birthmarks, and moles. Ari spent her childhood complaining about the skin tag under her armpit. She never threw her arms into the air at concerts or school dances because the lump embarrassed her. I shove my own hand down my shirt and run it across the stubble. Across a slight bump.

"No no no no no," I say, unzipping my jeans. I wriggle out of the denim and crumple to the ground in ratty, cotton boxers. Fresh scabs cover my kneecap, but the self-harm marks on my upper thighs are missing. So is the clump of freckles on my ankle. And the scar on my knee.

My throat shrinks to a pinpoint. I have trouble breathing, trouble swallowing. I try to calm myself down with the grounding exercise Dr. Quinta taught me, combing the room for things I can see, hear, smell, touch, and taste. It doesn't help. None of the senses are mine. I can see black, rumpled jeans through the eyes of my sister. I can smell bleached hospital blankets with her nose. I can taste salted tears dribbling onto her tongue.

I gasp through my (her) lips and exhale through my (her) nostrils, on the verge of hyperventilation. Rhea lied about the chopped hair, the fake nails, the chemical burns. She lied about my accident, my recovery, my sister.

Still stripped to my underwear, I minimize the viewed video. I click the circle bouncing on the doc, launching a livestream conference. *Boston*, MA hovers in the corner along with a running timestamp.

Rhea stands in the center of a crescent stage. The sight of her—wearing the same outfit she wore this morning when she woke me from my coma—makes my stomach churn. I resist the urge to switch off the stream, to make her disappear. I force myself to pay attention.

"Smells can trigger memories better than any other sense, which means they also trigger emotion better any other sense," she says. Old-fashioned index cards sit untouched on her podium. She must have given the speech to enough audiences to know the marks and beats by heart. "When someone smells the scent of cinnamon, for instance, they might remember the cookies their late grandmother used to bake and get misty-eyed. When someone smells the perfume their ex wore, they might get aroused. This happens naturally every single day."

The speech builds up to an explanation of how her new scent-based device works. She gives step-by-step instructions, complete with diagrams. The components sketched onscreen look like the bits and pieces in the medical cabinet.

I tug its handles, but the doors stick. A thick brass padlock protects the stash. I consult my stolen security pass, skimming door codes and computer passwords. I can't find anything about cabinets.

I jiggle the lock. It's sturdy, indestructible, but the four-digit slider is manual. Incorrect entries aren't going to lock me out.

I scroll through numbers, guessing and checking. I input our graduation year and wrench the lock. It rattles. I try the morning we met in freshman health class. More rattling. The day we first kissed. The day we first slept together. The day we first uttered those three little words. Rattle, rattle, rattle.

I nibble my lip. I can't come up with any more happy memories, but maybe this older, unhinged version of her set codes to painful memories. I think back to our worst fights. None of them stick out enough to recall the specific date. I remember the night we risked sleeping in the cabin, though.

It was her parents' anniversary. Rhea refused to return home and listen to them argue about unmade reservations and undelivered flowers. She begged me to keep her company, so I reluctantly lied to my own parents about a sleepover with Marzia. I wasn't thrilled with the idea of sleeping in a roped-off area known for its midnight drug dealings. Rhea, on the other hand, would've moved into the cabin permanently if I agreed to join her. She wanted nothing to do with her parents, their mansion, or their money.

I roll the numbers to match the day and month they got married. The lock snicks open.

I unhook the lock, part the doors, and rummage through the cardboard box for all the components. I tug on my jeans and shove each piece into my waistband.

In the prerecorded video, the surgeon mentioned erased memories of a breakup and a suicide. With the right scent, the device should recover my missing past.

Outside, the fallen guard wheezes on the pavement. I stretch his security pass onto his hand and park my wheelchair within his reach. Someone could trace the chair back to me, but covering my tracks would be a waste of energy. The swiveling camera over the door has already captured my face, caught me red-handed.

I return to my resort room with my bladder beating against my stomach. I toss the Memory Scent components onto the coffee table and waddle to the toilet, squeezing my eyes shut to give my sister some semblance of privacy.

I rinse my hands across from a blank wall. While toweling myself dry, I realize why Rhea wanted to keep me away from mirrors. She didn't want me to see the face staring back at me.

"I'm sorry," I say aloud, in case a piece of Ari can hear me. "I'm so sorry you're going through…whatever this is. It won't be for much longer, though. I'm going to find a way to get you back to normal. I'll convince Rhea to reverse the surgery. I'll force her if I have to. This is your body. Not mine. Mine's in the dirt somewhere. Or burned to ash in a furnace."

Tears collect on my lashes. I can't imagine abandoning my family, regardless of whether my girlfriend broke up with me. Dad would've forgotten to pop his blood pressure pills without my reminders. Mom would've had trouble weeding the garden on her own with such bad knees. And Ari would've flunked chemistry without my homework help. I wouldn't have left them to fend for themselves. Not a chance.

Desperate to learn what made me change my mind, I line up the Memory Scent components. I add my cold mug of coffee into the mix. If memories involving Rhea are lodged in the unconscious area of the brain, hazelnut vanilla should be the scent to loosen them.

I follow the steps outlined in her livestream, starting with the wire. I insert it into the tube like a pair of headphones and wiggle the opposite end into my nostrils. Then I trickle the coffee into the attached compartment and snap it closed.

I ignore the tightness in my chest warning me to be careful, to stop asking questions, to live in ignorance. With a trembling hand, I press the activation button. A fan hidden deep inside the device whirs.

The blades spray the sweet, milky scent through the wire. It burrows into my nose, burning my nostrils.

I grab a pillow and chomp an edge to keep from screaming. A strong, metallic tang coats my tongue. A shrill ringing pricks my eardrums. My cheek twitches. My brow drips sweat. Every pore on my skin scorches as my lost memories come into focus.

They arrive in flashes at first, snapshots of the past. The cabin, the camera, the brain scans. Our breakup, our graduation, our reunion. At first, I struggle to make sense of each snippet, to put the timeline in order, but as the ache grows deeper, the story grows clearer.

When my pain hits its highest peak, the device sputters to silence.

I rip the wire from my nose and sprint to the bathroom. I spew vomit across the toilet rim, my stomach churning, my heart beating hard against my ribcage.

It's a struggle to calm myself, to control myself, now that I remember the memories stolen from me. The months missing from my mind. The stepping stones leading to my death.

CHAPTER 14

The day Rhea Laman ruined my life, I torched lavender candles. I unloaded cookies and chips. I spread a blanket across key scratches in the floorboards (SATAN WAS HERE, NY SUCKS, LOVE IS DEAD).

I felt comfortable in our secluded little cabin, even though I'd been hesitant to make it our hideout at first. I'd worried someone would stumble upon us so close to the beach, but the rotting wood and mildew stench warded off visitors. Concerned parents herded their children into cleaner areas free from stray needles and cigarette butts. Our classmates planted themselves near shirtless, toned lifeguards who looked the other way when they snuck a case of beer onto the sand. Junkies were the only ones with any interest in our clubhouse, but they saved their deals for after dark.

We only intersected once. The evening we stayed overnight. A twitching meth head beat at the door, his skin covered in pockmarks, a switchblade poking from his bunched fist. I cowered in the corner with my phone set to 911. Rhea warned me not to dial—she had a thing against cops—and confronted the man face-to-face. I listened through the walls as she persuaded him to leave with a wide fan of bills. Whether she was answering SAT questions or marching in rallies, she always stayed calm under pressure. It took a lot to fluster her.

Knowing that, it should have bothered me when she staggered into the cabin, chewing flakes from her lip, scratching at her sideburns until dandruff collected in a snow pile.

"You know how I belong in more advanced classes, but I keep refusing to skip grades?" she asked. "Do you remember me telling you I could've done that?"

I *mhmed*, distracted by the oversized sweater skimming her thighs. Only her knuckles peeked from the sleeves. "You must be boiling in that thing."

"Listen to me." She propped a white umbrella against my duffel bag. "High school is simple. Our classes? They're nothing. I like it that way. It makes it easier for me to focus on my neurochemistry program. I told you about that, too. The program."

"Yeah, whenever you tell everyone you're going to your book club or meditation meetups or private piano lessons, you're really going to work for this *mystery program*." I pronounced the last part the way a camp counselor would pronounce *the boogey man*, with wobbly vowels and fluttering fingers. Then, with another glance at the drooping sweater, "You're not skipping meals again, are you? I brought snacks."

"I'm not hungry. The company running the program, they've been doing extensive research on the brain. They're called Endellion. Endellion Enterprises. After Endelienta, the saint. King Arthur was her godfather. He had a man killed and she revived him when…"

I tuned her out, growing concerned. She trusted me with personal stories no one else knew about—her struggles with anorexia, her serial cheater mother, her con artist father—but whenever I asked about the neuroscience program, she shushed me with words like *classified* and *confidential*. If she was suddenly volunteering the name of the company, something must be wrong.

"Stingray. You're making me nervous. Can you get to the point?"

"You know our brain scans from tenth grade? Those machines were made by Endellion. My boss, Dawson, created the technology. Our school was chosen as one of the test locations because of me." She dropped to the ground. Her knees brushed against mine. "We had to sign permission slips to be eligible, remember? In the fine print, which no one read because they were too excited about our school getting picked, it included an agreement granting Endellion permission to use any private information collected. At our offices, we have a program that gives us a more detailed look at the neuron connections than what students received on their papers."

"That's kind of creepy."

"I avoided looking at yours. At anyone's from our school. It felt like an invasion of privacy. I went through a few batches from other locations to avoid a conflict of interests, but it didn't further my research. Eventually, I got frustrated and I got curious and we had swapped scans to hang in our lockers, so I felt like you'd be okay with me taking a closer look."

She squeezed my palm. I didn't squeeze back.

"It only took me a little while to realize all the information I learned from your brain was information I could have provided on my own because I know you so well. That got me thinking. I ended up designing an experiment where we invited family members to answer a set of questions about a loved one. Broad range questions like 'what will their reaction be when placed in a high-pressure situation?' and more specific questions like 'what will they do if a homeless man asks them for change?' We inserted the subject into corresponding scenarios and compared their actual reactions to the predictions from their loved ones. Then we compared their success rates to the success rates of the MRI evaluation."

"Okay." I elongated the word.

"We learned that, although most of the information overlaps, close interpersonal relationships are a slightly better predictor of a person's future actions than the information gleaned from brain chemistry. Isn't that fascinating?" She smiled wide enough to flash her gums. "It made me realize, instead of analyzing brains from strangers, I should be analyzing someone I know well. That's when I started to look deeper into yours. It made the process much easier. I knew what I was going to find before I found it, so I was able to uncover new ways that different sections of the left and right hemispheres interact. My findings have the potential to lead to manipulation of brain tissue in ways never imagined before."

I reeled my hand away. She didn't notice.

"Of course, in order to develop technology based on those findings, they need a participant for run-through procedures. They want you. You're the only brain I've dissected this intricately right now, so it would make the most sense."

My cheeks burned with embarrassment, then anger. Private, personal information appeared on my brain scan. My allergies. My mental disorders.

My genetic risks of developing alcoholism or depression or a suicidal ideation.

"I'm confused," I say. "You're asking me to do a favor for a place you refused to talk about until today?"

"It's an honor. You're part of a major breakthrough."

"You're not serious? You haven't told me a single thing about this company. Whenever I ask, you shut me down. But these people, these strangers, get to know everything about me? Tell me how that's fair. Tell me how you're smart enough to get valedictorian but stupid enough to think this was going to be okay with me. You think I want to be some guinea pig? What would happen to me during these studies? What would I have to do?"

"Dawson, my boss, is working on an intrusive thought solvent. To help patients with OCD. You would be put under a small dose of anesthesia and your senses would be tampered with using nearly imperceptible electric pulsations. We would keep a running log of your brain waves, so I could see how you reacted to different stimuli. That way, we could help advance both his projects and mine. Two birds. One stone."

I sprung from the blanket, leaving her on the ground alone.

"Domino, please don't be upset. I would do this any other way if I could, but it would take me ages to achieve the same results with another brain I'm less familiar with. We have to finish unlocking yours, so we know what we're doing. Then the rest of the brains will be easy. The studies shouldn't take long. They'll pay you. And we'll get to hang out more."

"You invaded my privacy. Do you get that? You used my personal information without permission. And now you want me to take part in some kind of electroshock therapy? Can you hear how out-of-your-mind psychotic you sound?"

"I understand how crazy it seems when you're hearing it all of a sudden like this, but I'm trying to make the best of the situation. I don't want you mad at me. But Dawson could do so much for my career. I don't want him mad at me, either."

"Why? What's the worst he can do? Break up with you?"

"He could take away my funding for…" She sputtered to a stop, registering the weight of my words. "Don't joke about that. I understand you're annoyed with me, but if I'm being honest, I'm kind of annoyed with you, too. You know how much my work means to me. You could at least consider what I'm asking instead of saying the most hurtful thing that pops into your head. You don't want to break up over this. We need to talk some more. You can't just say things like that without talking."

"I don't know. My brain scan said I have *an impulsive nature*, remember? Your friend Dawson could tell you that." I yanked my promise ring and chucked it. It rolled across the floorboards, upturning a pile of dust in the corner.

Rhea scrambled to her feet. "No. This isn't happening. We're not broken up. I have a say in this, too."

I shouldered my duffel bag without bothering to pack. It knocked over her umbrella, coating the white canopy with dirt.

"Domino, every couple has rocky moments. This is ours. We'll figure it out. We just need to talk some more." She chased me into the ocean mist. Her boots crunched across glass shards, deepening their cracks. "Domino, please wait. We'll figure something out. You're not being fair. Come on, Domino, seriously."

Her begging failed to slow me, stop me, change my mind. It only reminded me how much I hated that damn nickname.

*

Hiding a breakup took more effort than hiding a four-year relationship. I faked frail smiles. I cried beneath covers. I rapid-fired lies about my sudden lack of a social life. Luckily, senior year was coming to an end along with volleyball season. It made sense for me to become a homebody.

I could have gotten away with hibernating in my room until June, but the loneliness drove me stir-crazy. I missed the cabin. I missed Rhea. I wasted all of my energy thinking about her—or ways to avoid her. I mapped out my routes before leaving each class. I deleted her whiny blocks of texts. I muted her on social media.

I needed a distraction to hold me over until graduation, so I spent weeks organizing a charity volleyball tournament. Our last match. The end of an era.

On game day, stands of two-dollar pretzels and hot dogs lined the hallway leading to the auditorium. Mom wore a homemade T-shirt printed with my jersey number. Ari snapped action shots from her phone. Dad swore in excitement when the ball whooshed toward me—and in concern when I tripped and sliced my brow bone. I scrubbed the blood, patched the wound with a Band-Aid, and rushed right back onto the court. Physical pain I could handle.

When the bleachers thinned, my teammates bear-hugged like we would never see each other again. Of course, it would only be a few months until we reunited. Every single one of us enrolled in a community college dubbed Grade Thirteen because of how many students in our town enrolled. The low-income kids. The homesick kids. The kids without any ideas for their major.

Meanwhile, Rhea earned a full ride to an Ivy League school. We would've broken up in a matter of months, regardless of our clash in the cabin. No relationship lasted through long-distance. As soon as high school ended, our days would have been numbered anyway.

*

After the final bell rang, releasing us for summer vacation, I swung open my locker to dump my old, unneeded textbooks and binders. A delicate origami heart sat atop the pile. It had been dropped from the vent.

My own heart fluttered. Before exchanging numbers with Rhea, we traded love notes every weekday. I thrust my handwritten letters into her locker as quickly as possible to avoid being seen, crinkling and crunching them in the process, but she turned hers into artwork. A swan. A butterfly. A shooting star.

I unfolded the heart, flattening it against a random page in my yearbook printed with senior trip photos. Part of me hoped for an apology worth accepting, a good enough reason to forgive her. Another part wanted to rip the heart straight through the center without reading.

I read anyway. The looping words said, "The meeting is the night after graduation. Please come, Domino. I know you're not happy with me right now, but you can trust me. You've trusted me with the biggest secret in the world for four years now. I've never said anything, right? I've never broken your trust. I understand I made a mistake, but I hope you can forgive me for it. I hope things can go back to normal soon."

"Unbelievable," I muttered.

I slammed the yearbook shut, smothering the message. I swept my stack of books into my backpack, banged my locker, and stormed to the hallway I had been avoiding.

Rhea leaned against her own locker, deep in conversation. I marched toward her, prepared to cause a scene, but the person standing across from her stopped me in my tracks. Antoni Tan.

I watched as he laughed at something she said, as he leaned toward her, as he brushed a strand of hair from her cheek. She didn't close the gap herself, but she let it happen. She let him kiss her.

I shuffled to the bathroom in a daze. I planned on sobbing in private, but I felt numb as I locked myself inside a rusted red stall. I only felt something once I jammed my house key into my thigh.

I dragged the ridges against my skin, scraping hard enough to trace a white line but not enough to cut, to seep, to scar. The scratch was only temporary. The discomfort was only temporary. Just like my heartache would be in the end. Temporary.

*

Height determined our seating arrangements at graduation. Our vegan, Tesla-driving principal thought it was problematic to split us by gender. She rewarded the short kids with front-row seats and banished the lanky kids to the back. I got crammed in the middle, sandwiched between a blue-haired girl from the volleyball team and the infamous Antoni Tan.

Our principal introduced the commencement speaker first. She had earned her five minutes of fame on such an irrelevant dating show that a TV junkie like my mom hadn't even heard of her. The woman gave a long-winded, rambling speech about how small opportunities could snowball into bigger and better things. She encouraged us to embrace any chance, accept any risk. When she finished plugging her social media handles, she introduced our valedictorian.

Rhea stepped onto the stage in a messy bun. She layered long-sleeves and leggings under her red robe, which must have been stifling under the stadium lights. When she greeted the class of 2019, Antoni nudged a friend in front of him, a silent brag.

I swiveled toward him. A tasseled cap rested on his crotch. Green felt letters spelled out *Breaking Grad* with marijuana leaves on the side. If he watched the show, he would have known it was meth.

"I heard you two are dating now," I said, trying my best to sound casual. "How'd that happen?"

"She's hot. I noticed. That's the short version. I'd tell the longer one, but it isn't PG."

"How romantic."

"Don't look so jealous, Diaz. I could probably convince her to make it an open relationship if you're feeling left out." He snaked an arm around me and cupped my breast.

I shoved him. Hard. He crashed into another kid, creating a domino effect down the aisle.

Antoni's friend, who had turned in his chair to watch the scene play out, oohed like someone was called to the principal. "Bro. She shot you down *and* she beat you up."

More heads turned toward us. A few of them recorded on their cells, expecting a fight.

"It's okay. I like it rough," Antoni said, loud enough for the surrounding rows to hear. "I'm taken, though. I don't need her. I already have the hottest girl in town. You should see what's under those baggy clothes. She's not as tiny as you think. But she's as tight as you'd think."

His friend reached out a fist to bump. The blue-haired girl fake-gagged. I tried my hardest to ignore him the rest of the ceremony, but Rhea kept glancing in our direction. He smiled a cocky smile each time, but I could tell she was looking at me.

*

Ari snapped photos after the ceremony, professional grade ones with sunshine and shadow landing in all the right places. I swiped through the digital album on the car ride home.

"You should be a photographer," I told her. "I bet you'd make a lot of money."

She rolled her eyes, which were lidded in gold glitter. "I don't think so."

"Why not? You like it. And you're good at it."

"I'm nothing special. I'm better than Dad, but that's not saying much."

"If you're trying to insult me, it ain't working," he said from behind the wheel. "You're supposed to be better than me at everything. Means we raised you right."

"Apparently we did." Mom dabbed a tissue under her nose. "I'm proud of you girls. You both deserve to have some fun tonight."

Each year, graduates gathered at a local diner for unlimited apps and underaged drinks their parents gave them permission to sneak. My teammates drove straight there to snag tables by the bar, but my family made a pit stop at our house to prepare for the night ahead.

Mom excused herself to touch up her tear-streaked makeup. Dad refilled his to-go cup of Jack and Coke. Ari transferred pictures from her phone to her laptop.

I needed to change out of the tank top and shorts beneath my gown, but I lingered in the backseat to call Marzia. Graduating without her felt wrong. All throughout elementary school, we obsessed over getting our licenses, losing our virginities, and leaving our hometowns. When she dropped out to raise her firstborn, it put a life-sized wedge between us. We still invited each other over for cake on birthdays, but we stopped texting every weekday, stopped planning sleepovers every weekend.

"Dom, it's good to see your face," she said when she answered. Her second son, who looked identical to the first, suckled her breast. "I hope you don't mind him joining the call. We spend 24/7 together these days. It's nice finally knowing boys who stick around. Anyway, what's up with you? Aside from being a high school grad. You can get a job at McDonald's now and everything. Lord knows GED looks better on a resume than *mother*—even though I'm doing way more work now than I ever did in school. But really, congrats."

"Thanks." I played with the tassels resting on my lap. "I can't believe that's your kid. He's gotten huge."

"So have I. And guess what? I don't care anymore. Magazines should replace those mommy-shaming, post-pregnancy workouts with articles on which energy drinks have enough of a kick to keep you running on an hour of sleep. Really, though. What's up with you? How's the fam? The love life?"

"My parents are good. My sister's good. I can't say the same about my love life. That's actually what I wanted to talk to you about. There's this person I've been seeing for a while." Her eyes spread wide, so I rushed to clarify. "We broke up. And it's fine, I'm fine with it. But they really screwed me over and now they want my help. They want me to go to this…place with them that's going to be packed with all the people they pretty much chose over me."

"You should stay away from him. You don't want to text him. You don't want to walk into the same room as him. And you definitely don't want to help him with some batshit favor. That's the smart thing to do." Her son finished feeding. She adjusted her top. "Now, the *realistic* thing is to go wherever this event is and find out how much this douchebag screwed you, whether he did anything else you don't know about. Because if you don't find out the details, you're going to spend the rest of your life wondering whether any of your relationship was real. Been there before. You might think you're better off moving on without answers, but whatever guesses run through your mind are way worse. Especially with how anxious you get."

I nibbled on a thin, stubby thumbnail. "You're saying I should go? I don't know. I'm not entirely sure these people are safe to be around. I don't want to get into too much detail, but the whole scenario sounds kind of…creepy."

"I get it. I've dated jailbirds, potheads, cokeheads, meth heads, you name it. I'm not saying you should go anywhere near someone who's trouble. I'm just saying you're gonna."

"Right."

She itched a chin pimple. "I guess you're not gonna correct me? I thought we were better friends than that. But it's been forever since we've hung out. We're not as close, I guess. You don't trust me anymore."

"What are you talking about?"

"Come on. *This person I've been seeing? This person screwed me over?* I don't talk to anyone from school except you. It's not like I'm gonna spread rumors. What's her name? I don't care if you like vag."

My teeth nipped my tongue, speechless. Strangers had seen us swinging hands at the aquarium two hours away from town. Classmates with their own secrets to hide had caught us getting intimate beneath the staircase. But the only person in my actual, physical life who knew about my girlfriend was my sister. I came close to spilling everything to her on a dozen different occasions, but before I got the chance, she admitted to spotting me in the cabin. She never delved into details, but she must have seen us cuddling, kissing, stripping. She cut me off mid-explanation like she had no interest in hearing my story, so I never tried to tell it again.

"We don't have to talk about it right now," Marzia said. She picked at her teeth with a nail. "I'm sure today is crazy busy for you. You've got to get to the diner, right?"

"Rhea. It was Rhea. Laman." The name whooshed out of me before I had the chance to change my mind.

"No shit? That's your type? We worked on some project together in middle school. Seemed like a prissy bitch."

"We actually met while working on a project. I thought the same thing at first. Then I dated her for four years."

"That long? I couldn't keep my pregnancy a secret for four hours."

"It wasn't like I never talked about her. I just did it with my therapist."

"Hmm. Maybe I should get one of those. Instead of running my mouth on Twitter."

Our laughter was cut off by clanking. I jumped toward the sound—my father drumming his knuckles against the window.

"Are you doing a Clark Kent outfit change in there or running into the house before we leave? Your friends are going to be vomiting up their breakfasts before you order your first Fireball. Come on, you know Louanne ain't carding."

I held up a finger, *one minute*, and spoke into the phone. "Marz, I have to get going. You should come. Kids get a color mat at the diner, don't they?"

"They'd need to throw a grand on top of that to get me to sit in a room with everyone from high school. The best thing about having a baby was getting away from those people. You'll see how nice it is soon. You'll be much happier. A hundred percent."

"You promise?"

"Pinkie."

"And promise you won't say anything about...what I just told you? I haven't exactly talked to anyone else about it yet."

"For sure. I don't need any more drama in my life. These kids give me enough of that. Trust me, both sets of lips are sealed."

*

The night after getting tipsy off warm diner wine, I lied to my parents about seeing a movie with Marzia. While they thought I was pulling up to our local, three-theater cinema, I parked outside a chipped brick building. Loops of graffiti swirled across the box trucks in the parking lot. A strip of dead grass separated the property from a boarded-up Laundromat. I texted Rhea to double check the address.

"You're at the right place," she said with a beaming, blushing emoji. "I see your car."

I unhooked my pepper spray bottle from my clutter of keys. I clutched it in a sweaty palm and stared out the rearview, waiting until she entered my vision to step onto the muddy gravel. My combat boots suctioned to the sludge.

"Thank you so much for coming," she said, wobbling toward me in open-toed kitten heels.

She had ditched her high boots. Her oversized sweaters. Her maxi-skirts. She exchanged them for a pair of thin black tights. A pleated skirt. A form-fitting sweater. She still sported her trademark, schoolgirl look—just with a little more skin, a few less layers.

The change was a big deal for her, the girl who sobbed in dressing rooms, who shook her head at compliments, who turned mirrors toward the wall. She squeezed into an outfit outside her comfort zone to impress me, to win me back, but she also betrayed me. She sold my mind to Endellion. She regifted her heart to Antoni Tan.

"This doesn't mean we're suddenly back on good terms," I said when she tried to embrace me.

She dropped her arms. And her smile. "Right. I realize that."

She took the lead, guiding us toward a set of cracked concrete steps. She knocked on the rusted door at the top with a slow, purposeful rhythm. Morse code.

A ball-capped woman unchained the latch and joined us on the cramped patio.

On cue, Rhea spread her arms wide. Like wings. The woman waved a metal detector wand over her curls, her neck, her chest.

"This place looks like a serial killer lair," I whispered as the wand lowered to her legs. "This is where you run off to whenever you're not in the cabin?"

"They deliberately make it look beat-up on the outside, so it fits in with the aesthetic of the town."

She meant my town. She lived on the opposite side of the ocean, the side with three-story houses and boats docked in backyards.

"And you wonder why I never invited you over to my house," I said.

"Come on, I didn't mean it like that. You know money means nothing to me."

"Mhm."

The security lady redirected her wand toward me. It beeped on a closed fist, the one palming the pepper spray.

"Weapons are prohibited," she said. "Leave that in your vehicle."

Rhea shook her head. "It's pepper spray, not a gun. How much damage could she do?"

The guard stared at her for a beat.

"If it makes her feel more comfortable, she's bringing it with her. Dawson is really excited to meet her. If she walks back to her car, she isn't coming back."

I braced for the woman to fire back, but the argument got the door opened. Rhea must've held some serious weight at the company. Either that, or they were more desperate to tinker with my mind than I'd thought.

We advanced into a spacious white lobby. A coffee pot, cooler of cucumber water, and slushie machine churned with drinks. In between, men and women in lab coats sat on cream couches with charging ports built into the armrests.

"There are some papers we need you to sign," Rhea said, steering me toward an elevator bank. She thumbed the button for the lowest level. It sent us chugging down, underground.

"You work in a basement?"

"Dawson offered to move me, but I declined. I like it better where it's quiet. It's easier to think."

The doors coughed open, releasing us into a musty concrete hall. Naked bulbs dangled from the ceiling. Wires slithered out from exposed holes in the walls.

"I thought this place was only supposed to be shitty on the outside," I said.

"I've always thought of it as cozy."

We walked single-file to a windowless brick office. A phallic security camera swiveled in the corner. A set of monitors perched on a desk along with a stack of paperwork. Neon pink and yellow page markers poked from the edges.

Rhea jabbed at the blank lines on each page. "If you signature here, here, and here, and then initial on the rest of the spaces, we can get started with why we brought you in today."

"You expect me to read all this right now?" I fanned through pages upon pages of tiny print.

"I can recap it for you. I read it front to back. I have the whole thing memorized."

"Why would I trust you?"

"Because if I did two stupid things in a row, I would lose you forever. And I'm not letting that happen."

I rolled my eyes and waved a hand, waved her on.

"I had a long talk with Dawson. I told him using electrical impulses on you is off the table. If you sign, you would be consenting to have pictures taken of your brain. A *bunch* of pictures, but that's it. Most of them wouldn't be taken here. You would never have to come back. I would use the pictures to further my research and then, when we're prepared to go public, I would use a different example brain. No one would ever know you were involved.

Your name wouldn't be attached. But you'd still get paid, of course. I convinced Dawson to bump the price to one hundred grand."

"Just for pictures?"

She nods. "Here. Let me show you. I don't think I explained it well enough in the cabin." She rubbed a trackpad. All three screens stirred with light. "Human brains are similar in nature, but none are identical. Not even fingerprints are identical." She brought up a side-by-side image of two brains, both labeled as females of the same age. They were the same shape and size, but the squiggles sketched inside curved differently. "Just because I know how certain areas of *your* brain interact doesn't mean I can pinpoint those areas in someone else. With the limited information I have right now, I would have to analyze their entire brain and piece the sections apart. It could take months to do that for a single person. Years, more likely. But I know you personally, so I've been able to make leaps easier. If I had a few more pictures to analyze, I could complete the work and backtrack, so I could do the same thing for everyone else in a much shorter period. It needs to be you because I don't know anyone else as well as you. Maybe my parents, but they would never agree to this."

"Then why do you expect me to?"

"Because they don't love me. You do."

I dropped my eyes to skim the contract. Or to avoid looking at her. "You're serious about the money?" I asked.

"It's right here." She flipped to a pink tab. The number was bolded. Six digits. Five zeros.

With that much cash, I could afford my own tuition. Dad wouldn't be forced to work past retirement age to pay off two separate student loans. Mom would stop feeling obligated to make side money selling crocheted hats and scarves at craft fairs. If I budgeted right, I could probably put aside a few extra bucks for a digital camera, a fancy high-definition one, to surprise my sister.

Endellion already had one scan of my brain in their database. What difference were a few more? I unzipped my tattered cross-body bag, dropped my spray into a pocket, and replaced it with a pen.

"Thank you, Domino," Rhea said as I scribbled and flipped, scribbled and flipped. "Before you finish signing, I should probably explain what's going to happen in a little more detail. Unlike your last scan, the photos are going to be taken internally. A camera is going to be inserted into your skull so we can take pictures on the go. The procedure is painless and should only…" Her eyes flicked toward the doorway and stuck there. "Dawson. I wasn't expecting you until half past."

I followed her gaze. A man in a pinstripe suit stood on the threshold, half in, half out.

"I canceled a meeting," he said. When he outstretched his hand, the diamonds on his watch glittered like an engagement ring. "You must be Miss Diaz. I feel like I already know you."

"I don't know you at all," I said, training my gaze on the space between his brows. A trick Dr. Quinta taught me to make it look like I was holding eye contact whenever I was too nervous to handle the real deal.

"My name is David Dawson. I'm the head…"

"I meant *you* as in the company."

"Of course." He flattened his tie to play off the dangling handshake. The clip fastened to the silk tapered into a sharp, bloodthirsty point. It resembled a sword. A katana. "Most people are surprised to learn how little researchers know about the human brain. Like outer space, it's vastly unexplored. But here at Endellion, we have been striving to work out the details. Once we learn what type of information every cell holds, we'll be able to manipulate them. Right now, my focus is on intrusive thought patterns in OCD patients. Theoretically, if we learn enough about all types of human brain behaviors, in the future we could add memories, retract memories, alter personality traits, and so on and so forth. In theory, we could reprogram an entire human being."

"That sounds dangerous."

"It could save lives. Picture a child who has been through severe trauma. Instead of going to therapy every week to deal with their issues, they could have the traumatic memories removed with one simple surgery."

"What about that moth story?"

"Come again?"

"She means the folk tale," Rhea said. "A man snips open a cocoon to help a moth emerge. But it dies shortly after because it needed to struggle to gain enough strength to survive in the wild." She pivoted toward me.

"Think of it the opposite way, then. We could take an abuser and remove their memory of abusing, so the behavior doesn't become a learned pattern. The first crime is always the hardest—it gets significantly easier to cheat or lie or kill after getting used to it—so if they don't remember there *was* a first crime, it reduces the chances of repeating the offense. Of course, we would consider pairing our operation with therapy because some behaviors are ingrained, and we wouldn't want to take chances. And we wouldn't be working with murderers and pedophiles. We would try to help average people with bad habits. Married cheaters. Teenage shoplifters. Something along those lines. We won't work out the finer details until we complete our research. We don't want to get ahead of ourselves."

"It sounds like you want to give bad people a second chance without them earning it."

She tossed her head. "Not at all. We would be giving both victims—and *bad people*—the chance to heal. With your help, we'll be able to develop the technology to lower suicide percentages, to assist the mentally handicapped, to break bad habits."

"You really think that's what's going to happen? What about the whole *those who don't learn history are doomed to repeat it* thing? We learned that in like second grade."

"I know you must have plenty of questions because this was sprung on you so quickly, but I've dedicated my entire career to this. I've considered all the different angles and am going to be mindful of them moving forward. But I really believe in what we're doing."

"And we believe in her." Dawson patted her on the back like a proud father, which was more than her real dad ever did. "Why don't you get back to your research, Rhea? I can handle our guest from here."

"I'm not comfortable leaving her alone, sir. This place is still new to her. I would prefer to stay with her."

"Right, I think you mentioned that earlier. Then I suppose you can both follow me."

He marched us six stories higher, into a minimalistic room with the chemical stink of bleach. Thick, multicolored cords plugged into a strip outlet. Green-tinted monitors scrolled HTML. Standing printers chugged out 1s and 0s.

Dawson motioned for me to stretch across the metal slab in the center of the room. A small oval hole was carved into one end like a massage table. I poked my face through the gap, careful not to lean against the cut on my brow. The skin had begun to stitch itself together, but I was worried about reopening the wound.

A screen installed in the floorboards presented a third-person view of the area, recorded from a security camera. It captured Dawson from above, tugging on black latex gloves. He grabbed tweezers with the same material on their tips and used the tool to pinch a transparent sheet printed from a console. It looked like a tab of LSD.

With careful movements, he rested the slice against my scalp. "This is going to have a slight chill," he said after the chill had already hit.

My teeth grinded. "What is that?"

"An Endellion brand dissolvable camera. It has the ability to soften to a liquid, seep through pores, and harden back to its original form. It will take photographs of your brain every half hour on the hour."

I brushed my fingers along my hairline, searching for a lump, a bump, a scar. The skin was smooth, but my heartbeat went wild.

"I was starting to tell you that back in my office," Rhea said. "We thought an internal camera would work better because the scans can be taken at your house, while driving, anytime, anywhere. Otherwise, you would've had to keep coming back here and I knew that would make you uncomfortable. Besides, this way the photos will record your brain functions throughout the day while you're engaged in different activities and using different sections of your brain, so it works better for everyone involved."

I propped myself onto my elbows. "You've done this before, right? You're sure it's safe?"

She scratched behind her ear. "Not personally, but Dawson has assured me the risks are minimal, inconsequential. I wouldn't have invited you here if it was dangerous. The worst part is over."

I glanced at him for confirmation.

"See for yourself, Dominique." He pressed a series of buttons. The results appeared on his screen as numbers, nonsense. "We're taking a picture now. You shouldn't feel a thing."

I peeked through the hole without lowering my head. The screen grew fuzzy for a count. A new image developed, pixel by pixel. It sketched my brain with more lines and squiggles than my original scan, a deeper dive into my subconscious.

"Verdict?" he asked.

I rubbed my scalp some more, frizzing my hair. "I couldn't tell. It didn't hurt or anything."

"Excellent. The manual functions are working as designed. If you don't mind, I'd like you to stay for at least a half hour to make sure the automatic functions are working as well. There are beverages in the lobby."

"Or you could wait in my office," Rhea said. "It will give us an opportunity to talk. There's a lot more we should discuss, personally and professionally."

I swung my legs onto the floor. "No thanks. I would rather get home. My parents are waiting for me. If the camera doesn't work, you can text me to let me know. I did what I needed to do for my money, right? When do I get it?"

Dawson stroked his skinny tie. His fingers glided over the sword clip. "We'll pay you in small increments, week by week."

"How small?"

"A few thousand. We can get the first installment to you tomorrow."

"Okay. Good."

I nodded a goodbye, swiveled on my heels, and booked it toward the elevators. Rhea scurried after me, but I smashed the *close doors* button to block her. Like I had told her in the parking lot, showing up didn't mean we were suddenly back on good terms.

CHAPTER 15

My first payment pinged into my email the following morning. I cashed every cent as a test. It worked. The money was real. Endellion was legit. I folded the fresh bills in my wallet for a celebratory solo shopping trip. I splurged on cinnamon buns and fresh headphones and a red leather pocketbook.

On the drive home, I worried my parents would question how I could afford the haul—or how I could afford to drive to the mall without bumming gas money.

I snuck my bags through my bedroom window, stashed my remaining money in a drawer, and unfolded my laptop. I hunted through websites for part-time work at a supermarket, bowling alley, cinema, anywhere experience wasn't a requirement. I scrolled through dozens of multiple-choice applications, answering with white lies. *Do you consider yourself a team leader? Can you handle criticism well? Do you enjoy working with others?* I clicked the bubbles with the right answers, not the real answers.

I refreshed my inbox every hour on the hour, but no one requested an interview. Every teenager in town applied for the same summer positions. The spots had been taken.

Until I could find someone willing to hire me, I lied to my parents about securing a secretary position at the library. It was the perfect cover story. I could hang out there without getting in trouble for loitering, use their computers to continue my job search, and sign up for free programs taught by

the staff. Quilling classes. Chess club. Button making. Meditation. I hoped the trials would give me a better idea of which major to choose, which direction to propel my future. My junior year brain scan encouraged me to become a fitness trainer or massage therapist, but I wasn't so sure.

The day of my first free class, I dressed in plain black slacks with a black blazer in the hopes it looked like a uniform. After driving through windshield wiper weather, I parked in a spot visible from the main road. If Dad checked for my Thunderbird on his way home from the power plant or Mom took a detour on her way to the deli, it would support my lie.

I hopped from the car and raced through the rain with my head ducked to keep my makeup from smearing. Inside, I scrubbed my Converse against a storybook-themed welcome mat, scuffing a strawberry blonde princess.

I joined an elderly couple in the activities area, a carpeted room with a circle of collapsible chairs. I chose the seat furthest away from them and fished my e-reader from my new bag.

I opened *Drowned By Brown Sugar*, an autobiography written by the ex-drummer from my favorite band. At the start of a chapter, he said: "I tried to rip my wires out when I got my stomach pumped at seventeen. When it happened again at eighteen, I cursed out the nurses. One of them recorded it. You've probably seen the video. THE WORLD IS CHANGING. By my twenties, that shit started feeling like a part of my routine. Like it was no big deal. Just something that happens every once in a while, like cavities, like chlamydia. HUMANITY IS CHANGING. Whenever I woke up in a hospital bed, someone—a doctor or sister or uncle—would tell me how lucky I was to be alive. I would tell them to go fuck themselves. YOU ARE CHANGING. I could never take that word seriously. Waking up with a tube stuffed down my throat wasn't lucky. Having paparazzi outside my hospital room wasn't lucky. Luck was bullshit. At least, good luck was. ENDELLION IS CHANGING IT ALL."

My heart slammed against my rib cage as I reread the capitalized portions. *The world is changing. Humanity is changing. You are changing. Endellion is changing it all.*

I bookmarked the page and highlighted the text, surprised the touchscreen picked up my fingerprints with all the sweat. I swiped forward, skimming paragraph after paragraph for more hidden messages.

I hit the acknowledgement section without finding anything suspicious. The rest of the story flowed without interruption.

I scrolled back to the bookmarked page, nearly skipping over it. The capitalized sentences had disappeared. The neon yellow lines highlighted ordinary, unedited text. It was like I had imagined the whole thing, hallucinated it into existence.

I pawed for my cell phone and punched the first number on my contact list. It only took two rings for Rhea to answer.

"I need to talk to you," I said into the receiver. "I'm at the library. Get over here. Now."

The elderly couple shot me nasty looks, shushing me. I slung on my pocketbook and escaped to the hallway.

"What? What's wrong?" From her side, footsteps thudded. Keys jingled. She was already on her way out the door.

"I'm not sure. It's not good."

"Are you going to have a panic attack? Stay on the line, so I know you're okay."

"I don't want to talk."

"You don't have to talk."

I slid down the wall, hugged my knees to my chest, and rested my phone on my crotch. I counted my breaths, practicing my grounding exercises while staring at the storybook mat. A streak of mud smeared across the castle. A sopping-wet green leaf covered the princess. A tiny speck of an ant crawled across the sun.

The outside doors split. The wind whistled and spat mist at me. Strangers offered generic *good mornings*, but nobody asked whether I was okay.

When the mist struck for the third or fourth time, Rhea flew through the doors with her cell crammed against her ear. Her boots squeaked on the tile. Her hair fell frizzy and damp. She must not have thought to grab an umbrella.

"Are you okay?" she asked. "What's going on?"

I rose in one clumsy lurch, like a puppet with too many joints. "Your boss threatened me."

Her green eyes stretched wide. She scanned the hall, cursed beneath her breath, and dragged me into a single-stall bathroom. Once she snicked the lock, she said, "What do you mean? When did you talk to Dawson?"

"He sent a message. In the middle of a chapter." I thrust my e-reader toward her. It was still set to the bookmarked page.

"He hacked into this? What does it say?"

"Stuff about how Endellion is going to change the world."

"That doesn't sound like much of a threat." She flicked back and forth through pages. "Is this the right section? I don't see anything here."

"I know. That's the problem."

"I don't follow."

"What if it wasn't hacked? What if I was seeing things? What if the camera made me see things?"

She scanned the page again. Her lips peeled back in a concerned grimace. "Domino. When was your last session with Quinta? I know you stopped going as much as you used to. Maybe you should talk to her about this."

"Jesus. Wow." I snatched my book, stuffed it into my bag. "I love how you're allowed to go on and on about screwing with human brains and you're completely sane. But I bring up a valid *threat on my life* and I'm the psychotic one who needs therapy?"

"I'm not trying to imply anything like that. I'm just saying you're not in danger. No one is coming after you. I promise. Even if he was tampering for some reason, the message sounds harmless. I'm sure there's an explanation."

"I don't know why I called you. I don't know why I thought you'd help." I wrestled my keys from their clip and stormed out the bathroom, through the hall, into the parking lot.

Rhea sprinted to keep up with me. "Domino, think logically. Do you really think I would work for someone who would hurt you? He's a good guy. I've known him as long as I've known you. He wouldn't do anything dangerous."

"How do you know that? You're so quick to defend this place, to defend this guy. But did you ever think that maybe his teen intern doesn't know everything about his big company?" The wind swept bangs into my eyes. My hair curled from the downpour. "That place might feel like a family because your own family sucks, but it's a company. Dawson is not your father.

He doesn't care about you. He cares about your research. Maybe he's planning on using it for something you don't know about yet. Maybe he's using you, Rhea."

My car chirped as it unlocked. I folded myself inside, soaking the seat covers. I didn't bother to strap on my seatbelt or adjust my mirrors, too angry to care about whether I crashed. I shot into reverse, gunned the gas, and peeled onto the road, leaving Rhea drenched in my rearview mirror.

*

I swerved into the muddied parking lot and killed the ignition. I had planned to pound the door and demand to speak to the man in charge, but now I tap-tap-tapped the wheel, too anxious to take the next step. Ten minutes passed. Fifteen. Twenty. The guard must have recognized my car because instead of kicking me off the property, she summoned Dawson.

He strode through the rain, which had thinned to a light drizzle. "I assume there's a reason you're sitting in our parking lot," he said, muffled through the glass. He wore a checkered suit with the same sword clip holding down his tie.

I cracked the window a sliver, enough for him to hear me but not enough for him to reach an arm through. "I want to know what your camera is doing to my head," I said.

"We discussed the details yesterday. It's taking timed, internal photographs of your brain activity."

"What else?"

"That's the primary function."

"Are there other functions making me see things? Because I'm seeing things."

"I've heard. Rhea called in a fit not long ago. She wanted to make sure our written contract still stands, that I'm not going off-script."

"Are you?"

He stroked his dark pinpricks of stubble. "It wouldn't be in my best interest."

"Then what's happening to me?"

"It must be some sort of glitch. I'll review your brain scans and get back to you. Or you can ask Rhea to double-check them if it makes you more comfortable. She's been getting each scan delivered to her email as they arrive in the system. If there was any funny business, I'm sure she would alert you."

I nodded but didn't buy it. He said he'd been researching intrusive thoughts. And now I was having them. "Why are you funding this research anyway? You really think your findings are going to help people?"

"I certainly hope so, but I'm not as convinced as Rhea. For someone in a scientific field, she can be quite a dreamer. She wants to save the world, play the hero. While we can try to use our findings for philanthropic practices, there's no telling where it will lead. In the end, we'll use our data in a way that aligns with our company ideals—but also financially compensates us. Our equipment doesn't pay for itself."

"Are you saying you'd turn to the black market then? Because Rhea was instructed to hide the name of this place for years. And it doesn't pop up on Google. It seems weird you're not advertising yourselves to get investors. Like you said. You need money for your fancy equipment."

A single brow raised, a silent question.

"My sister is big on conspiracies."

"You have a sister?"

My hands tightened on the wheel. "I never mentioned this place to her. I was just trying to think how she thinks."

"Dominique, I see why you're close with Rhea. You have the same good intentions. But no one can tell where inventions will lead. People die from texting and driving. People build websites to profit off kiddie porn. Bill Gates and Steve Jobs never predicted these things would happen. It's not their fault. And those incidents certainly don't mean smartphones or the internet in general never should have been invented."

"Are you saying I shouldn't feel responsible if people die from your research? Or are you saying you're not going to feel bad if I die from your research?"

He placed a hand on the roof of my car. "I'm saying you're getting paid. More money than a child your age could ever dream of getting paid. You should enjoy this opportunity. You don't want to ask too many questions.

And you don't want to upset my best researcher. I can't have her losing faith in me, in Endellion. We need her. Do you understand that?"

I twisted my key in the ignition. The engine growled. "Yes," I said, understanding he had threatened me for the second time that day.

*

I dumped my damp shoes on the porch, flopped onto the couch, and kicked my feet onto the coffee table. Ari grabbed sappy handfuls of caramel popcorn from a bowl in between her thighs, her eyes trained on the television. On screen, a camouflaged man raved about a cryptid killer seen wandering the waters of Scotland. His eyes bulged like grapes.

"I thought you had an eight-hour shift," Mom said. Her fingers weaved a crochet hook between loops of a half-finished blanket.

"They let me leave early," I said. "Because of the rain."

Ari shushed me. We sat in silence until the commercial break.

"Do you really believe those conspiracies?" I asked as a tampon spokesman twirled across the screen. "Or are you watching this like a horror movie, for entertainment?"

Ari tossed a puff of popcorn into the air. She caught it on her tongue and spoke between crunches. "I don't believe in most of the monster stuff. But some of the more political ones turn out to be true. Like how the government poisoned alcohol supplies during the Prohibition. It killed a bunch of people." She tossed another piece. It bounced off her chin, onto the floor. "And the CIA, they did actual mind control experiments. With hallucinogens. Have you ever heard of Project MK-Ultra? They tried to rebuild personalities with fake memories. On involuntary test subjects. Super controversial. Turns out, they do a lot of sketchy stuff for their own benefit. Or just to see what happens."

"How do they get away with that?"

"They have deals with the police, the president, sometimes mobsters. If you tell the truth about what happened, they'll threaten your family. Or they'll make you look crazy and throw you in an institution." She handed the bowl to me, the remote to Mom. "Let me pee quick. Pause if it comes back."

As she wandered out of earshot, Mom folded her bright yellow blanket into a square. She scooted toward me, swatted my feet from the coffee table, and said, "It's strange for a library to close because of rain. Isn't that when most people want a new book?"

"I didn't say they closed," I stumbled. "I just said they…"

She raised a hand. "I might be old, but you can still talk to me about whatever's bothering you. You just might have to stop once in a while to explain the lingo."

"Slang."

"You might have to stop once in a while to explain the *slang*. See? I'm a quick learner." She brushed a damp curl of hair behind my ear. "I can take you to an Al-Anon meeting this weekend if you want. We haven't gone in a while. It would be good for me, too."

The meetings, held in church basements and YMCAs, taught us the only person we could control was ourselves. We couldn't change an addict— but we could change our own reactions, our own behaviors. Our workbooks held statistics about how common it was for children of alcoholics to inherit self-destructive traits. Low self-esteem. Irresponsibility. Impulsivity. Extreme loyalty. Like the kind I seemed to have toward my ex.

"We can go if you want to go, but you don't have to worry about me. Dad hasn't been bothering me lately. He's barely been home." I chewed on a hangnail, ripping it with my teeth. "I really am fine. I just haven't been getting a lot of sleep lately."

"Go check the bathroom cabinet. There's some lavender lotion there. When Ari had trouble sleeping, Quinta told her a sniff would soothe her." She fumbled with the remote. "Shoot. Which button is pause again? I don't want her causing a fuss."

I glimpsed the television, which had returned from its commercial break. I could hear the host raving about Loch Ness, but static mushroomed across the screen. Red pixels clotted together on a black-and-white background. It reminded me of the color-blind tests at the eye doctor, the ones with hidden numbers. Except these pixels formed a word. KILL.

I squeezed my eyes tight enough to see spots. My heart bobbed its way up my throat, gagging me. I swallowed it back down along with sour chunks of vomit. When I gathered the courage to peek between finger webbing, the image had disappeared. A man in camo treaded knee-deep through the marsh, perspiration pouring from his forehead, bags bruising his cheeks.

"Seriously? I asked you to pause it," Ari said over her own footsteps. She trailed off toward the end, head tilted. "Whoa, are you okay? What happened? You look as bad as that dude."

The room spun. "I'm fine. Just seeing things."

"She hasn't been getting sleep," Mom said.

"Oh. Makes sense, then." Ari plopped onto the couch and tucked her legs beneath her. "Sleep deprivation can make you hallucinate. Driving tired is more dangerous than drunk driving. If you're stressed, that can make it worse. But you don't have anything to be stressed about. I'm the one still stuck in school, broke as hell. Do you think the library would take me? No one around here is hiring. I might have to strip."

Mom clucked her tongue. "Let your sister rest. Graduating is stressful in a whole different way than high school is stressful. You'll see next year." She wrapped an arm around me, hugging me to her chest. "Go get some rest, honey. You'll feel better once you sleep."

*

I sprawled across my mattress, hoping my new noise-isolating earbuds would soothe me to sleep. In the meantime, I mouthed the lyrics to my favorite playlist, a pop-punk blend of nineties bands. I knew the order by heart, I could predict which song would play before the opening notes, but I stumbled over a chorus. I paused with my lips trapped around the wrong words.

It took a moment to register my memory wasn't the problem. The lead singer had the song wrong. Instead of crooning about darkness turning to light, he sang rubbish, gibberish. It sounded like the song had been sped up or reversed or translated to a dead language.

I tried to convince myself I was overreacting, that the batteries had simply lost their juice, but the charge in the corner was still set to three bars. I was about to reset the player when I saw it. The song title scrolling across the screen.

On a loop, with all the letters squished together, it said *murderer-murderer-murderer.*

I tugged the white wire with a fist. The buds ripped from my ears, scraping them, stinging the flesh. Heaving, I launched the device at my window, cracking its screen to spider webs.

I rolled toward my nightstand, reeled open the top drawer, and dug for my clonazepam bottle. I dry-swallowed a tablet, coughing as it went down.

Before the medication could take effect, I bounded into the hall in my pajamas—an oversized band T-shirt and a baggy pair of shorts. I paused at the living-room entrance to look in on my family. Dad had come home and fallen asleep on the couch. Ari had switched to munching on pretzel rods. Mom had switched to scrapbooking. The television blasted at its max volume, so they must not have heard my meltdown.

I ducked into the bathroom, the only room with a working lock. I filled the tub to add an extra layer of noise and redialed the most recent number. While it rang, I removed a tube from the medicine cabinet. I pinned the phone against my cheek, slathered myself with lavender lotion, and cupped a palm over my nose to sniff the scent deep into my lungs.

"Are you feeling any better?" Rhea asked. She didn't bother with a hello.

"No. I'm not. It keeps happening. I'm pretty sure it's getting worse. It's coming closer and closer together."

"That doesn't make any sense."

"Well, it's the truth." I balanced my butt on the lip of the tub, cradling my head in my hands. "Dawson said you've been getting my scans sent to your email. Have you looked at all of mine today? Every single one?"

"I looked them up on my phone after you left the library. There was a missing scan that lined up with when you called me. I talked to Dawson about it as soon as I realized. He said it was a fluke. He said not to worry about it."

"Check again. I bet there's two more missing now. Dawson is keeping them from you, Rhea. He doesn't want you to know he's doing his own research behind your back."

"If it was a glitch, the pictures might have deleted themselves. Or...or they might never have been taken in the first place."

"Do you seriously think it's a glitch when he's admitted to researching intrusive thoughts? I doubt he's trying to help people. Or whatever bullshit reason he gave you for why he's doing what he's doing. What if he's trying to put thoughts into people, Rhea? Could he do that?"

"I suppose brainwashing is possible. OCD patients don't typically act on their troubling thoughts, but hypothetically, he could compel someone to purchase a specific product or develop a certain craving. Technically, he could compel anyone to do anything." She pushed out a long, wobbly breath. "There must be some sort of other explanation, though. I can't imagine Dawson doing this. I believe you. I do. I just...I don't understand what's going on."

"Can you get rid of the camera or not?"

"It's built to disintegrate. Even if there was some way to extract it, I'm a researcher, not a surgeon. Dawson is the only one who would know which steps to take. I would have to talk to him."

I tapped my nails against the tub. "Fantastic. Thanks anyway."

"Wait. Don't hang up. I can figure something out. He just started training a new girl. Cara. She might be able to help me. I'll call her right now, okay? I don't want to say too much over the phone, though. If you're right about all this, that means Dawson is okay crossing ethical—and legal—boundaries, so who knows if he's bugged our phones? I should go, but I promise, Domino, I'll fix this."

"I hope so." I punched the red button, ending the call.

With the lavender lotion in hand, I slunk back to my bedroom. I squeezed another squiggle onto my palm and rubbed the cream into my neck. The scent tickled my nose, but it didn't soothe me or send me to sleep.

I tossed the container in my drawer and switched to a more reliable method. I packed a glass bowl and blew streamers of smoke out my cracked window. The marijuana loosened my limbs, lowered my lids. When the embers dimmed to ash, I latched the window and drew the blinds. Sleep sucked me under like quicksand, slow but steady.

The calm lasted until midnight, until a chime broke through the silence. A text message. I groped the nightstand and yanked my phone with too much force, releasing the charger from its outlet. The wire dangled like a tail.

I squinted at the screen, adjusting the dimmer. A pop-up box glowed with an airdrop notification: "Endellion would like to share 3 photos with you."

My heart stopped. Ariadna airdropped photos to me after tournaments, but they could only be sent from short range. We sat side-by-side on the couch, our arms smushed together, to get the service to work. That meant the sender currently squatted within a few feet of me. If they actually existed.

I tiptoed to the window and parted the blinds, searching for headlights slanting through our fence or shadows blackening our bushes. Wind rustled leaves. Branches slapped against siding. A raccoon scampered between our garbage cans. Nothing out of the ordinary.

I checked my phone. The files were still there, still waiting. I accepted the download and swiped through the images. Each one captured a different angle of my sleeping body. The first was snapped through my window slats. I could barely see my bed, only my trophies reflecting moonlight in the background. The second was clearer, snapped from a gap in my closet. A thin, silver tool was clenched in my palm. It glinted like the trophies. The last was snapped inches away from my face, close enough to make out the blade in my closed fist, close enough to read the engraving on the handle. FOR MY DEAREST ARI.

The breath squeezed out of me. I mentioned a sister to Dawson. I never used her name, but it wouldn't take a sleuth to track her down. Our social media accounts overlapped. Only a few days ago, I had posted graduation shots with her tagged as the photographer.

I scrambled out from my covers and swung my door wide. A shoebox propped her door directly across the hall. I could see her rummaging through her closet, hangers clinking. A beat pulsed from her headphones. She sang along in a low, whispery voice.

Everything was okay. My sister was safe. No one could harm her. No one had access to her.

Except me. I could creep into her room at any time.

Every one of the messages looped through my mind. *You are changing. Kill. Murderer. For my dearest Ari.*

If Dawson could manipulate my senses in a matter of hours, what could he accomplish in a matter of days? Rhea said it herself. He could compel anyone to do anything. He could compel me to hurt someone, slaughter someone.

My cheeks swam with hot, helpless tears. I stumbled back to my bed to pop my last clonazepam in the bottle. It didn't help. Between the weed and the pills and the camera ingrained in my brain, my intrusive thoughts picked up speed. Disturbing visions streaked across my mind—of my sister stabbed, bruised, bleeding, burned. Whenever my eyes closed, there was another gory scene waiting for me, showing Ari splattered across pavement or mud or her own bedroom carpet.

I didn't know what to do, where to turn. Talking to Dawson hadn't helped. Running to my ex hadn't helped. There only seemed like one solution. Solve the problem on my own. Stop myself before I could do something dangerous.

I had considered different methods before in theory, but I had never thought them all the way through. Our bathroom razors were clogged with underarm and leg hair, their blades too dull to impart any serious damage. I would need a prescription refill to overdose on my anxiety pills, which would take at least a week. And Mom refused to stash guns in the same house as an alcoholic. Hanging, then. It had to be hanging.

I unhooked a studded black belt from my closet. I dragged it to the bed along with my darkened cell phone. As expected, the airdropped photos had vanished from the system. Proof my neurons had misfired. Proof my mind wasn't to be trusted.

I typed out a message to the number still smuggled beneath *Antoni Tan*. "I don't want to do this to you or my parents or my sister—or myself. But my brain is messed up and I'm worried about what I'm going to do and I'd rather hurt myself than hurt any of you. I know you're going to blame yourself for this, but if you want to make it up to me, be there for my family. Help them get over this. Don't let them wonder whether this was their fault. Just don't tell them about Endellion because it could put them in danger and the whole point of this is to keep them safe. If they knew, they would sue or go to the press and I have a feeling your boss wouldn't like that. I need you to make something up for them. You're good at that. Or tell them a version of the truth if that's easier, tell them we were together, anything to make them feel better. Do whatever you have to do. Just don't let anything happen to Ari. Please, Stingray."

I reread my rambling lines and backspaced in chunks. Like she'd said earlier, Endellion might be listening. Even if our phone call hadn't been recorded, they would probably hack into my messages after hearing the news about their latest guinea pig dying. They might not like the idea of their best researcher choosing me over them.

I rewrote my note with her boss in mind, saying, "I hope you know this is entirely your fault. I hope you spend the rest of your life blaming yourself for this. I hope what I'm doing makes it clear that I don't love you and never have."

The goodbye made it seem like she chose Endellion over me, like we ended on bad terms. It protected my best friend and my parents and my sister, everyone who mattered.

I smashed *send*, trusting her to read the letter the right way, to understand the sentiment was meant to be reversed. *I hope you know this isn't your fault. I hope you don't spend the rest of your life blaming yourself for this. I hope what I'm doing makes it clear I still love you and always have.*

I powered down my phone, dimmed the lights, and climbed onto my whining mattress. I secured one side of the belt to my ceiling fan. The other drooped into my palms. With shivering fingers, I squeezed the loop around my throat and tightened the notches.

As I shuffled to the edge of my bed, I tried not to think about whether Mom or Dad or Ari would find me. I tried not to think about who would speak at the funeral, what they would say, how long it would take them to recover after the urn screwed shut. I tried not to think about a million missed milestones—moving boxes and diplomas, wedding veils and adoption papers.

I tried not to think. And then the thoughts stopped on their own.

CHAPTER 16

I pace the boardwalk, sneaking peeks at the guards clustered on the dock. I try to piece together their schedules, their lunch breaks, and their shift changes, hoping to discover an opening where I can make my escape.

"It's not going to work," a rasping voice says. I flinch, expecting a goatee, but am met with wisps of blond scruff. The officer from the bar, Elliot, drifts to my side. "Have you ever been inside a submarine before? There's no private space. Just a few racks where the guests sleep on the trip to the island. They don't knock them out on their way to the mainland, which means extra people bustling around. If you found a way to sneak past those guards— who never leave position while the sub is docked—there are supply boxes that you could try to squeeze into, but underway watchers check the valves, equipment controllers, and boxes before each trip. I'm not authorized to perform routine maintenance. I only board the sub to get here and back between shifts, so I couldn't help you stow away if I wanted to."

I stumble to a stop, unsure whether he's on my side or getting ready to bust me. My pupils dart from his tanned cheeks to his pale, naked hand. He catches the unspoken question.

"My security pass is being repaired. I told them I dropped it in my driveway and my roommate ran it over. I don't even have a roommate." He keeps his neck on a swivel, scanning for eavesdroppers, but no one seems suspicious. It only looks like he's doing his job. "Tell me what's happening here. You were kicking back drinks one day and Laman was pushing you in a wheelchair the next day. Your wrist is all bandaged. You said something about a coma. I couldn't ask too many questions at the bar because our gloves are always recording, but…" He wags his empty wrist. "How much trouble are you in, Ariadna?"

I fidget with my ring, twisting, twisting, twisting. I'm caught between choices. Scramble for a believable lie? Or tell the hard-to-believe truth? If he went through the trouble of ditching his security pass to talk to me, maybe I could trust him. At the very least, I could swap information with him. He might know how to help me get home, get my body back to normal.

I run my tongue along my gums, brainstorming my best approach. I can't come up with an eloquent way to phrase what's happened to me, so I take the most straightforward route.

"Ariadna is my little sister. I'm Dominique. I'm supposed to be dead."

His head cocks. His lashes beat. "So…that means…what does that mean?"

"Rhea—and some woman named Cara—performed a surgery on me. On Ari. It replaced her memories with mine. So, if you saw someone drinking the other day, it was her. But I was the one you spoke to about the wheelchair. That's when we met."

"Jesus." He rubs a hand across his jaw, muffling himself.

"This isn't my first run-in with Endellion. I died because of them. Right after my high school graduation."

"This place never should have opened," he says, shaking his head. He veers toward the edge of the boardwalk, wraps his callused hands around the railing, and throws swears into the ocean.

"You believe me? Just like that? Does everyone working here know about these operations? Have you had one?"

"Whatever surgery she did on you is new, but we know about the others. We get them for free. All the guests vacationing here have had Memory Cleansings, which are temporary things. Memory Transfers are permanent. The public doesn't know about those. They're part of our employee perks. I was scheduled to have one my first full week working here. I wanted to forget about, well, pretty much everything before my twenties."

"But you decided you were better off remembering?"

"Not really. I would have gotten it. I showed up for it. But then they brought this girl out, Number Twelve. They strapped her into one side of the machine and me into the other." He clears his throat, stalling as another guard passes. They exchange grunts and head nods. When the other man becomes a pinpoint in the distance, he continues. "Yeah, so, Twelve was screaming like someone severed her arm with a bone saw. If there was a wall separating us, or a curtain, I probably would have gone through with it. But being right there next to her, looking at her flailing around, I had to call it off. Laman had a one-on-one with me when she heard. She let me keep my job, but she took away my ticket to a big conference she's holding as some sort of punishment, I guess."

"Why didn't you quit right then?"

"I mean…" He shrugs. "The paychecks are unreal here. My hospital bills were insane before I switched to Endellion's insurance. I've been looking for another job, but not many people are hyped about hiring a guard like me. Interviews are over as soon as they see my license. It takes a fucking eternity to change your gender marker. I can't afford to be unemployed right now and it's not like I can go to the police to rat. They work with Laman. She gives them surgeries for free, too. I guess it's so they don't shut her down. This place isn't exactly squeaky clean."

"If you want to keep your job so bad, why would you risk helping me? What changed?"

"The people they usually do surgeries on are criminals. Not that they deserve it, either, but you're a guest. You're innocent." He cuts eye contact, like he's leaving something out.

I let it drop. Whether or not he helps matters more than the *why*. "I just want to get out of here. I'm not safe on this island. Ari isn't safe."

"There are scuba lessons on the beach tomorrow. Anyone vacationing here can sign up." He gestures to a faint line on the horizon blending with the clouds. "The island's blocked off by a wall. Like from *The Truman Show*. Nobody's able to jump over it or pass through it. You have to go under. That's why we have submarines."

"Why would they risk having diving lessons here, then?"

"Most people aren't in your position. Why would a paying guest escape after spending thousands of dollars here? Even if they did, the contract requires you to fork over the payment prior to your trip. Endellion wouldn't be losing money, so what's the difference?"

"I don't even know if diving would work. I might not be able to swim very far. I have a gash in my wrist, my sister was never super athletic, and I think she likes to drink. Look at my hands." I raise them, knuckles up. I fight to hold my palms steady, but they tremble and twitch. Dad showed the same symptoms whenever he took a break from chugging whiskey. Just a few hours without it would give him the shakes.

Elliot peeks at the docked submarine bobbing behind us. "If you schedule it right and leave a few minutes before the sub does, you can swim up and latch on. There are metal bars at the top. You can ride it back to the mainland. You won't need a crazy amount of stamina."

"Won't the driver or the conductor or whatever see me?"

"There aren't any external cameras. And it's dark under there. It'll be hard for them to spot you through portholes. I only did the dive once or twice, but I'm pretty sure the tanks last about an hour. A little less depending on how far down you dive. But the sub trip only lasts forty minutes, so you should be fine. As long as you complete the training session early in the morning, you can use the equipment all day."

I run a hand through my hair, almost forgetting it's chopped so close to the scalp. "I don't know if I can wait until tomorrow," I say.

"Why? I don't think anything is going to happen to you. I'll keep an eye on your room."

"It's not that. There's a guard. Around the back of the big horseshoe building. I needed to get inside and he was blocking me. I don't know if anyone found him yet or if he woke up or radioed for help..." My lip wobbles. So does my voice. "I shouldn't have done it, but I wasn't sure what was happening to me. Rhea made me think I was in a coma. She told me my sister was dead. She said we were in a car crash. She lied about everything. Literally everything. I wouldn't have hurt the guy, but I was confused. I didn't know if he was dangerous."

"It's cool. I get it. You were scared. I'll take care of him."

"You're not going to hurt him?"

"I'm going to bribe him." He shoves away from the railing. "Head back to your room. Use your band to request medication for your arm and maybe some alcohol to stop your shaking. Just don't step outside. Don't let anyone catch onto what you've caught onto. I have to put on a new glove, so I won't be able to talk to you until we're off the island. I'll take the same sub as you. The first one in the morning. Until then, try to get some rest. Tomorrow's going to be kind of nuts."

CHAPTER 17

The door creaks, letting in the sunrise. And Gomez. He waddles into the living room with a medical kit beneath his armpit. His loafers have been swapped for sandals. A price tag clings to their side.

"How is your arm feeling?" he asks. "I know you mentioned wanting to try swim lessons yesterday. I dressed for spectating."

"It's scuba diving, actually. I think I can handle it after one more dose."

Last night, after my conversation with Elliot, the goateed man brought me fresh shampoo and razor blades along with my medication. He administered the needle himself since the medic was currently off-island, unavailable. He apologized for not offering sooner, but *Miss Laman* hadn't briefed him on my treatment plan. He was as surprised to see my burns as me.

Just like last night, he unlatches his medical kit and pulls out an Endellion brand bottle. The label curling around its edges claims to *numb the area, increase movement, and advance the healing process.* A single dose worked better than the drugs pumped into me after my tonsils were taken out. Or after I'd tumbled in the driveway and had ten stitches sewn into my knee. Rhea easily could have taken the company in a different direction. She could have used her research to help people, *really* help people, but she chose a selfish route.

Gomez sucks the liquid into a thick needle and pricks the wrong place twice. When he finally finds a vein, the pinch is lightning quick. Only a dribble of blood escapes. He swipes the spot with a damp cotton ball and applies a fresh, waterproof bandage.

"Are you ready to go, Miss Diaz?"

"Soon. Give me five more minutes."

I wriggle a sweatshirt over my bathing suit. It cascades down my freshly shaven legs like a dress. I duck into the bathroom to grab a few more things, then make a final stop in the kitchen.

I pop open the fridge. Elliot suggested a drink to calm my shakes, but the last thing I want is to turn tipsy, clumsy, inept. I stand in the chill, unsure which risk is best. My fingers shake against the door handle, making it hard to think, hard to keep hold. Which could be a problem. I won't be able to reach the mainland without a sturdy grip on the sub.

I unscrew a baby liquor bottle and force it down in one swallow. It burns a trail through my throat like a flaming match.

Gomez watches my coughing fit from across the room. "Are you okay, Miss Diaz? Is there anything else you need?"

"I'm fine," I say, flapping a hand. "Let's go."

He escorts me to the secondary beach, the one built for activities. I plop my butt in the sand, cross-legged, along with sunscreen-streaked classmates. Gomez hovers in the background, hands clasped at his groin. Our instructor arrives last with her wet suit unzipped to her stomach. She greets us in a thick Boston accent and asks our names. I stutter over *Ari*.

When introductions are complete, she rattles off safety information. She gives us warnings about every possible risk, some of which I hadn't considered until now. Decompression sickness. Defective equipment. Animal bites. Air embolisms.

"If you push air into a vein, it can cause a seizure," she says. "You've probably heard about this happening during medical procedures when air gets caught in a needle. But what most people don't realize is the majority of air embolisms take place during scuba diving. To reduce your risk, you should resurface slowly and avoid alcohol. It's early, so hopefully none of you have had a Sex on the Beach just yet."

She winks at a couple with their arms roped around each other. Everyone except me chuckles.

"Now we're ready for the fun stuff. Technique. You can't get away with doggy paddling down there. In fact, you're not going to be using your hands at all. You're going to be using your legs only. Keep your arms crossed in front of you." She mimes the correct movements. "Now for those legs. When you're wearing flippers, you need to keep the natural spacing of your hips, but since you're beginners you might want to keep a little extra space for better stability. This will prevent you from rolling. In order to move, you're going to bend your knee, move your thigh forward, and extend your ankle."

I repeat each technique, term, and emergency protocol in my head. If I forget to *tighten my buoyancy compensator* or *miscalculate my oxygen* or *misplace my alternate air source*, I'll miss the sub.

Our instructor closes our training session by quizzing us. Correct answers are rewarded with a wet suit. I earn mine during the first round but struggle to strap my gear into place. Everyone else stretches into their suits and heaves packs onto their backs like it's second nature, committed to muscle memory.

Before boarding the boat, we pair up with a buddy to double-check our equipment. There's an uneven number of students, so Gomez acts as mine. "It looks secure," he says once he finishes tugging at straps. "I think you're ready to go. I can hold onto your things until you return." He nods at my sweatshirt and shoes, abandoned in the sand.

"I appreciate it. Thanks." I crouch for the pile, strategically angling my pack toward him to block his view. I dart a hand into my sweatshirt pocket and palm the razor blade hidden inside. I wiggled it loose from its handle after shaving, then pocketed it after my injection. I figured it would be easier to conceal than the bulky sack of soaps.

I pass the shirt and shoes to Gomez. He wishes me luck on my dive, unaware he won't be seeing me again.

"Come on, everybody! Let's do some exploring," the instructor says. She pumps her fist as she parades us onto a miniature moored boat.

A motor purrs as we glide through gentle currents. A thin mist sprays my cheeks. Gulls squawk overhead. I squeeze my knees together to take up as little bench space as possible, but my thigh still smushes against the man beside me.

"You've got the look of a newbie," he says. Yellowed teeth move beneath salt-and-pepper whiskers. "Am I right, are you popping your cherry?"

His wife sits at his opposite hip, swiveling her head like an owl to take in the scenery. The poor thing probably had memories of his cheating erased. He probably stumbled home at three in the morning, stinking of booze and bar-bathroom cologne.

"I know what I'm doing," I say, staring straight ahead.

"Ah. That's good to hear. I like experienced women."

Our instructor kills the conversation by bringing the boat to a halt. "Remember," she says, "breathe normally when the regulator is in your mouth. Never, I repeat, never hold your breath." She continues rehashing lessons we learned on land while distributing a box of clown-shoe flippers.

Getting nowhere with me, the married man resets his sights on his wife. He fondles her tiny, naked feet as he helps her into her fins. I slip into my own pair while eying his regulator, his primary source of oxygen.

I drop the razor from my palm, pinching the blade between my thumb and forefinger. I don't want to hurt him, but I didn't want to hurt the guard who dove through the dumpster for me, either. Of course, the guard turned out okay. This man would survive, too. He might swallow a splash of water, but the instructor will drag him back to land and resuscitate him.

I sweep my gaze across the boat. Some students are staring at their feet, still fumbling with their flippers. Others are staring at the instructor as she answers last-minute questions. No one pays me any mind.

I sip a shaky breath and rest the razor against his regulator. I wriggle my wrist back and forth, back and forth, until the blade punctures the hose. With our bodies pressed so close together, it looks like I'm adjusting my own equipment. No one suspects a thing—and since we already checked our equipment on land with a buddy, the small slice will go unnoticed.

I ditch my razor overboard. It plinks into the ocean and sinks out of view. My classmates do the same, vanishing into the ocean one by one. The instructor nudges them each into the water like a mama bird dumping babies.

Aside from the married couple, I'm the last to submerge. I secure my mask and climb onto the edge of the boat, facing backwards. My nerves should be gnawing away at me, but my chest rises and falls in a calm, steady rhythm. It could be the liquor. Or it could be the adrenaline.

"You make less and less sense the more I get to know you," Rhea said one afternoon as we scribbled bucket lists on the cabin floor. She picked practical things like *get a degree, put a down payment on a home, earn a high-paid position in my field*. I wrote out adrenaline junkie adventures like *bungee jump, sky dive, swim with sharks, scuba dive*.

"Domino, you have panic attacks whenever you have to give a class presentation. Or when you have to talk to a cashier instead of using a self-checkout line." Her pinkie skimmed the first item on my list. "But somehow *cliff diving from a 100-foot drop* doesn't bother you?"

I shrugged. "I don't think it's that weird. I get the same type of rush when I raise my hand in class as I do when I snowboard down black diamonds. Except the adrenaline feels good when I'm snowboarding. In class, it sucks."

"I still don't understand it."

"I'll take that as a compliment. I'm the one thing Rhea Laman doesn't understand."

The memory evaporates as the instructor knocks me into the water. I break through the surface, feeling as weightless as an astronaut in space. The critters even look alien. There are whiskered fish and spikey fish and fish with veiny, bulging eyes.

I camouflage myself with a cluster of divers. They gawk at a more mundane, plain-looking school of fish as the final two students dive. The instructor joins us last. She makes eye contact with each of us, giving us a chance to flash the 'okay' symbol she taught on land. Everyone takes a turn folding their thumb and pointer finger together.

Except the married man. He chokes, thrashes, puffs his cheeks, cups his throat. The teacher torpedoes toward him to help. A few students follow. A dozen hands drag him to the surface.

I fumble through coral and seaweed and algae, hoping to reach the sub before anyone notices me missing. My awkward, jerky movements make it hard to move fast. My own body—my teenage body—could have swum several miles easy. I earned extra credit sophomore year for lapping the gymnasium pool faster than the school average. Rhea would've been in my class, but she forged a medical note about asthma to skip the swim unit, to avoid baring her body in a swimsuit.

She spent her P.E. periods in the library poring over a thick, glossy biography. *Walt Disney: The Man Behind The Mouse*. She said the subject had something to do with her mystery internship, with a seedling of an idea. That semester, she learned every detail about the park's robotics and ride mechanics. She was especially impressed by smellitizer machines. They worked like air cannons, spraying the scent of salt water or barbeque sauce or orange blossoms to create an *all-encompassing experience*. I asked her why she would want to ruin the magic by reading behind-the-scenes secrets, but she said those details were the magic.

I will myself to stop thinking about her, to avoid adding emotional pain to the physical.

My hamstrings sting. My calves burn. Each inhale scalds my throat. I hope my body will survive the trip. Ari has always been thin, but she had Dad's metabolism to thank. She never stepped foot in a gym. She wheezed on two-story staircases. Her elbows buckled from a single pushup. She had no stamina, no muscle.

Luckily, the spindly legs of the dock come into view, giving me a chance to rest. I float in place and wait for the sub to lower. The break is a relief at first, but it ends up giving me too much downtime to think, to play out worst-case scenarios.

I worry the sub will leave late. I worry my oxygen tank will run out early. I worry the alcohol will slow my reflexes—and worry why Ari drank her muscles to mush in the first place. To cope with missing me? To relieve some sort of guilt over being the sister left alive?

Rippling water snags my attention. The swollen underbelly of the sub sinks into view. It chugs forward as the rest of its body pushes into the ocean.

I uncross my arms and stretch toward the railing, but the fat, hulking machine moves faster than expected. I reach out too late. My fingertips graze the railing and close around water, around an empty palm.

I propel forward, groping, scrambling. I latch onto the metal with one hand, my good hand. I swing out the other, but the water creates too much resistance. I keep aiming wrong, slapping at nothing. As the machine picks up speed, I lose my hold. The sub continues course without me.

Panic tightens my chest. I pump my legs harder, faster, but my pace stays the same. Frantic, I make wide sweeps with my arms the way I would above water, exerting every muscle, pushing forward with every limb.

The change in technique disrupts my balance. It tips me in the wrong direction. Extra bubbles gurgle from my mask as my breathing grows more and more ragged.

The sub shrinks in the distance as snippets from our training session whoosh through my head—tips about buoyancy and arm positioning and leg movement. When the solution hits, I feel stupid. The angle of kicks increases speed, not the frequency.

I hug my arms across my chest and reposition my torso. Bit by bit, my speed increases. I slowly gain on the sub. Every muscle below my waist burns, but I refuel myself by running a single word through my mind, shaping it into a chant. *Ari. Ari. Ari.*

I wait until coming within a foot of the sub to risk unlocking my arms again. I stretch toward the railings and fasten on with both fists. I grip the metal tight, too tight to slip, but my biceps throb. There's no way I can survive the whole trip with my arms extended pin-straight in front of me.

I use every ounce of strength to tug myself closer in a horizontal pull-up. The water tries to drag me backwards, to uncoil my fists, but I fight against the current. I squeeze my arms in between the railings and choke the bars with wobbling elbows. It chafes the skin beneath my suit, but it provides a sturdier grip, one that should last.

Afraid to celebrate too soon, I check my oxygen. I sapped the tank faster than forecasted. It won't survive until the mainland unless I get my panting under control.

I try to calm myself with a grounding exercise, but the midnight-black ocean hums in silence. With every sense deprived, I fasten my lids to think tranquil thoughts. I picture Mom wrist-deep in soap suds, scrubbing silverware. Ari chucking water balloons across the backyard. Marzia chugging a thermos in between bong hits. Dad flicking his thumb on the garden hose, spraying me instead of the car.

The visions calm my breathing to a safe, steady rhythm. I think up more soothing memories as the sub drags me across the ocean with my legs trailing behind me. Dr. Quinta sipping from her plastic bottle with GROW

THROUGH WHAT YOU GO THROUGH printed on the side. My teammates recording an ice bucket challenge, dumping gallons of freezing water over their heads for charity. Turtles flapping their stubby legs in aquarium ponds, swimming, swimming, swimming.

I snap back to the present as my own legs dangle downward, signaling a change in direction. The sub must be ascending. We must have reached the mainland.

I untangle myself from the railing. Pins and needles prick my flesh. I flex my fingers to work blood back into them as the sub climbs to the surface.

The fewer bodies milling around the dock, the higher my chances of escaping unseen. I plan on lingering underwater until the crew disembarks, but a quick glance at my tank spoils the idea. My oxygen tips dangerously low, grazing zero. I need air, not in five minutes, not in five seconds, now.

I inflate my buoyancy compensator to drift toward land. I poke my head above the water carefully to avoid ripples or splashes.

Even through the mask, the sudden switch from pitch-black to blinding sunlight gives me an instant headache. I squint away the bright spots and scan the area. The returning family files into the neighboring building, but employees hover in every corner of the courtyard.

Maintenance workers unload equipment from the sub. Groundskeepers snip trimmers and shear grass. A group of guards cluster together in small talk, blocking the only exit.

Leaving now would guarantee getting caught, so I hold my breath the old-fashioned way and pray the guards scatter before my lungs give out. I have my nose dipped underwater, halfway to hiding, when shouts cut through the courtyard.

A stampede of black boots flock to the far side of the grass. Employees form a ring like high schoolers at a cafeteria fight.

I use the opening to swing a leg onto the dock. With thirty pounds of equipment anchoring me down, it's a struggle to heave up the rest of my body. All the flailing loosens my flippers. They vanish into the ocean.

When I drag myself onto land, I stagger onto pruned feet. One or two workers dart glances my way, but they dismiss me to elbow into the crowd.

A few men raise their phones, recording the chaos. Others whoop and holler. Through their weaving heads, I spot Elliot. He tussles with a lanky, porn-mustached man in a janitorial jumpsuit. A fist swings. A jaw cracks. Blood spits. A perfect distraction.

I shed my equipment, stripping down to my wet suit. Free from the extra weight, I zip across the courtyard and barrel through the double-door exit.

It dumps me in a crayon-colored shop selling magnets, keychains, and plushies. A cashier blocks a door behind the register but another leads toward a hall, toward freedom.

I limp across the padded rainbow floors. As my bare toes cross the threshold, my body gets jerked back. Broad, dark hands seize my waist.

I wriggle and kick, knocking my heel into a shin. "Don't touch me. Get off. Get off me."

"I need to call a manager," my captor says in a cool, collected voice.

I continue to thrash, scissoring my legs and chopping my arms. A family browsing knickknacks stares, noses raised. My captor apologizes to them about the 'fuss' and drags me into a backroom.

He waits until the lock is twisted to release me. The unexpected gesture sends me stumbling forward. I trip onto the couch, soaking the cushions with my silhouette. I right myself with loose, soupy arms and finally get a good look at him. His square body blocks the exit. His bald head shimmers with sweat. It matches the blotches my wet suit left across his button-down shirt.

"I need to get home," I say. "I'm not doing anything wrong. I just want to go home."

"Miss Laman gave you a personal tour a few days ago. And now you're back, sneaking around sopping-wet. I can't let you leave without checking with a higher-up. I hope you understand." He jabs at his security pass like a grandfather, using the same finger for every letter. "We'll have everything sorted soon. You should rest in the meantime. You're panting."

I consider my odds of overpowering him, then take another look at him. Broad chest. Thick thighs. Veiny arms. I don't know what I was thinking, trying to escape.

Running was shortsighted, a frightened reflex. If I want my surgery reversed, I need to keep the enemy close. I need to get in touch with Rhea so I can sweet-talk her into giving me what I want, manipulate her the way she manipulated me.

I flinch when the door rustles. A salt-and-pepper man strides into the office with a vacant smile. He perches on a stiff leather chair directly across from me. A white handkerchief peeks from his breast pocket. A gilded sword clip tethers his tie together.

"Ariadna Diaz," he says, reading from his security pass. "Do you want to tell me why you're ending your vacation prematurely? I'm looking at your profile right now. You're not authorized to be in this building for another few days. And that looks like an Endellion wet suit. Were you planning on leaving the property while wearing it? That's a count of theft."

I swallow the crater in my throat, unable to concentrate on whatever he's saying. I'm too distracted by the familiar face. Aside from the creases in his forehead and the slight hunch to his spine, he looks the same as ten years ago. As the day he inserted a camera in me.

"Ariadna. Do you understand the seriousness of this situation?

"I didn't do anything," I say. It comes out as a stutter.

"You crossed through a prohibited area and attempted to steal Endellion property."

"I left the tank in the courtyard. It's there with the mask. You can have the wet suit back, too, if you let me grab clothes from the shop."

"I would love to give you a change of clothes. If you would give me your story. What happened today?"

"I would rather talk to Rhea about it," I say, which isn't entirely true. The more I learn about the grownup version of my ex, the less I want anything to do with her.

Dawson drove me to suicide, but she still worked with him, still trusted him. *He keeps calling me the wrong name*, I remind myself. *He doesn't know everything. She's keeping him in the dark for a reason.*

Dawson strokes his graying stubble. "I'm afraid you're stuck with me. Miss Laman is currently unavailable. She's attending an important conference today."

"About Memory Scent technology?"

His smug grin falters. His eyes drill into me, unspeaking, unblinking.

"Excuse me, sir," my captor says, stabbing his pass with a single finger. "I think I better message her. I don't want her to get upset I went around her.

She said not to disturb her today, but maybe she would want to deal with this directly. It seems to be a unique case."

Dawson grunts, holding his focus on me. "Have we met before?"

"Me and you haven't met, no."

"Are you positive? *Ariadna Diaz.* It sounds familiar."

"It's a pretty common last name. There were a dozen Diazes in my school."

"What school was that?"

I lick my cracked lips, stalling. I already leaked enough info to scare them into summoning Rhea. Revealing more might backfire. I rummage for a safe answer, but my captor beats me to speaking.

"Miss Laman would like the young woman brought to the parking garage," he says, gesturing to his pass. "I have a family to attend to, if you don't mind escorting her?"

Dawson comes to a stand, smooths his trousers, and rebuttons his jacket. "Up," he says with a snap of his fingers. He shoos me ahead to keep an eye on me. He barks directions, turning us down a hall, into a glass elevator, and through a garage reeking of gasoline.

A white limo idles in a reserved space. A squat, muscular man emerges from the driver's side. His scarred face stays flat as he pops a door for Dawson, a door for me.

"You're bringing her with you?" Dawson asks. He ducks to make eye contact with Rhea.

She sits cross-legged in the backseat. A silky red dress drapes down to her ankles. Spider-like lashes are glued over her thin ones. "I should have been on the road by now," she says without bothering to look up from her glove. "I can't stay here, so I might as well deal with her on the way."

"Let me come with you. In case something happens."

"I have my driver. I'll be fine."

"You seem pretty confident about that."

They exchange a long, tense look.

Rhea flicks her wrist. "Go on, then. Sit in front. You have a ticket to the conference anyway. You might as well show up early and help with the setup."

Dawson drives my head down, shoves me in the cabin, and slams my door. When he drops into the passenger seat, he angles himself sideways to watch us through a wide, gaping partition.

Rhea raises a window with a *one-way* sticker, cutting him off from our conversation. He glares at the glass.

"Are you feeling okay?" she asks. "I heard you swam all the way here. You're lucky you haven't hurt yourself. You're supposed to be on bedrest. You're supposed to be recovering."

"From the surgery that turned my sister into me?"

She swallows, clears her throat. "I realize how horrible that sounds. I'm sure you hate me right now, but you don't have all the details."

"That's because you didn't give me any."

"I know. I'm sorry. And I'm sorry about your sister. I researched all your relatives. Accessed their medical records, tracked down their brain scans. Ari was the closest match. She shares your blood type along with an impressive number of DNA strands. And, I know you don't want to hear this, but she was a mess. Unfulfilled. Unsuccessful. Unhappy." She leaves space for me to speak, but I don't take the bait. "I never wanted to operate on her. I held off for as long as possible. I was looking at other options outside of your gene pool, hoping someone else would eventually work. I performed a few operations, but each one failed. I was going to keep testing strangers, but Ari emailed me once the resort opened and this conference was coming up, so it felt like fate, like I was supposed to use her after all. I wanted to make sure you were taken care of in case something happened to me, so I went for it. You wouldn't be here otherwise."

I dig my fingers into my thigh and inhale. Exhale. Inhale. Exhale. I fight against the urge to smack her; mindful violence won't convince her to reverse my surgery. "What you did in high school was an accident," I say, choosing each word carefully. "It was a mistake that snowballed. I get that. But I ended my life for two reasons. To protect you from Endellion—which clearly backfired since you're still working for them. And to protect my sister from them—but you pretty much turned around and killed her anyway. Did you really expect me to be okay with that? Really?"

"It's a lot to handle. I know. You would have acclimated better if you discovered the truth in steps. I didn't want you to find out this way. Not on your own. Not this early. Was it the nails? I told Cara to rip them off before waking you. I should have handled that myself."

"No. You should have left my family alone. They've been through enough. I'm not going to let Ari die because you feel bad about letting me die. You have to reverse the surgery."

A boom ricochets through the cabin. And another. Dawson beats a beefy fist against the partition, scowling.

Rhea continues as if she hasn't heard a peep. "Domino, I love you, but I can't deal with this right now. The conference is my main priority today. People across the world are flying through time zones to test our newest product."

"Yeah, I know. Memory Scent Technology. It turns scents into emotions. Why are you making such a fuss about it? Compared to what you did with me, it doesn't seem like such a big deal. Shouldn't you be flaunting me around if you want attention so badly?"

"This isn't about fame or a fat paycheck. It's about making things up to you. I've been gathering a group together. All of the businessmen associated with Endellion—the ones responsible for your death—and all the cops who have been keeping Endellion secrets since the beginning. I gave them all a chance to prove their morality. I tested them with Memory Transfers. If they turned down the operation, they didn't receive a ticket for the conference today. Unfortunately, most people are corruptible. The venue is going to be packed."

"What's happening at this conference?"

"All of the people attending believe in my vision. The Memory Transfers were a good way to build trust. I barely said a word and they signed up for the chance to test Memory Scent Technology. That's all that's going to happen. They're going to test it."

A shrill ringing interrupts us. A video call. Rhea excuses herself and answers with a polite, patient smile. "What is it you need, Dawson?"

"You closed the partition," he says, echoing in the tight space. He squints at the one-way glass, unable to see us. But we can see him.

"Is that a problem? I didn't realize you wanted to be involved with the conversation. If you could have handled her on your own, I wouldn't have been called to take over."

"You were called because she knew information that hasn't been released to the general public."

"I don't see how that's possible."

"Neither do I. Unless you're working with her. But that would mean you're lying to me, maybe trying to pull something behind my back."

Rhea frowns. "That's quite the accusation. What would make you think such a thing?"

"She's the sister. I recognize the name."

"Whose sister? What are you talking about?"

"You quit over that Diaz girl. You tried to pin her death on me. And now you're hanging out with her sister—and lying to me about it? Are you still trying to get me in trouble? After this long?"

"I don't know what you're going on about, but if I wanted some sort of revenge for her murder, I would have put you through a lot worse than a jail sentence."

"It was suicide. Not murder. I was experimenting with intrusive thoughts. You were the one who wanted us to place a stronger focus on mental health in the first place. Regardless, I gave up that line of research after her death. You've completed much worse experiments since then. On Antoni Tan. On your parents. For what? A commercial resort? And you're making me out to be the bad guy? It doesn't matter if you're my superior now. It doesn't matter if the police are friendly with you. They only have your back because of your *favors*. I have real friends in the force and plenty of stories about what you've done. If you want to get me locked up, you'll be in the cell next to me."

"I told you. I'm not trying to get you arrested."

"Why is the sister here, then? What else does she know?"

"She's none of your business."

"Bullshit." He whips toward the driver. "Pull over. Let me out."

"No, don't pull over yet," Rhea says, fiddling with settings on her security pass. "I'm activating the program now. Front seat only. Please prepare yourself."

The driver rustles in his collar, slipping his hand beneath a set of dog tags. He pulls out a mask strapped to his neck. He tugs the fabric over the bottom half of his face and cranks the air conditioning.

"What's with the mask?" Dawson asks, head swiveling between the driver and the partition. "What's going on? Rhea, what are you doing? What is this?"

He unbuckles his seatbelt, jiggles the door handle, pounds the window switch. A child lock separates him from the rolling highway. He swears as he rams an elbow against the glass. Only a tiny chink forms in the window, but blood snakes down his fingers, staining his suit cuffs. He winds up for another hit, aiming for the same fractured spot.

Before he makes impact, his energy wanes. Both arms slacken. He lies still for a beat.

Two.

Three.

When he twitches to life, he clutches his chest like he's having a heart attack. It takes a second to realize his fingers are working at his tie, loosening his clip. He unpeels it from the fabric and holds it level with his neck. It catches sunlight, the metal winking.

Without warning, he stabs the edge into his throat. Again. Again. Again. He slashes until blood sprouts and gurgles, until his body surrenders and slumps.

A scream sticks in my throat. Only a wheeze comes out.

"I'm sorry you had to see that," Rhea says, crossing to my side of the limo. "I know it's morbid, but it needed to happen. Ever since he put the camera in your head, it needed to happen."

I have trouble swallowing, speaking, thinking. "You didn't know he was going to be in the limo. You couldn't have planned this. You just have the car rigged for this? For murder?"

"We had to practice on an increasingly bigger scale to prep for a space as large as the conference room. Broom closets. Bathrooms. Cars. We've fine-tuned our prototype over the last few weeks. We don't need to use masks or tubes anymore like we did during trial runs. All we have to do is position a scented substance between a strong airflow—a fan or pressurized air—and an audience. That's the plan for the conference tonight. Everyone attending thinks they're going to experience a burst of euphoria. In reality, the scent will induce an intolerable sadness. For a little while, they'll feel what it's like to be your mother without her firstborn, to be your father so lost in his grief he tried to kill himself, too."

A pang hits my stomach, like someone punched me in the gut. "That's the real reason he's paralyzed?"

"Yes. I'm sorry. People do drastic things when someone they love leaves them." She cups my knee and squeezes.

I don't have enough energy to knock her hand, to scoot away. My imagination disables me. Did my dad ring a rope around his neck? Press a barrel against his tongue? Drink himself into a coma? Was it my fault, just like my sister and her drinking?

"I've been planning this since your death," Rhea says, still squeezing. "I'm hoping to make it look like a technical malfunction, an accident, but if authorities figure out the truth, they won't have any reason to continue protecting me. I have a safehouse ready, but who knows if I'll make it there? I might be behind bars tomorrow."

"Good. You belong there. That's where Dawson should be, too. Not dead."

"Domino. When you sent your goodbye text, I guessed what it meant. I drove to your block to check on you, to calm you down. I got there too late. I saw the cop cars. The ambulance. The gurney." Our limo crawls into a tunnel. It blankets her in shadow. "I talked to Dawson later that morning. I made a scene. I quit in front of everyone. The Endellion board pulled me in for a meeting almost immediately. They warned me against contacting the police. They told me I would only get myself in trouble. Dawson had connections to higher-ups in the government just like I do now. They convinced me the police would cover for him just like everyone at the company was doing. They all picked his side." The tunnel widens to a highway, rinsing her with sunlight. "The only reason I was able to make it a day without you, let alone a year or two or ten, was by holding onto the hope I could fix things. I always planned on making enough money to buy Endellion out, to kick Dawson out, to ruin the company from the inside. I *did* buy them out and it felt good at first, but I couldn't go through with firing Dawson. He manipulated me and murdered you. Losing his company wasn't torture enough. I decided he deserved to feel the same way I felt, and I felt dead. I still do. Especially when you look at me like that."

I search her lined face, trying to align the person in front of me with the one who cuddled and kissed me on a cabin floor. I want to call her a stranger, to pretend I don't recognize the face staring back at me, but she's eerily similar to the morning we met. Brilliant. Passionate. Persistent. Nothing changed. Except she's a murderer now.

"I don't get the point," I say. "Why would you bring me back? If you knew this conference was going to end with you thrown in prison or running from the police?"

"I wasn't being selfish. I didn't bring you back to live happily ever after with you. I did it because it was the right thing to do. Sometimes, the right thing looks like a bad thing at first glance."

She removes her hand from my knee. She plunges it under her flowing dress, bunching the fabric. A mask is strapped to her thigh like a garter.

My stomach lurches. I stumble backward on the bench, leaving a slug trail of water across the leather.

"It's okay," she says, muffled through the mask. "I would never give you what everyone else is getting. This one is only like taking a sleeping pill. Like what your sister was given before her sub ride to the island. Or in the bathroom before her operation. It doesn't hurt."

I clamp my lips tight as a vise, afraid crying or screaming or cursing her out will suck extra air into my lungs. I lunge toward the closest door and shimmy the handles, but they rattle and thump like they did for Dawson. Locked.

My attention climbs toward the sunroof, hoping it unfastens manually like the one in my old Thunderbird. I crouch, standing as tall as the cabin allows. Overhead vents shoot mist at me. The chill tickles my cheeks as I run my fingers along the glass edges, feeling for a latch. No luck. I try pressing both palms flat against the sheet to raise it myself, but that doesn't work, either. I resort to shoving my nails deep into a corner and prying. The window barely budges. It only moves a sliver.

"Damn it," I say, accidentally letting air into my lips. More air sneaks through my nostrils. The limo is inescapable. Fainting is inevitable.

But if the scent is going to knock me out, I might as well knock my ex out with me.

I whirl in her direction and leap toward her, my claws bared to tear the mask from her face. Just as my nails graze her cheek, I lose my footing. The anesthesia weakens my legs, buckles my knees. I careen toward the carpet.

Rhea catches me by the waist. She guides me into a seat and cradles my head in her lap. "It's okay. Everything is okay," she says.

The last thing I see before sagging asleep are her plump, puckered lips pressing against my forehead.

CHAPTER 18

I flutter awake to a penlight drilling its beam into my pupils. When it clicks off, a woman slips the device into her breast pocket. A gold band glitters on her ring finger. One of the diamonds is missing.

I remember her from the recording. She's the surgeon who operated on my sister, who took a blowtorch to her wrist.

"Wonderful. You're awake," she says with a clap. "Welcome to my apartment. My name is Cara. And I know your name. Your real one. Dominique."

I clear my throat to answer her, but my tongue tastes like sand.

"You don't have to speak if you're not feeling well. I have plenty to say anyway. Since you know what's going on now, there's no point in holding you on the island like we originally planned. Over the next few months, I'm going to help integrate you back into this big blue world. We can set up my equipment inside of your apartment and I'll visit once per week to administer Cleansings—which will scribble over your sister's memories for seven days straight. When I'm confident your body is healthy enough for a Memory Transfer, we'll get rid of those memories for good and you'll never have to see me again. Gosh, where are my manners? You must be parched."

She uncaps a water bottle from the bedside table and tilts it against my lips. I snatch it from her, able to control the flow myself. I gulp as much as my stomach allows and set it back on the counter. Beside a loaded syringe.

The unspoken threat looms over me. *Don't do anything stupid.* If I misbehave, she'll knock me out again.

"What if you don't do the Cleansings?" I ask with a rasp. "Will my sister go back to normal?"

She wets her lips, a serpentine dart of the tongue. "Hmm. You would both be living inside one brain. Cohabitating. Competing. It would be physically possible to sustain multiple personalities at once, but in all likelihood, you would be placed in an institution. Written off as mentally unstable. Hallucinatory. *Haul her off to the funny farm*, they'd say."

"Could you reverse it instead? Get rid of...me?"

"I don't think you understand what's happening here. You have a second chance. You should be dancing around in your underwear, popping pink champagne."

I rock myself into a sitting position. The bedsprings creak. "I'm pretty sure I know more than you. Did Rhea tell you? The real plan?"

"I know all the gritty, gory details, yes. To be honest, I was a bit nervous she would ask me to sit in the audience after the week we've been having. Since I'm her best surgeon, she lets me get away with Transfers, but she was steaming mad when I forgot to remove your nails. I know I made a whopper of a mistake, but I was preoccupied with your tattoo. And making sure your surgery was a success."

"You're okay with what she's doing, then? With mass murder?"

"Oh, I wouldn't call it *that*. My husband has a ticket to attend. Miss Laman did me a favor by slipping him onto the invite list." Her hand covers her gasp. "Gosh, that must sound awful. Let me backtrack. I skimmed through Transfer logs recently and counted my name more times than it had any business being on there. We're meant to leave a nifty little reminder note whenever we sign up for a Transfer. I scribbled HUBBY next to each one. There's something I don't want to know about him. Which means it must be bad."

"What if you were the one who hurt him? You could have cheated on him or something."

"He would have reminded me."

"Maybe he doesn't know. Maybe you got rid of the memory before you could tell him."

Her nose wrinkles. "He's my dream, my groom, my everything. I wouldn't have hurt him."

"You don't know that for sure. You took away your ability to know."

"I may have gotten rid of a few pesky memories, but I still have the same thought process. I'm still living in the same headspace." She crosses the room in purple socks and nudges a door with her big toe. "If you're awake enough for all those silly questions, you're awake enough to get changed. You'll get sick if you wear that suit for any longer. I scrounged up a spare outfit for you. You can drop your wet clothes in the tub."

I wobble on liquid legs, pressing a palm against the wall in case my knees give out. Her bathroom is spacious, wide as a trailer, with litter speckling the tiles. A lanky orange cat kicks up more clumps from a plastic box. A plumper black cat perches on a fuzzy toilet seat cover. They both watch me unpeel my wet suit. The zipper squeals.

I shrug into clothes Cara hung across the shower rod: a tacky jogging suit with skinny stripes running across the arms and legs. It swishes with the smallest movements, ruining any hope I'd had of acting discreetly.

I activate my messenger app anyway. I type out an SOS to Elliot, saying, "Rhea is out of her mind. She killed someone in front of me. And she's going to kill everyone at the conference tonight. We need to figure out where it's being held and stop her. You need to come get me."

A message pings back immediately. An error. YOUR ACCOUNT HAS BEEN DEACTIVATED.

My cursing startles the orange cat. He skitters into the tub, flapping the lion-in-a-swim-cap shower curtain. Cara must hear the thud. She calls inside to check on me.

"Sorry," I say. "I didn't realize you had pets. We scared each other."

I flush the toilet, hoping the burbling pipes drown out my snooping. I hunt through each drawer for an escape tool, a defense weapon, something sharp and easy to conceal. I can't find anything useful. Cara has hair-removal strips instead of razors, nail files instead of cutters, scrunchies instead of bobby pins. I unlatch a mini medical kit, but it's stuffed with trash. An empty pack of princess bandages. Crumpled smiley-face stickers. A broken stethoscope. She must stow her actual equipment at work.

"I'll give you ten more seconds in there, little lady," she says as she raps on the door. She counts backward like a camp counselor.

"I'm coming," I say, twisting toward the door.

A reflection freezes me. A full-length mirror clings to the wood, casting my sister back at me. Her hair is cropped close to her scalp, too close to see her natural curls. Piercing holes pepper her ears, her nose, her brows. Her almond eyes are the only recognizable piece of her, mainly because they look identical to mine. If I focus on their hue, I can almost pretend I'm looking at the real me.

"Two...one..." Cara swings the door wide, killing the reflection. "Oh good, purple suits you."

She smiles at me like she expects a *thank you*. I swish past her and plop onto the edge of the mattress.

"Someone is in a sour mood," she says, making herself comfortable on the other side. "Lucky for you, I have a surprise. I think it will get you on board with everything that's happening."

She withdraws a phone in a bunny-eared case. She dials ten digits at lightning speed, activates the speaker function, and rests the phone on the blankets between us. It rings. And rings. And rings.

"Hello?" a woman says right before we get sentenced to voicemail. "Who is this? We're on the no-call list, you know. That means no calling. Unless you want to chip in for my phone bill. I'd be happy to take a donation."

I miss a heartbeat. The next one throbs hard in my throat. "Mom? Is that you?"

"Oh. I'm sorry about that, honey. I didn't recognize your number." She chuckles. Other than the wheeze in her throat, she sounds the same as always. "You didn't lose another phone, did you? I heard they can track them now. That would have come in handy back in the day. Remember when your father lost his in that terrible snowstorm? It took us a whole weekend to find it."

I do remember. We only had one full-sized shovel, so Dad sent us into the yard with ladles and pans. It felt like a punishment at first, but Mom turned it into a scavenger hunt. When we finally dug up the phone, she rewarded us with s'mores toasted in the fireplace.

"Are you there, honey? Do you have a bad signal?"

My face puddles with snot and tears. I swipe the mess with my sleeve. "Yeah. Sorry. My phone is fine. I'm fine. How are you?"

"Oh, you don't have to pretend to care about me. I know why you really got in touch. You want to hear about Arrow. I can tell he misses you. He keeps staring at the door, whining. But we've been having fun. Don't be too mad, but he gained a few pounds. He likes my cooking more than you or your father ever did."

"How is he? Daddy?" I choke on the word.

"Your father? Well, Arrow is sitting at his feet right now. I've been reading to them the last few days. I borrowed books from the library. Graphic novels. I think he likes the pictures. And I like acting out the different parts. It makes me feel like a movie star."

"I wish I could see that. You were always good at acting out our storybooks."

She would go all-out when she read to us, donning silly accents and making goofy faces. I try to picture her doing the same thing now, two decades later. I wonder whether her looks weathered the years as well as her voice, whether time has bulged her cheeks or whittled them to the bone.

"Are you doing okay, honey?" she asks. "Do you need anything? If something is wrong, you don't have to hide it from me. I would rather know."

I must not sound like Ari. I must have strayed from their standard script. I make a mental note to be more careful with our conversations in the future, then remind myself there is no future.

"Stop your worrying," I say, trying to mimic my sister. "I'm perfectly fine."

"Okay. If you're sure. I don't want to rush you off, but your father has an appointment in an hour and I promised the pup I would walk him around the block before we left. I can talk to you after?"

"That's okay. I'll be back home soon. We can talk then. Love you, Mom."

"Oh? I love you too, honey."

The line goes dead.

I hunch forward and sob, cradling my head in my hands. Mucus drips between my fingers.

Cara waits for the hiccups to space apart, for the sniffles to slow. "If you want, you can see your mother in person," she says. "You can visit her. Bear-hug her. Have a mother-daughter day every single day. You deserve this life, Dominique. Don't question it too much."

I *have* to question it. Dad drank a twelve-pack per day but swore he was in perfect health once he quit smoking. Marzia cheated in every relationship, but she considered herself a good girlfriend because she put out. Rhea murdered my sister, but she didn't feel bad about it because she resurrected me in the process. Everyone rationalized their wrongdoings. I could rationalize this, too.

"You shouldn't feel guilty about putting yourself first for a change," Cara says, rubbing circles on my back. "Really, you would have more of a reason to feel guilty if you let this chance slip away. Miss Laman worked her butt off to get you here. It's pretty romantic when you think about..."

Across the apartment, a latch clicks. A handle jostles. A cat meows and paws at a door.

"Just a second. Excuse me," Cara says, brow furrowed. Her footsteps recede down the hall.

Unchaperoned, I hunt for a fire escape, a balcony, any gateway to the outside. Most of her windows are closer to prison slats, only letting in a sliver of sunlight. The widest one is in a connected office, installed above a cluttered desk. If I angle myself right, I should be able to squeeze through the gap.

"Where did you find that key?" Cara asks, dulled from distance. "Did my husband give that to you?"

I climb onto her desk, hovering over tiger-print notebooks and paw-print pencil cases. The plastic top dips with my weight. Careful not to fall, I flip the latch, ease up the window, and plunge my head into a wind gust. I crane my neck but don't see any ledge to step onto, any cushioning to catch my fall. Just sixty feet of freefall ending in a pebbled street.

"Cara, you swore you wouldn't do it again," the visitor says. I tip my head, recognizing the voice. "You don't have any idea what I'm saying, do you? You know what, it doesn't matter. That's not why I'm here. I need you to tell me about what's been going on. I know Laman is making you perform extra operations. I know about Dominique and Ari."

I scramble onto the rough wool carpet and peek into the hall. Cara faces the opposite way, wielding her phone like a cross, poised to dial 911. Elliot locks eyes with me over her shoulder. A bruise swells his nose, a casualty from helping me in the courtyard. He parts his lips to speak, but I smash my wrists in a handcuff motion. He must understand the meaning—*I'm here against my will*—because he resets his sights on Cara.

"I'm going to assume you're drunk, since you aren't making any sort of sense," she says to him. "If you give me the key right now, you can leave without blue and red lights flashing on your face."

"Fine with me. I don't want it anymore. You can take it. As long as you give me some answers. I'm not leaving until you tell me what's going on."

"That's my personal property. I have a right to it. You, on the other hand, don't have authorization to any information. It's classified. Off limits. Locked tight."

Their squabble continues, but I drown it out while I concentrate on an escape plan. With someone else on my team, I have double the options, double the hope.

I gravitate toward the untouched syringe on the bedside table. I could creep up to Cara and stab the needle into her arm, but she would struggle. Even with Elliot strapping her down, I might miss a vein. I might waste the dosage.

A cat, gray as a rain cloud, startles me. It weaves between my ankles, purring. I back away on instinct, but the real Ari would drop to the ground and stroke it. She begged our parents to get her a pet since she learned her ABCs. Dad refused to adopt anything bigger than a goldfish, but Mom mentioned a dog during our phone call. I bet Ari spoils him rotten. I bet she cares more about him than she cares about herself. And I bet Cara feels the same.

I duck into the bathroom to borrow the old, chubby, declawed cat snoozing on the toilet. He doesn't wriggle or nip when I scoop him. He lets me cradle him like a football and carry him into the office. With my arms full, I shimmy the desk away from the window with my hip. I scrape floorboards loud enough to be overheard.

Cara barrels into the room. She skids to a stop when she sees me, arms stretched out the window, dangling her cat over the sixty-foot drop.

"What are you doing?" she howls, rushing at me. "Put him down. Let him go."

Elliot restrains her. He hugs her to his chest like a human straitjacket, but he looks as mortified as she does.

"You're out of your minds. Both of you." Anger cracks her voice. "Dominique, I hope you realize I could have handled this visit very differently. I didn't handcuff you. I didn't drug you. I brought you into my home. I let you sleep in my bed. I put you in touch with your mother."

"And killed my sister."

"So you're hoping to get payback by killing a part of my family? What I did to your sister *brought you back*. It traded a life for a life. You should be thanking me, not threatening me. You're not thinking clearly. You need to give him to me. Right now. I'm serious. Give him to me."

I nod at the syringe through the open doorway. "After you inject yourself."

"Excuse me?"

"Inject yourself. Then you can have your cat."

She pauses. Her nostrils flare. "No. You're going to put him down either way. There's no benefit to hurting him. What would be the point?"

"To show you I'm serious. Then I'll grab another one. I've seen at least three."

"Hold on," Elliot says. He pokes his head out from behind hers. "We don't need to get crazy here. If Cara lets us leave, then we're all cool, right?"

"She'd call someone the second we're gone. We need her asleep, so she doesn't rat us out to Rhea. Whatever is in there can't be that dangerous. If it was safe enough to use on me, it must be safe enough for her."

I force myself to lock eyes with her, to appear threatening. My nerves tempt me to look away, but I channel my anger about how she kidnapped my sister, operated on my sister, killed my sister.

"I'll give you ten more seconds," I say, parroting her threat from earlier. "Ten…nine…eight…"

"Fine, fine, fine," she says. Veins burst from her forehead.

Elliot stumbles across the room, clumsily dragging her like a couple in a three-legged race. Near the nightstand, he loosens his hold. He gives her enough slack to lean forward and pluck the needle. I worry she might attack him with it, but that would mean risking her kitten, her baby.

"You were right before," she says, tapping the sides to dispel air bubbles. "Miss Laman never should have brought you back. You don't deserve to walk this planet. You're just a wasted experiment."

She drives the syringe into a vein and rams the plunger. The liquid drains into her. She stares at me through the doorway as the tube empties, waiting, brows raised. I reel the cat through the window and clutch him against my chest. He purrs into my tracksuit.

Her muscles relax. It could be relief. Or it could be the drugs. As she loses consciousness, Elliot guides her onto the mattress. He props her head with hairy, purple pillows. I plop the cat on her stomach and rub between his ears as an apology. He kneads her shirt and falls asleep with her, unfazed by his big adventure.

"Think you can fill me in on what the hell is happening?" Elliot asks, following me into a walk-in closet.

I toss aside polka-dot heels and ballet flats. I cram my feet into neon sneakers a size too small. "I tried to message you before. I talked to Rhea. She's going to use her new Memory Scent Technology to kill everyone at the conference."

"Wait, what? I thought tonight was supposed to be a private thing for employees and the police force? Why would she kill them?"

"She thinks *they're* bad people for using technology *she* created. She's out of her mind. She killed someone in front of me on the limo ride here. You should look through Cara's cell or her security pass for the conference address. We have to get there before anything happens."

He taps on his own security pass. "I was supposed to go to the conference before Laman took my ticket away, remember? I have the address saved in an email. I just have to find...oh shit."

"What? Did you delete it?"

"I don't think I need it." He crouches to my level. "News headlines pop up on my email's main page. Look at this one. About Endellion. Apparently, there's a protest outside the conference hall."

He clicks the link, activating a livestream. A pair of redheads lead a crowd in a chant. They thrust homemade, anti-Endellion posters outside a domed building. The street sign behind them says *Enchantment Avenue*. The watermark below them says *Twins Spilling Tea*.

"Enchantment Ave. is only a twenty-minute drive from here," he says.

"Do you have a car?"

"A truck. It's parked outside."

"Then let's go."

"All right. You can tell me about your limo ride on the way. Who did Laman kill? What did he look like? Do you know his name?"

I pull in a shuddery breath, not wanting to relive my trauma, but not having much of a choice.

CHAPTER 19

We jostle and bump down a potholed road. Elliot dangles a cigarette out the window, his third since hearing about the limo incident. I tip my head back and close my eyes, exhausted. I could sleep for an eternity—and that's exactly what will happen when my surgery gets reversed. The thought jolts me awake.

"Thanks for helping me with Cara," I say. "And helping me with the sub ride. I saw your fight in the courtyard. I'm surprised you didn't get in trouble for it."

"I got written up, but it's cool. I already quit in my head."

"You'll find a better place to work, I'm sure. A safer place at least."

He flexes the hand holding the wheel. Bruises darken his knuckles. "The dude I punched was her husband, you know."

For a split second, I think he means Rhea and my heart drops. Of course, he's talking about Cara. He knew where she lived. He had a key to her apartment.

"Is she the reason why you've been helping me?" I ask. "Because you feel bad someone you love is behind this? Is that why you knew I was in trouble in the first place? No one else on the island did. Not even Gomez, and he was glued to my side."

"She didn't tell me much. Only a few things here and there. She knew it bothered me—or knew Laman would kill her for snitching—so she didn't go into detail. If she did, I would've been more helpful. You wouldn't have watched Dawson die in front of you, for starters."

I'm tempted to interrogate him about how much he knew, how long ago he found out, whether he could have stopped the surgery before it was set in motion, but the details don't matter. He could lose his job by helping me. He could lose his life. But he's still steering the wheel.

I twist toward a trunk bed covered with vinyl. "Do you have a gun in there? Or a taser or something?"

"I have extra tires, jumper cables, a bunch of tools, stuff like that." He flicks his cigarette. Its tip sparks when it hits the road. "Why? Were you thinking about shooting Laman?"

"Talking to her hasn't seemed to work."

"We don't have to talk to her. We don't have to go anywhere near her. She told you how it's going down. She's pumping the scent through the auditorium, right?"

"The mist came through the vents when we were in the limo. I guess she'll do the same at the conference."

"Makes sense. I watched a documentary about Smell-O-Vision once. In the 50s, or maybe 60s, movie theaters tried to infuse the theater with smells to match whatever was happening on the screen. They pushed the scents through their air-conditioning systems. If that's what Laman is doing, we just have to track down the main AC unit."

"And break it?"

"As long as we don't breathe it."

I spend the rest of the drive staring out the window in a daze. A forest blurs past. A homeless woman wrangles a shopping cart overrun with bottles and plastic bags. Another woman juggles three separate strollers at a bus stop. Every mile, there are more strangers struggling, suffering, assuming they have it the worst.

As our destination inches closer, the scenery transitions to crisper, cleaner buildings. We ease to a stop at a traffic light stationed beside a chic strip mall. I browse its shops. A tanning salon. A bait shop. A masseuse parlor. A sporting goods store. I squint at the final storefront display. It feels like fate. Or a slap in the face, warning me to plan better, to think two steps ahead.

"Hey, can you pull into that parking lot quick?" I ask, pressing my thumb against the seat belt buckle. "And can you lend me your credit card?"

*

We park in a public lot and cross onto Enchantment Avenue on foot. My tall, bulky backpack curls my spine like a question mark. Elliot bought a matching one, but the weight doesn't bother him.

"We're either the last ones here or the early birds," he says as we approach the entrance.

Guards flank a velvet rope maze, scanning security passes. A dozen middle-aged men and women wait for their turn to trickle inside. A group twice that size surrounds the ropes, mostly teens and twenty-somethings. They carry flimsy, makeshift signs. END ENDELLION. NEVER FORGET WHO YOU ARE. ERASING YOUR MEMORIES WON'T ERASE YOUR PAST. Fresh paint drips and smears across the cardboard.

"We're early enough," I say, hitching my bag higher. "We have to be. They would have stopped letting people inside if it started. The doors would be bolted."

We thread through the protestors with muttered *excuse mes* and *sorries*. At the head of the herd, the two redheads from the livestream pump their fists in a chant. *LAMAN IS A CON. LAMAN IS A CON. LAMAN IS A CON.*

A man with a bun records the scene on a handheld camera. When the viewfinder lands on me, his arm drops to his side. He charges through the throng of people, nudging and shoving and scratching the lens.

"Ari, thank Christ," he says. "Are you okay? What do you need? Do you need water? Do you need to sit?"

The redheaded woman breaks her chant. "Are you insane? Cassidy, pick up the damn camera. We're live." She double-takes when she spots me. She hurls her megaphone at her brother and jogs over, shaking her head. "You little bitch. You could have called. We've been sweating our balls off, thinking you were kidnapped or brainwashed or...where's all your piercings? You look like a fetus."

"Sorry," the man in the bun, Cassidy, says to me. "I had to tell her. I know we were going to keep your Endellion visit between us at first, but as soon as that little boy called with your SOS, I blabbed to everyone. You said not to trust the police, so I wasn't sure what to do. I redialed the resort until sundown, but they wouldn't put me in touch with you. I figured you were gone for good. I never should have pushed you to get in touch with that Rhea woman. It's my fault."

The redhead makes a zipping motion in the air. "Shut it. Something's wrong with her. Look at her face. Her memory might be screwed up still." She rests her hands on my shoulders and speaks in slow motion. "I'm *Harper*. I'm your *favorite* at work. You *film* me. Much better than *Cassidy* does."

Despite everything, my lips crack into a smile. Rhea lied when she called my sister unsuccessful. Ari had a life. She had a career. She had friends. If she sent her coworkers an SOS message, she must have trusted them. And I trust her.

"You're right," I say, massaging my temple. "My head is still a little foggy. I'm not really myself. Elliot—this is Elliot—he helped me escape the island. And now he's helping me again. We have to get into this conference. A lot of people are going to die in there."

I recap the limo ride and revenge plot without explaining the reason Rhea wanted revenge in the first place. Elliot jumps in with details about the top-secret surgeries offered to Endellion employees and law enforcement. Neither of us mentions my real identity.

"Repeat that. Word for word," Harper says when our tag-team story ends. "I'll interview you about it. On air. The people inside will see it on their phones and leave. Boom. Perfect plan. The day is saved and we've gone viral."

I shake my head. "That won't work. Someone on Rhea's team might see it first, figure out we're trying to ruin her conference, kick us off the property, and take down the video. We can't let them know we're here. We have to sneak inside and destroy the air control system. That's the plan."

Cassidy eyes Elliot. "You're wearing a uniform, bud. Can't you just stroll in?"

"I don't have a ticket and I'm off the clock." Elliot rotates his wrist. Dried blood clings to swelling, yellow knuckles. "They'd be able to tell from the glove I'm wearing."

Harper pushes out an over-dramatic sigh. "Leave it to me. I'll sneak Ari inside, no problem. I've been talking my way into bars since I was fifteen."

She spins toward Elliot. "Officer, which one of your little friends do you know the best? You must have been stuck working with at least one of them before. Give me all the dirt. Everything you've got."

We reposition ourselves for a better angle of the entrance. The rope maze is empty aside from a lone straggler, so most of the guards have clumped together to chat.

Elliot gestures toward an older man with Swiss-cheese bald patches. "The guy on the right is Sean Williams. He grew up in Kansas City. He's married to his third or fourth wife. He's turning fifty soon. Oh, and he goes to some bar called *Sip And Trip* after every shift. He's nuts about their vodka tonics. He's invited me out with him, but I've never gone."

"Wow, what a good listener," Harper says, nodding her approval. She flicks her curls, shimmies her bra, and reapplies a stick of highlighter. "Come on, Ari. I'm ready for my close-up."

Cassidy and Elliot camouflage themselves in the crowd while we make a wide arch around the ropes. I cover my face with my hood in case Cara woke up and warned anyone about me. I use Harper as an extra shield, shadowing her movements. When we reach the velvet rope separating us from the cluster of guards, I keep my head dipped.

Harper calls out for *Seany* in a flirtatious baby voice. The female guards stare daggers at her. The male guards nudge rib cages.

"Are you lost, miss?" Sean asks, wading through his friends to greet us.

Harper cocks her head. Her glossy lips purse.

"Miss, this event is restricted to passholders. You're not permitted beyond this point without a ticket. If you *have* a ticket, you can walk through the ropes like everyone else."

"You're kidding, right?" she says. "You're screwing with me?"

"I don't like repeating myself. You're going to have to step back."

She drops her jaw. Her brows hitch to her hairline. She looks like a Broadway performer, overacting for the audience in the back. "Seriously? I can't *believe* you're doing this again. You got another one of those damn surgeries, didn't you, Sean? You don't know who I am."

His chin rises. It shows off the apple bobbing in his thick, veiny throat.

"We hooked up at the *Sip And Trip*? More than once? You normally get your little surgery after seeing me, but you promised you were going to keep the memory after what I did to you in the bathroom?" She barks out a dry, sarcastic laugh. "You know, I said I'd never do this again, but you told me, you swore to me, that it would be different. You said you were going to call your divorce lawyer. You said you'd take me back home to Kansas City for your 50th to meet everybody. Oh my God. I am such an idiot. I always do this."

He speaks over her last few lines, shushing her. "Hey. Listen. Calm down. I was supposed to head in after my shift. Take my seat. H10. Sit there. We can talk about the rest later. In private. Okay?"

He hoists the rope. She slips to his side.

"Thank you, Seany. But next time we stay out until four in the morning talking over vodka and cheeseburgers, you better keep the damn memory." She motions for me to duck under, to join her. "I brought a friend, by the way. Like you said I could. She can sit on my lap if she has to, but I'm not leaving her out..."

"Cheeseburgers?"

"That's what I ordered, at least. I don't remember what you had. Maybe just the vodka. I was pretty drunk."

She tries to step around him, but his tank of a chest blocks her. He prowls toward her, backing her against the rope. The velvet bulges toward me. A post topples onto the pavement.

"You're one of them," he says, dropping to a deep growl. He wrenches her arm, twirls her, and cuffs her. "You should have stuck to waving your signs."

Harper's brother comes running. The other protestors follow. They stream into the spaces surrounding me, chanting and swearing and demanding her release.

Cassidy bulldozes his way to the front of the horde. Harper locks eyes with him and mouths *record this*. To me, she mouths, *go*.

I push upstream, smacking passersby with my backpack. A steady breeze fans my face, but sweat suctions to my cheeks from my nerves. Each minute stranded outside the venue is a minute closer to the guards bolting the doors, sealing their own fate.

"What happened?" Elliot asks when we reunite on an out-of-the-way sidewalk. He paces the concrete, spewing smoke, as I fumble through a watered-down version of the conversation.

"He was going to let us through," I say. "I don't know what changed his mind."

He dumps his cigarette, stomps the stub, and types something into his security pass. "Apparently, *Sip And Trip* is a vegan bar," he says. "Apparently that's a thing now."

"How do you know?"

"It's in big letters on their website. I bet Sean said something about it before. I should have thought of it."

"I meant, you have internet right now?"

"Yeah, worker passes aren't like guest passes. We can access an uncensored version of the web anywhere. As long as there are hotspots, obviously. These gloves won't work at all without internet."

I glance at the screen still strapped to my hand. "I messed with mine on the island so that Gomez couldn't track my location. Maybe that would work again."

"How would breaking our passes help?"

"Not ours. Theirs. They're scanning people to get in. If we can shut down their hotspots, maybe we can slip inside. You're wearing a uniform. And you have a good reputation, right? They'll assume you belong there." I tilt my head back, cupping a hand on my forehead. "Shouldn't there be telephone poles? We could climb them and snip the wires."

"There aren't utility poles on this street. They must be underground. In a junction box. We use them over on the island, too, but it's not really my area. I don't know too much about them."

"We might as well try, right?"

I peer at the thinning protestors, the scattered guards. Only one worker remains at the rope maze, scanning the occasional security band. Harper has vanished along with everyone else. Sean must have stowed her inside somewhere, sentenced her to death.

We retrace our steps to the parking lot, moving as fast as we can without drawing attention to ourselves. Elliot points out a junction box along our route, embedded in a dirt patch between the sidewalk and street. "That one should be close enough to impact the stadium," he says. "We'll set up there on our way back."

It takes another two blocks for us to reach the truck. Elliot tosses me an extra uniform lying across the backseat—a green jacket and slacks, a carbon copy of his current outfit. He shoos me to the passenger seat to change behind tinted windows. I wriggle into my costume while he rummages through the trunk for bolt cutters.

I'm the first to finish. He tells me to get a head start and he'll catch up, but I loop back to his bumper anyway. I immediately regret it. His trunk bed is crammed from corner to corner, cluttered with a cooler and grill, deodorant and toothbrush, pillow and sleeping bag.

He reattaches the cover, stretching it over his temporary home. "I told you I wouldn't have worked for Endellion unless I really needed the money," he says.

We U-turn to the junction box in silence. Our uniforms trick onlookers into thinking we have the right to tamper with the equipment, so Elliot drops his kit and crouches to work the vault cover loose. It takes three separate tools, but he successfully detaches the grate. It lands on the pavement with a clatter.

"I hope, after you get the operation reversed, she doesn't remember any of this," he says.

He means my sister. He must see her whenever he looks at me, but there are moments when I forget, when her body feels like mine. I *have* to think of it as mine in order to breathe, to blink, to function.

"We'll figure that part out after the conference," I say, flittering around him, keeping lookout. A woman rolls a garbage can. A man screams into his cell phone. Neither of them pays us any attention. "We don't really have time to worry about stuff like that right now."

"I get that you don't want to talk about it. I can't imagine how hard it would be to sacrifice yourself after getting a second chance. I wouldn't blame you for wanting to put it off as long as possible."

"It's not like I'm procrastinating. I wasn't going to let everyone here die when there was nothing I could do about Ari anyway. Rhea refused to reverse the surgery. So did your girlfriend."

"I just want to make sure you do the right thing. I'm sure you love your sister, but the longer you're walking around, living life, the harder it'll be to leave."

"I made the decision as a kid. I can make it again when this is all over."

"Yeah, but if you have regrets—"

"Can we focus on our plan right now? Please?"

"Right. You're right." He redirects his attention to the junction box. He studies the exposed wires, grasps his bolt cutters by their rubber handles, and wraps the tip around an orange cable. Frowning, he switches to gray. He fusses with every single color in the box before committing to the thickest of the bunch. When he cracks the handles together, the wire easily snips in two, like scissors on a string.

He checks his security pass. I wait for confirmation we succeeded, but his face stays blank, unreadable.

"Did it work?" I ask. "Are we good?"

He replaces the vault cover and restocks his tool kit. A subtle, silent *yes*.

I set the pace, speed walking back to the stadium. As we draw near, we weave between what remains of the protestors. They yell obscenities, tricked by our uniforms. Each insult raises my hopes we can pull off our charade, sneak our way into the auditorium.

The entrance proves me wrong. The maze is dismantled. The doors are fastened. The guards are long gone.

"Shit. Shit. Shit." I swivel toward Elliot. "What do we do? Where do we go? There must be a back door or a basement or something, right? There has to be."

"I don't know. I've never been assigned to work over here before."

"Do you have any friends you can call? Or blueprints on your security pass?"

"The one we just disabled?"

I swing my head in every direction, taking a few steps right, a few steps left. I stop short when I spot someone in uniform. The woman who passed us at the junction box earlier. She returns an empty can to the entrance and grabs another, filled to the brim with trash. She slaps on a lid and rolls the clunking can across sidewalk cracks.

I follow close behind, stalking her around the curve of the building. She vanishes behind a row of thick, overgrown shrubs. It reminds me of the hidden path on the island. That one led to the storage room where I woke from my coma. This one must lead somewhere important, too.

I follow the woman up the path, through an unhinged, chain-link fence. Dumpsters are arranged in a straight line across the grass. Across from them, a small bin props open a side door.

"If you have a ticket, you got to go through the front," she says when she catches us creeping. She hauls a bulky contractor bag like a mall Santa.

"They closed the doors, but we were scanned through the ropes earlier. We were doing maintenance work and got locked out." Elliot rattles his toolbox. "I worked sixty hours last week. I don't want to argue. I don't even want to be here. I'd rather be sleeping."

Her lips peel back to expose stained, yellow teeth. "Ugh, I hear you. I'm enjoying my stint here while it lasts. I'm scheduled to mop the island cafeteria five days in a row next week. I'm going to barf from all those sub trips. But they know we'll do whatever they ask. I always say Miss Laman hired broke people on purpose. I thought it was to help us out at first, but now I wonder if it's 'cause she knew we'd be stuck."

"I just hope she's not pissed about us missing this thing. I know everyone wanted a ticket. She might fire us for wasting two."

"Nah, I won't let that happen." She pitches the bag into the dumpster, dusts her palms against her pants, and checks her security pass. "Eh, it's not scanning. The net must be down. Oh, well. As long as you've got yours on, nobody should mind. I'll be in right after you. I'm pretty sure I'll be the last one. They should be starting soon. Oh, and be careful with the can. Laman wanted the doors locked. God knows why, but I won't be able to get in if you knock it." She wrangles another sopping-wet trash bag into the dumpster, her back turned.

We squeeze through the gap. Elliot carefully sidesteps around the doorjamb, but I kick out my heel on purpose. The can topples. It rolls toward the dumpster, overturning stray coffee beans and sugar packets. The woman whips toward me as the door slams, clueless I saved her life.

We emerge backstage. A craft service table is littered with stray poppy seeds and snapped, plastic knives. Traces of coffee swirl in a see-through pot. Containers of cinnamon and sugar and creamer are staggered around the machine, some shaken dry and others unopened.

The area is tumbleweed quiet. No one toils behind the scenes with clipboards or makeup brushes or brooms. Every employee on the clock earlier, like Sean, must have received a ticket and taken their seat. The only sound in the auditorium comes from the thumping speakers. Rhea has already begun her speech.

"Whether you're in the front row or the nosebleed section tonight, I want you to know you have the best seat in the house," she says from the opposite side of a ribbed black curtain. "There are individual dispensers on the back of every chair. Scents are going to be generated at a central location and piped into those dispensers. That way, the odor will travel evenly throughout the room. No one will be left out. Everyone will experience the same sensation."

A machine hums in the corner. Horizontal vents run across each side like an outdoor AC unit. A thick black tube protrudes from the backend and buries itself into the floorboards. It must split underneath us like tree roots, branching to each chair.

I run a hand along the slats in the machine, groping for an *off* switch. Elliot unlatches his toolkit, but I stop him from driving a screwdriver into the metal. If this is the central generator, breaking it might release the scent instead of containing it.

"Is there any way we can just unplug it?" I whisper, hunching to view it from every angle.

"Someone would just plug it right back in again. I can't tell where the wires lead, anyway. We might have to pull up floorboards."

"That would make way too much noise. Can you do what you did with the internet with the lights? Kill the power?"

"We'd have to find the fuse box first."

He parks himself in front of a closet and runs his screwdriver between the hinges, jimmying the lock.

He could be wrong. The fuse box could be hidden in another room, so I continue exploring. A side door leads to a maze of forking hallways. The layout looks eerily similar to our old high school. There are rows upon rows of meeting rooms that could be mistaken for classrooms. There are trophy cases with neurochemistry medals and plaques. There are even employee lockers. The auditorium sits at the center of it all, just like the assembly room where we got our original brain scans.

Rhea resurrected more than me. She brought back her whole childhood.

Backstage, a lock clicks. The closet door folds inward. Elliot nudges a switch on the inner wall, illuminating a fuse box—and a woman handcuffed to an overhead pipe. A purple bulb shines on her forehead. One of her shirt-sleeves is torn.

"God...Harper. Are you okay?" I ask, scrabbling to her side.

She spits a glob of blood. "I got to say, I've been better. You sure you don't want these fuckers to die?"

I trade an uneasy glance with Elliot.

"Get her down," he says. "I'll figure out the fuse box."

I dig through tools, clueless about how to pick a lock. I settle on using the longest, narrowest nail in the kit. I raise onto my tiptoes, jam the tip inside the handcuffs, and wiggle it in zigzags and circles. My fingers keep slipping as my eyes track to her forehead, her swelling bruise.

"I didn't create this technology for myself," Rhea says through the speakers. "I created it for all of you. You all deserve to feel the same way I felt back when I was eighteen, when I developed the starter technology that led to Memory Cleansings. You each belong in the pages of history."

I lose hold of the nail. It bounces beneath a wheelable bucket of slosh-ing brown water. With three of us crowding the space, there's not enough room to roll it away, so I drop to my knees and thrust a hand underneath.

Elliot must be as flustered as me because sweat drizzles down his nose. He mutters swears as he flicks switches inside the fuse box.

"I don't want to keep you waiting any longer," Rhea says. "The scent you're about to experience is called Endellion Rose. This trademarked odor will bring you the ultimate feeling of peace. Serenity. Nirvana. Now, I need you to all lean back and close your..."

The lights sputter and fade. The hum of the machine dies.

Harper squeaks. Elliot pumps a fist, creating a shadowy streak in the dark. I tuck my head into my knees, drowning in relief.

Beyond the curtain, the audience rustles in their seats. Legs uncross. Jackets crinkle. Grumbles and gasps swirl into a tornado of noise.

"Calm down. Everything is fine," Rhea says. She thunders even without her microphone. "We have a backup generator. It should kick in shortly. Remain in your seats, please. The doors are locked, so you won't get far any-way. You're stuck with me for the next half-hour. You can't escape."

The audience chuckles as the ceiling click-click-clicks. Harsh fluorescent lights switch on in rows, one after another after another. The machine behind the curtain reactivates, humming with power. Chairs creak with weight as the audience settles back into place.

"No no no no no," I say, stumbling to my feet. I break from the closet in a clumsy lurch, skittering in one direction then the other. "Where's the generator? We need the generator. Where is it?"

Elliot shakes his head. "It's not back here. It could be on the roof. Outside by the dumpsters. In another closet. Anywhere."

"So we're screwed," Harper says. She thrashes to free herself. Her handcuffs grind against the pipe, carving grooves into her flesh.

Elliot grabs the bolt cutter and wraps its blades around the steel. The chain crumbles in one crunch, leaving her with a bracelet on both wrists.

"What are we going to do with her?" I ask. "We only have two backpacks. And there's three of us now."

Elliot shakes a cigarette from his pack. "It doesn't matter. She'll be fine. She's never been to the island."

"What do you mean?"

"The scent can only impact people with scent-association implants. The cops out there signed up for them. The guards got them when they started working for Endellion. And visitors get them during their Memory Cleansings. Cara pretends she's only inserting a fake memory into guests, but she's really putting in a bunch of associations. She told me that a few weeks back, which is why I knew something sketchy was about to happen. It's why I wanted to help you." He lights his cigarette, sucks, and puff-puff-puffs. The smoke swirls down my throat.

Harper coughs into her elbow. "Do you have to do that here? You're gonna kill us before she does."

"Sorry." He kicks his heel back to snuff the flame.

"Hold on." I reach out, swipe the stick, scald my fingertips. "This could work. We could get everyone out of here safe. This is perfect. This is all we need."

"My cigarette?"

"Smoke. We could start a fire. To mask the scent. And set off alarms. People will run out. The fire department will come. Give me your lighter."

"I don't know how much good it would do," he says, but he digs in his pocket. He tosses me a lighter with a fading, discolored tiger on the casing.

"Actually, that little thing can light up this whole place," Harper says. She drifts to the craft service table and scans labels while she speaks. "I was an extra in an indie movie some fuck-boy-frat-boy put together. He only asked me on set because he was trying to sleep with me. It didn't work. He was a piss-poor director. Turned me right off. Anyway. The budget was low. They used flour for the action scenes. To make explosions. Coffee creamer should work, too. It has something to do with the fine—"

"Now that the excitement is over, let's try this again," Rhea says, echoing. "I want you all to lean back and rest your eyes. Let the sensation wash over you."

I drop to my knees and shrug away my backpack. Elliot does the same. We unzip compartments, strap oxygen tanks to our backs, and fasten masks against our ears. The diving gear cost Elliot a few paychecks, but the splurge will be worth it if we survive.

Above us, vents hiss. A thin veil of mist spreads through the stadium. The toxic scent sweeps across the air, but clean, clear oxygen pumps into us.

Elliot uncaps the coffee creamer while I uncap the lighter. I roll my thumb against the flint wheel. Once. Twice. Three times. Low on fuel, it struggles to maintain its flame. It pops and fades. Sparks and sputters.

A deep, guttural scream cuts across the auditorium, freezing me. A symphony of death follows. Gasping. Wheezing. Gargling. Sobbing. It's mixed with sounds of attempted escape. Pounding walls. Shattered glass. Pleas for help, help, help.

"You can't afford to freak out right now," Harper says. "Come on. Move your ass, Ari."

The name snaps me back. I squeeze harder on the wheel, scrolling my thumb again and again. It took Dawson seconds to butcher himself in the limo—and most of the workers behind the curtain are younger, faster, stronger.

At last, the lighter catches. I thrust my wrist forward, extending my arm as far as it can stretch to avoid getting burned.

Elliot shakes a dense cloud of coffee creamer into the air. I wince, waiting for the explosion, but only a small dusting lands on the flame. Sparks sputter, tame as a sparkler.

Harper grabs his waist, then shoulders, then arms, posing him like a dummy, repositioning him for a better angle. "Jesus. I have to do *everything* around here," she mutters, but she lingers a second too long before letting him go.

Once she backs into a safe space, I ignite the lighter again. He shakes the container again.

The creamer hits the flame. A burst of fire sprays onto the curtain, gobbling the fabric.

Heat beats against us. The steam fogs our masks. I scrub the mist away with my sleeve as Elliot shouts something about checking locks. I only half-hear him over the wailing fire alarm, but I catch him bolting to the back entrance, holding hands with Harper.

I swing the opposite way to stagger around the blazing curtain. On the other side, lifeless bodies slump in chairs and sprawl across aisles. Their skulls are dented. Their wounds ooze dark, syrupy blood. Somehow, the conscious ones are even more unsettling. They claw at their eye sockets, choke themselves, and bang their heads against chair backs, grunting and groaning with each blow.

"Domino?" Rhea says, muffled by the alarm. She stands at the podium, but she faces sideways, faces me. Hair sticks to her wet cheeks. Nose plugs peek from her nostrils. I wonder why she bothered to give herself the scent implants in the first place, whether there was a point when she considered ending her life tonight, too.

"How did you get here?" she asks. "What happened to Cara?"

She brushes away a strand of hair. Or swipes away a teardrop. I'm not sure which. I'm focused on the security pass twinkling on the backside of her hand. It must be connected to a private hotspot. It must control the scent in the auditorium, just like she controlled the scent in the limo.

I don't think. I spring off the balls of my feet, lunging at her, seeing red. She twists sideways and guards her face on instinct, unsure what's happening. I lock my arms under her pits to disable her, to hold her in place. I raise to my tiptoes and bite at her glove like a rabid dog, yanking the screen with my teeth. I tug hard enough to snap one of the loops.

"Stop it. Domino. Please, this is ridiculous, I don't want to hurt you," she says. But once I tear another loop off another finger, she thrusts her arms down to break my grip, takes a single step forward, and snaps back. Her elbow strikes my ribs.

I double over, my lungs sucked dry. She darts to the other side of the podium. The crimson train on her dress skims the floor like a wedding gown.

"I'm sorry," she says over the screeching alarm, the rumbling fire. "Are you okay? Please say you're okay."

I force myself upright and swing at her over the lectern. She catches my forearm, but I extend my opposite hand, my bad hand, and rip at her glove. I snap the remaining loops. The device flings across floorboards.

Rhea tightens her grip to stop me from chasing the screen. We grapple, hands wringing elbows, the podium caught between us. My stomach digs into the lip extending from my side of the wood. Her side, the side facing the audience, is smooth with more space to maneuver.

The extra room gives her an advantage. She stretches her leg sideways, trying to scoot the screen closer with her foot. It's still slightly out of her reach, so she crouches for a better vantage point. The movement is too fast, too unexpected. As she drops to the ground, she launches me down with her.

I crack my forehead against the podium rim. The blow knocks me onto my back.

"Jesus, God, I'm sorry," Rhea says. "I didn't mean to do that."

Spots dance on the ceiling. Embers drip from the curtain like raindrops, lighting the stage around me on fire.

"You have to fix this," I say, but it hits the air as gibberish, garbled and slurred.

The impact must have whacked my mask off-center because a sweet, citrusy scent tickles my nostrils. Visions swarm me. My mother, blowing snot and tears into a handkerchief. My father, slack-jawed in a wheelchair. My sister, falling over, drunk off her grief. My fault. My fault. My fault.

My nails cleave red stripes into my chest. I sink my teeth into my bandaged hand to stop myself from gouging out my eyeballs, plucking off my lids, pulling out my veins thread by thread.

It would be easy. Ending it would be easy. Half the audience already went through with it. I wonder whether the ones like me, loaded with trauma, were the first to give up—or whether they held on the longest because they were used to this feeling, to this overwhelming sense of sadness. Maybe minds well-acquainted with pain were better equipped to fight it, but not forever, not for...

Rhea readjusts my mask. Through my clouded vision, she looks like an apparition, glowing at the edges.

I test a breath. Safe, untainted oxygen flows into my lungs. The knots in my stomach loosen. My limbs sag against the floorboards.

"Are you going to attack me if I try to carry you outside?" Rhea shouts. She stands at a distance to protect herself. "I want to get you someplace safe. Can you let me do that? Please?"

I ignore her, hypnotized by the ruin above me. The beam bearing the charred, flaming curtain slowly detaches from its hinge. The wood around it splinters, losing support. As it tilts, the curtain bunches to the slanted side. The metal groans, but it's hard to hear over the competing sounds of death. I only notice because I'm stranded on my back, staring at the ceiling.

And Rhea is staring at me. "You're going to hurt yourself. What are you doing?" she asks when I tuck my arms and roll.

My oxygen tank disrupts my balance, trapping me on my side. I slip out of my backpack straps, hug the tank to my chest, and fling my weight again. It works. I propel myself off the stage and plunge six feet to the carpeted aisle.

The beam topples, shaking the ground, sending vibrations through my spine. The collapse opens a crater in the stage. The curtain falls across the crumbled wood, blanketing it in fresh flame.

It works like kindling, feeding the fire, spreading its blaze. Thick waves of smoke crash through the auditorium, shading the world gray. Screams are replaced with gasps and deep, hacking coughs.

The survivors, bleeding and bruised but alive, cover their noses with collars and shirtsleeves. They book it for the exit, some on their own, some dragging mangled, mutilated friends.

The smoke must have overridden the scent. It must have gotten the misery out of their systems.

A form emerges from the fumes, hooks their arms under my pits, and heaves me to my feet. Elliot. I can barely see his eyes beneath the layer of ash smeared across his mask. "The alarm automatically unlocked the doors," he says, wrapping an arm around my waist. "We can get out of here."

"Wait. We need to bring her with us," I say, screaming to hear myself over the ringing in my ears.

"Harper? I got her out earlier."

"No. Rhea."

I shove myself away from him with a weak push. I trip toward a section of stage flattened to our level and crunch through the rubble. Burning chunks of debris rain from the rafters. Flames lick the ceiling and walls, peeling them bare.

Rhea sprawls dangerously close to the crippled beam. One of her heels has snapped its stem. The other has gone missing. A shard of wood, wreckage from the crushed stage, juts from her chest.

"She's either going to die or get arrested here," I say, craning toward Elliot. The movement sends a stabbing pain through my neck. I must have sprained it when my skull cracked against the podium. Or when it thudded against the aisle. "I need the operation reversed. I need her."

"We can get Cara to do it. She's the surgeon, anyway. It makes more sense."

"Elliot. Please."

The flames spread, pooling closer and closer. Elliot shakes his head behind the mask, but he hobbles toward Rhea. He scoops her beneath the neck and knees, careful not to disturb her injury. I do the same as I strap my own mask over her dribbling makeup and roll her gown up to her thighs. I pray no one recognizes her as we stagger outside.

Fire trucks, police cruisers, and studio vans clog the street. A dozen different crews position cameras on the hunt for the perfect shot. *Twins Spilling Tea* is the only station already prepared, ready, rolling.

Cassidy points his lens toward Harper, cuddled in a shock blanket. Her brother sits somberly beside her. Bloody marks curl around her wrist. A bandage slants across her forehead. In the background, smoke wafts from the building in thick, black globs.

Men in uniforms, fresh on the scene, instruct us to remain on the property to fill out police reports. Everyone else in uniform—the men and women who made it out alive—wheeze and cough up phlegm as medics stitch their wounds.

Firemen weave their hoses through the crowd. EMTs wheel gurney after gurney. Reporters shout invasive, insensitive questions.

The crime scene is crowded enough, hectic enough, to stagger down the block unnoticed. We make it halfway to the truck, nearing the busted junction box, when an SUV creeps up to us. I worry it might be an unmarked police car sent to arrest Rhea, but when it parts its tinted window, I recognize the driver. He jerks his head, an invitation inside.

"Where's your limo?" I ask, stiff as a deer in headlights.

"Boss wanted to leave with new plates."

"She said something about a safehouse?"

"Got it plugged into the GPS."

"You're not going to hurt us?"

"You help her, I help you."

I peek over the hood, through the wire fence encircling the public parking lot. We could tear apart the truck bed to make space, but Rhea would bump and roll beneath the tarp. Worse, we would need to scout out a safe place to drive her, to hide her.

Sirens howl. Another fire engine races toward the venue. But the next burst of lights could belong to a cop.

"Okay," I say. "We'll go together."

A door glides open, exposing a middle and back bench. Elliot straps Rhea into the last row, bending her knees to fit her in the cramped space. I circle around to the other side, untangle her mask, and chuck it onto the floor. Her eyeballs shift and flinch beneath the lids. The wooden shard in her chest moves along with each breath.

I crawl into the middle row, beside Elliot, and strap myself in place. The locks swish shut. The window rises. The driver leans across the dashboard and rifles through the glove compartment. A part of me expects him to whip out a handgun and waste two bullets, but he flings a plastic bottle between us. It rattles with pills.

I shake three aspirins onto my tongue and gulp the batch dry. The tablets flay my throat.

"What happened to you in there?" Elliot asks.

"I fought with her. And fell off the stage. And my mask came off for a little while."

"Jesus, I should have stuck with you. I ran out the back with Harper. Then got a few friends I recognized out. Then came looking for you."

"That's good. That you helped some people." My neck stings too much to stay twisted toward him, so I stare at the headrest. "Did you see all those bodies? How many do you think died? It must have been two or three hundred. Minimum."

"We saved at least the same amount. We did enough. The whole world is going to know about this. Endellion will get shut down. Laman will get life in prison."

"Do you think the police are looking for her? I'm surprised no one followed us."

"They might think she's trapped inside with the others."

"Or they might think it was an accident. She said she set it up to make it look like one."

"I'll check if it makes you feel better. I'm sure she's trending."

He scrubs the soot from his security pass. When the touchscreen functions again, he recites news articles about the conference. I have trouble following along with the police statistics and social media speculation, rumors and reality. As my adrenaline wears off, the stress from my dive and the limo ride and the fire catch up to me. My system shuts down.

I don't realize my eyes have shut until Elliot jerks me awake. He applies a little too much force, like it's not the first shove.

"Sorry. You were really out," he says. "I think we're here."

We bump down a wide, winding side road. It loops us around lush trees and overgrown weeds, wild turkeys and white-tailed deer. The street ends at a crumbling, weather-beaten motel with a paper CLOSED FOR BUSINESS sign taped over a marquee WELCOME sign.

The driver parks between faded blue handicap lines. He disengages the locks but keeps the engine idling.

"You're not coming?" I ask.

He grunts. "Did what I was paid to do. Bring her here. Not sticking around to get arrested. Company ain't coming back from this."

The front door unfolds as my sneakers touch gravel. A pair of hairless workers, a man and a woman, shuffle toward the SUV with a stretcher. They transfer Rhea onto the slab and strap her in place.

I follow their lead, crunching through the deserted parking lot. The sharp red pebbles remind me of our driveway at home. In first grade, I fell onto a pile during a game of tag and gashed my knee. When Mom saw the damage, she babied and bandaged me. Dad told me to walk it off. They both thought they were doing the right thing.

Right now, I pray entering the motel is the right thing.

The workers ferry Rhea up a steep ramp leading to the entrance. I climb a trio of chipped concrete steps to their side. The railing wobbles beneath my palm, coming loose from the concrete.

The aesthetic shifts as we advance into the main lobby. The crumbled cement evolves into crisp white tiles. Cream leather couches flank an elevator bank. A standing directory lists floors and services. I think back to what Rhea told me when she first brought me to an Endellion building in our hometown. They deliberately make it look beat-up on the outside to deter visitors.

The workers maneuver around the furniture, guiding the gurney into the elevator. I whip out a hand to catch the door. "Can we come up?" I ask. "We brought her here. We're the reason she's alive right now."

They exchange looks. "Not right now," the woman says with the gentle drawl of a nurse. "But if Miss Laman wakes up, and wants you to know she's woken up, we'll come get you right away."

"Is anyone going to try to kick us out?"

"No one else is here."

I reluctantly remove my hand. The elevator doors slide together with a chirp.

With nothing to do but wait, I stretch across the sofa. My catnap in the SUV only made me more exhausted. My neck stings. My wrist throbs. My stomach writhes, desperate for a drink. Part of me would rather be unconscious, oblivious, spared from pain.

Elliot is the only thing keeping me awake. He hovers over me, saying, "I'm not sure how long we should stay here. I checked social media, news sites, everything, while you were sleeping. There are reports EMTs found the old owner of Endellion unresponsive less than an hour before the conference. That means Dawson. They think Laman had something to do with what happened to him. They're helicoptering everyone off the island to be safe. There are already a bunch of petitions to shut the resort down. Apparently, a bunch of workers came forward on social media. They told the public about the secret procedures, about what Laman lets them do. Most of the people were officers—the ones who made it out alive and watched their friends die—but Gomez was on there, too. Everyone is turning against her, jumping ship, like the chauffeur said. I mean, look how empty it is here. Someone probably knows about this safehouse. They're going to mention it to save their own ass, get reduced time, get revenge, whatever. I don't know if it'll be days from now or minutes from now, but the police are going to raid this place. If you tell them about what happened to you, they might help you. Or they might shoot without talking first."

"None of that matters," I say, gesturing toward the directory. It lists operating rooms, laboratories, and equipment storage areas situated on each floor. "I think they should have enough stuff here to reverse my surgery. You should leave before anyone else shows up, but I need to stay. You were the one who said I shouldn't keep putting it off."

"I don't think you should wait too long. But I don't think you should risk getting a bullet, either."

"If we walk away now, and Rhea and Cara and everybody involved ends up in prison, no one is going to be around to do the surgery. It's never going to happen unless it happens today. I need to stay."

He shakes his head but doesn't protest. He must realize I'm right. "Are you ready, though? To leave again?"

I don't have a reassuring answer for him. Like the night my life ended, I try not to think about what my sacrifice means, how many milestones will be missed. I never stepped on a college campus. I never leased an apartment. I never worked a real job. I never got my tattoo.

"Did you see it?" I ask, tracing the wound on my arm, the lost traces of ink. "See what?"

"Ari had a tattoo. Do you know what it was?"

"I only saw it for a second. The day I helped her back to her resort when she was…out of it. They were dice, maybe. Some sort of squares and dots."

Growing up, Ari refused to play with my temporary, sponge-on tattoos. She wouldn't even tack stickers onto her cheeks or scribble pencil on her palm. If she put herself through the pain and permanence of a tattoo, the design must have meant a lot to her.

Slow as a sunrise, the answer dawns on me. "Were they dominos?" I ask.

"Could have been, yeah."

Guilt churns my stomach. I wish there was a way to explain why my belt and ceiling fan felt like my only option that night. Endellion was too dangerous to tell her about ten years ago, but without Dawson around to threaten her, with the entire company crumbling, the truth wouldn't put her in danger anymore. It might help her heal, give her closure.

"Are you all right?" Elliot asks when the silence overstays its welcome.

"I just miss her."

"If you want, I can keep in touch with her? Make sure she's okay? I'm sure she can handle herself, but you know what I mean."

"I know what you mean. I appreciate it."

Another ten minutes—and two sets of hugs—convince him to leave me to face my fate alone. When he unhinges the door, a breeze rustles papers at the front desk. A few slices float across the tile.

I stumble onto swelling feet and collect the scattered pages. Some are crammed with numbers from margin to margin. Others are blank, unprinted sheets of computer paper. I shuffle the plain pieces together, plop onto a receptionist chair, and rummage through drawers for a pen. At the top of the first page, I scrawl my sister's name.

I write to her about my days at the cabin, my brain scans, my hallucinations, my suicide. I save more recent events for last, explaining how I escaped the island, watched the man who caused my murder mutilate himself, and set the conference hall aflame.

I hope surgery will erase those memories, save her from the nightmares. But I still want her to be aware of what happened. She deserves the unedited story.

I keep scribbling until a voice echoes across the lobby. "Miss Laman is awake," the nurse says. She pokes her smooth head out from the elevator. Her frail hand holds back the door.

I crease my letter along the center, folding again and again. I condense ten sheets into a thick square and cram it into my tracksuit pocket.

"Thank you," I say when the woman swaps positions with me. She sets the elevator to the correct floor so it moves as soon as her hand does.

The carriage glides ten stories and dings at a medical wing. Each room along the vacant hall is transparent, wrapped with glass. The most spacious one, with computer monitors along the side wall, is reserved for Rhea. Her crimson gown has been replaced with a paper one. Wires snake into her wrists. A bandage is taped across her chest, in the spot where the wooden shard impaled her.

"I heard you were up," I say, slipping through the wedged door.

Her back is flat, so she stares at the ceiling as she speaks. A slur ties her words together. "I thought you hated me. You could have left me to burn."

"I only helped you so you would help me."

"Domino. Please. Not this again. It took me ten years to get you here. I don't want you to give up after a day."

"It won't be long until the police find you. They know you killed a bunch of them. They're not on your side anymore. They're going to lock you up. Before that happens, you have to set things right with me. I'm not living like this. Endellion is finished. This experiment is finished. You're fixing what you've done to my family. You're not putting them through any more pain. You're reversing the surgery."

She shuts her eyes. Tight. A tear rolls toward her chin, but she licks away the salt. "You're really not happy you were brought back? You really don't want to stay?"

"Obviously I want to stay. I never wanted to leave in the first place. But what I want doesn't matter. What you want doesn't matter. We have to live with what we've done. You belong in prison. I belong—"

"Alive."

"No. I'm not screwing over my little sister."

She nudges a button on her bed railing, slanting her mattress to angle. Her bloodshot eyes meet mine. "What if we made it so Ariadna was okay? But you still got to live?"

"What are you talking about? You said you needed to use her body to bring me back."

"That was for a full Transplant. But we could do something different. Combine consciences."

"What, so it would be half-me, half-her? I told you I'm not ruining her life any more than I already have."

"That wouldn't be it. Not exactly. I've been thinking about it since our limo ride. If you activate the computer on your right, I can show you."

I narrow my eyes, skeptical, but I stagger toward the monitors. "Make it quick. I don't know how long we have."

She instructs me on which keys to press, which files to click. Data fills the screen. She presents her idea while we pour over brain scans, spreadsheets, and diagrams. She outlines the potential risks, the benefits, the short- and long-term side effects. She makes sure I understand what I would be getting myself into if I agreed.

When she completes her proposal, she says, "I really do think this will work. If you trust me. If you want this, too."

I tense my jaw, chew my tongue. The answer should be easy. It should be no.

But for some reason, whether it's a survival instinct or my impulsive nature or a flaw in my DNA, I say, "I do."

an

CHAPTER 20

— ONE YEAR LATER —

"This heat is killing me," I say, downing the last drops of my virgin sangria.

My mother nods from across the table. "Maybe we should head back to the resort room? I'm ready if you are."

I pluck an apple slice from my glass and slip it underneath the table for Arrow. He gulps it whole, tail thumping. "Yeah. Let's go. I'm boiling. It feels like we're on another damn island." I loop the dog leash around my wrist. My skin is crinkled with scar tissue, but the moisturizer Marzia lent me is slowly smoothing each line.

We reconnected after she saw internet headlines splashed with my name. She unblocked me to apologize for sending me the email address that started it all, that gave me access to the head of Endellion.

It turns out, we have more in common than missing my sister. Twice a week, we carpool to Twelve Step meetings at churches and rec centers while my mother babysits. Marzia can't afford to pay much, but playing nanny helps my mother get the baby fever out of her system. Besides, it's not like she needs the cash. My settlement checks paid off her mortgage and medical bills. She refused to accept money from me at first, but the spike in views at *Twins Spilling Tea* left me with more than enough to pay my own rent.

We milked the Endellion situation for months. We replayed clips of Harper in handcuffs, police officers fleeing from the fire, bloodied bodies spread across gurneys. We invited ex-workers like Elliot and Gomez for exclusive, never-before-seen interviews. I even sat on our updated soundstage to tell a version of my story. I workshopped my answers with the twins prior to the taping, careful not to give away too much. I censored large chunks, namely the parts about Dominique.

The world has no idea she borrowed my body. They have no idea most of my stories come from a long, elaborate letter instead of a memory.

One year ago, I woke up on an operating table with a stack of papers on my lap, scribbled in my own handwriting. They revealed what happened from the moment Laman knocked me out on the island until the moment I returned to my old self. They went on to fill in the blanks from when we were kids, answering ten-year-old questions about the cabin, the secret stash of money, and the suicide.

I didn't see any reason to expose the truth about my sister, to turn us into a spectacle. Laman was already set to serve two lifetime sentences. Most of her colleagues were put on probation, assigned community service, or sentenced to jail time of their own. Endellion was destroyed, its doors locked tight. There was no coming back from the nationwide backlash. The internet freaked when they first learned about the mass murder plot, the unwanted scent associations, the memories being dumped into nonconsenting criminals.

Those criminals suffered the worst. With nowhere to deposit their extra memories, they were shipped to rehabilitation centers for intensive therapy. A small group reported noticeable progress. The rest suffered aneurysms, including Antoni Tan.

I wanted to confess everything to my mother, to explain Antoni and Domino never dated, to reveal what really caused her to end her life. But it was best to keep her in the dark along with the rest of the world. She bawled when she heard the televised version of what I had been through on the island. Telling her the entire, unedited story would break her heart all over again.

"I really wish you would let me pay for the tip," she says as she rises from the table. She shrugs into her puffy jacket, a size too big since she shed thirty pounds. "You paid for the resort. You drove me here. I like being spoiled, but this is too much."

"Calm down. You've spoiled me my whole life. If anything, I'm late returning the favor."

We step into the chill, following a shoveled path that connects the restaurant to our resort rooms. Arrow veers off track to play, pouncing in snow piles. The same crisp, white powder dusting his fur also blankets mountaintops in the distance. Their peaks glitter beneath the sun, like they're made of diamonds.

"You should take more pictures," my mother says, admiring the view. Little clouds puff from her lips. "I want all your aunts to see what they're missing out on."

"I took enough to last three months on social media. And people are going to get bored after a week."

"Nonsense. No one could ever get bored of a place like this, honey. How did you even find it?"

"I don't know." I flip my hood over my chin-length hair, stalling. "I saw it online somewhere. It had good reviews. And said it was dog-friendly. It seemed like the perfect fit for us."

Technically, every word is true, but I leave out the most important reason we drove hours upon hours to a resort upstate.

I scheduled a visit with someone.

*

My car crawls through a barbed wire fence. Several signs warn against loitering, but I linger in the parking lot to video call Elliot anyway. He answers from a marble top island in his new apartment. A nicotine patch clings to his bicep. A pair of glasses glint on the counters in the background.

"What are you celebrating?" I ask.

He does a double-take over his shoulder. "Shoot. Sorry. Those are from last night." He snatches the champagne bottle and stows it on the ground, out of frame, like the sight alone will knock me off the wagon. "I have news. Big news. Harper is moving in with me."

"Wow. Congrats. It's about time she pays rent. She's been sleeping over there for how long now?"

"Hah. Hah. Very funny."

Harper asked Elliot out on air during his interview as a *thank you* for saving so many lives. In the last year, she's been happier than I've ever seen her. Just like the rest of the crew. Her brother leased a new car so he could stop pedaling his bike to set. Cassidy welcomed a healthy, red-cheeked daughter into the world. Mr. Ritter rented a one-bedroom within walking distance of the studio. I restarted therapy.

"I really am happy for you guys," I say. "I never thought she'd find someone who could handle her...energy."

"I'll let her know you said that. I'd call her in to yell at you now, but she's sleeping. Shouldn't you be doing the same thing? You're supposed to be on vacation."

"I was hoping to get out of town and back before my mother's alarm went off."

He smirks. "Why? Does she still give you a curfew? Or wait. Wait. Is that today?"

"I'm about to walk in right now."

"Shit. Are you going to be okay by yourself? I should've made the drive with you."

"It's going to be weird, but I'll be fine. We've been writing letters and talking on the phone. I think seeing her will be good for me."

"If you say so. I just want you to be careful."

"I can handle myself."

"Why'd you call, then?"

"I could still use a little luck."

He forces a small, cautious smile. "Good luck, Ariadna. Love you, buddy."

"Yeah. You, too."

I cut the call, cut the engine, and cut across the parking lot to the hulking, gray penitentiary.

*

I slip off my snow boots. I unclasp my piercings. I untangle my belt. I stuff everything in a mustard-colored box along with my cell and car keys. A guard guides the container through lead-lined flaps while I pass through a metal detector. Another guard leads me past an administration office, around an *out of order* vending machine, and into a room with old-fashioned wall phones.

I sit opposite prisoner number 1015. A sheet of glass dissects us.

"How are you doing?" she asks. Her brown hair falls limp on her shoulders, frizzy and unwashed.

"Pretty decent. I brought Mom up here for a vacation. We've been hanging out a lot more. A couple of weeks ago, we went to a zoo in the city and saw sea turtles. Those ancient ones who live a hundred years."

"I hope you took pictures." One pupil focuses on me. The other floats toward the ceiling.

"Of course. I'll send you a few. I even took some of Dad. He's been doing better. I hired a full-time nurse for him. He's never going to be able to speak, but he can ding a bell to answer questions now and he smiles sometimes."

Her crooked eye refocuses on me. "Do they know you're here, visiting?"

"No. I'm not telling them about either one of you."

"That's for the best, I think. Just don't get wasted and spill everything. They'd send you to a psych ward."

I fidget with my naked earlobe, unsure who said it, one or another or a mix. "I'm sober again, actually."

"Oh, that's so nice to hear. I'm proud of you. Have you gotten more chips?"

"I have piles of white ones, the 24-hour ones. I have to keep restarting from scratch."

"Red is next, right? If you collect enough of those, you can make your own checkerboard."

I snort out a laugh. The guard snaps toward me, so I drop my volume. "Do you have those here? Board games? They tell me you haven't been interacting with the other prisoners. You barely speak. You sit in a corner alone."

She quirks a brow at the word choice. She's never alone.

She explained it at the bottom of her letter, a PS beneath her signature. She didn't want to say goodbye again, so she spilled her consciousness into a machine at the safehouse. That machine transferred her consciousness into Laman, pooling their memories into a combined mind. My own memories were unlaced sometime in between, reverting me back to myself.

"Sorry. I'm still trying to wrap my head around this," I say. "I got used to you being gone and now you're gone in a completely different way.

Sometimes, it feels like a worse way. You're never getting out of here. You're stuck. All the things you missed out on after you died, you're still missing out on now. You can't play volleyball anymore or smoke weed or eat dinners with the family. What kind of a life is that?"

"A real one."

"Is it?"

"Yes. *I'm alive.* That's all that matters to me."

"Not to me. I want you to be happy."

"I know it's hard to understand, but I'm not lonely, I'm not sad. I promise it looks worse than it feels. I really am okay. I chose this. I just hope I didn't do the wrong thing by telling you."

"No," I mutter. Then with more force: "No. I'm glad you didn't shut me out. I'm glad you trusted me."

She raises an asymmetrical smile and streaks the glass with her handprint. A shaky blue prison tattoo is carved onto the side of her pinkie. I press my own hand against the glass, in line with hers. A matching tattoo runs across my finger. A single domino, still standing.

— THE END —

HOLLY RIORDAN is a senior staff writer for Thought Catalog who is living in Long Island, New York. She is a prolific author of dark and chilling science-fiction tales and has penned several novellas that examine the complexities inherent in human nature and our relationship with technology and metaphysics. She is also a poet and kind human being.

TWITTER.COM/HOLLYYRIO
INSTAGRAM.COM/HOLLYYRIO
FACEBOOK.COM/HOLLYRIORDANWRITING
THOUGHTCATALOG.COM/HOLLY-RIORDAN

MORE BOOKS BY HOLLY RIORDAN

Severe(d): A Collection of Creepy Poems

Before The Farmhouse Burned Down

Lifeless Souls

Badass Broken Girls

Anxiety Ruins Everything

If You Were Still Alive

**THOUGHT
CATALOG**
Books

THOUGHTCATALOG.COM
NEW YORK · LOS ANGELES

```
THOUGHT
CATALOG
Books
```

Thought Catalog Books is a publishing imprint of Thought Catalog, a digital magazine for thoughtful storytelling. Thought Catalog is owned by The Thought & Expression Company, an independent media group based in Brooklyn, NY, which also owns and operates Shop Catalog, a curated shopping experience featuring our best-selling books and one-of-a-kind products, and Collective World, a global creative community network. Founded in 2010, we are committed to helping people become better communicators and listeners to engender a more exciting, attentive, and imaginative world. As a publisher and media platform, we help creatives all over the world realize their artistic vision and share it in print and digital form with audiences across the globe.

ThoughtCatalog.com | Thoughtful Storytelling

ShopCatalog.com | Boutique Books + Curated Products

Collective.world | Creative Community Network